THE SILENT SALESMAN

THE SILENT SALESMAN

MICHAEL Z. LEWIN

ALFRED A. KNOPF

NEW YORK

1978

C. 2

THIS IS A BORZOI BOOK
PUBLISHED BY ALFRED A. KNOPF, INC.

Library of Congress Cataloging in Publication Data

Lewin, Michael Z.
The silent salesman.

I. Title.
PZ4.L6713Si [PS3562.E929] 813'.5'4 77-7936
ISBN 0-394-40433-5

Manufactured in the United States of America

First Edition

THE SILENT SALESMAN

ONE / I spent the first half-hour after breakfast counting my money. My cash money. The two thousand dollars that made up my Never-Touch Fund. It came to $938.

For money belonging to me, that's not a bad survival rate over nearly three years. Especially considering I keep it in a box I don't even lock against myself. I can't afford a lock. The only restraint I use is an otherwise friendly candid picture of my woman giving me a stern glower. It's to inspire self-discipline.

The money came originally in a lump with a letter from a grateful client. A free and unsolicited gift. I honored the letter by giving it a file folder of its very own. And I resolved to keep the money intact until I really needed it.

I needed it.

All June I'd sat in my office, doing nothing but hand-to-mouth work and wondering why nobody in the whole of Indianapolis wanted to hire a value-for-money operative like me.

With my contacts, intelligence, integrity . . . cheapness.

But then I realized. It's marriages in June.

In July I realized it was still honeymoons. . . .

But by August at least the divorce side of the detective business should have picked up. It hadn't.

On Monday, the eighth, I had decided to act. One of my strong points is that I'm willing to take action. If I can't think of anything else to do. I went to the *Star,* to the advertising department.

> GIGANTIC AUGUST DETECTIVE SALE
> 20% off your private detective on all inquiries,
> including divorces, if started in August.

It seemed like a good idea at the time. The ad appeared Tuesday morning.

But of course Tuesdays are usually quiet anyway. Because all the housewives and househusbands do their washing on Tuesday.

Or is that Monday?

On Wednesday morning, I went to the bank to get my money, first thing. Then I came back to have breakfast. The ad was set to run for the rest of the week, including Sunday. It was my first ad since the week I started in business in 1863. My mistake, 1963.

Things had been bad for me since I opened, of course. That's the way I run my life, going from bad to bad. But being more than a thousand bucks down on what I wouldn't have had but for an unexpected gratitude . . . That's bad.

At 10:15 the phone rang.

"Albert Samson. May I help you?"

A man's voice asked, "Are you Albert Samson?"

"I am."

"That put this ad in the paper saying 20 percent off if I start my divorce now?"

"That's right."

"Are you on the level?"

"I don't quite know how to answer—"

"Either you're on the level or you aren't on the level. Is this some kind of joke or isn't it?"

"It's no joke. It's perfectly serious."

"Well, I think it's a terrible joke, Samson. I think it's in very poor taste, if you want to know what I think." He hung up.

The light bulb of my consciousness flickered for the rest of the morning. When I was off, I dreamed about doing some other form of work. Being . . . anything. Being something. Earning enough, after expenses, to pay tax.

When I was on, I passed the time trying to remember the names of the 1969 Mets. The ones who came from nowhere to win the National League Pennant, the World Series.

We had a lot in common, the Mets of 1969 and the Albert Samson of 1977. We both started the summer at the bottom.

At twelve, I retired to my back room for lunch. At twenty to one, I heard the unmistakable sound of someone trying to open my door. I paused, I listened. I put down the orange juice bottle and dashed the eight giant steps from my dining-room chair to my office door. I lifted and pulled. It flew open.

"Hi," I said from behind my best smile.

A middle-aged woman in a long brown raincoat was halfway down the stairs. She turned and looked back up at me.

"Can I help you, Ma'am?"

She said, "I . . . I . . . I . . ." Then hurried down the stairs and out onto the street. Advertising sure pulls them in.

I went down the stairs, but not to pursue her. I had noticed a letter in the wire basket that catches things pushed into my mail slot. I'm not usually overeager for my mail, but last week's letter had been from my daughter. I hadn't seen her for twelve years, and she'd written to say she might visit me. Her mummy and rich new daddy were spending the summer in Connecticut, which was, after all, nearly next door. I opened the envelope on the spot, at the foot of the stairs.

It was an eviction notice from my landlord.

They were demolishing my building to put up offices. It didn't seem fair, considering that the same thing had already happened to me. The site of my previous office—where I'd spent ten years —was now a multistory parking lot.

But Indianapolis is that kind of city, reaching for the sky on the sites of yesterday's men. And redevelopment is not the kind of thing you can get inoculated against without money. I had until mid-October to vacate.

I went back up. I'd been depressed before, but now I was just sad. "These lovely splintery rotting wooden stairs," I said to my-self. "Ahh, well."

But by the time I'd returned to my lunch I'd seen the bright side. If I had no work, I'd have plenty of time to do the moving. Everything is good for something.

Of course, if I went that long without any work, then I'd have to boil up the other shoe. . . .

I was getting manic with depression.

The phone rang. I sat and listened to it for a moment. Shrugged.

"Albert Samson. May I help you?"

"I am Mrs. Dorothea Thomas," said a woman. "I need someone to find out the why of something for me. Do you do that kind of work?"

"Yes," I said, hoping she was talking about the kind of job I could do. The last of the last shoe hadn't tasted sole good.

"Do . . . do you make house calls, Mr. Samson?"

"Yes," I said. I added, "Within a reasonable distance of Indianapolis," because I didn't want to seem too eager. She might think I wanted to eat her.

But her house turned out to be in Beech Grove and she wanted me at eight. I consulted my schedule and found I was available.

"Before you hang up, Mrs. Thomas, may I ask whether you called me because of my ad in the *Star* today?"

"Ad?" she said. "No, I just picked the smallest ad in the list of detectives in the yellow pages."

"Oh," I said.

"See you tonight, then," she said.

Beech Grove is a suburban community, about six miles closer to downtown Indianapolis than most. The house was a substantial brick structure and had been there for quite a long time. It seemed the building to house a comfortable ambition. A big beech tree towered over its left shoulder, and I wondered what the occupants of such a settled place could possibly want with me.

Perhaps they didn't; the porch light was off and I could see no other lights from the front of the house. I waited in my van because I was five minutes early. As I watched, I saw a woman move silhouetted along the side of the house to the front porch. But she didn't go in. She stood by the door and looked at her wrist.

I got out and walked up the path.

"Mr. Samson?" the woman asked, in a hushed voice.

"Yes."

"Come this way, please." I followed her back along the house in the direction from which I'd seen her come.

We turned the corner and walked past the garage to a small

aluminum trailer mounted wheelless on a concrete pad. The
trailer windows were filled with light and Mrs. Thomas held the
door for me as I went inside. "I'd have told you to come here
rather than the house," she said, "but it takes so much explaining."

We settled in two compact chairs. She was about forty, I
guessed, but she'd worn badly. Her face hung from her hairline
like layered leather flaps.

"I feel so foolish," she said.

"Please don't," I said, as if it meant something.

"I suppose I shouldn't have asked you to come all the way out
here without really knowing if you could do anything."

I did my best to look understanding. "The TV wasn't very good
tonight anyway," I said. "On the phone you said you had a problem?"

"I . . . I . . ." she said. "I am being foolish, aren't I?"

"It's hard to know where to begin," I offered.

"Oh, I know where to begin," she said. "I'm only trying to find
out what to do for the best. You see . . . my brother is not well. He's
been in Entropist Hospital for nearly seven months."

"I'm sorry."

"Yes, well, so am I," she said.

"Is he very sick?"

"Very; that's what they tell me. He was in an accident at work.
He's a salesman for Loftus Pharmaceuticals. There was some kind
of explosion in a laboratory and he got hurt."

"It sounds like very bad luck. Has the company been difficult
over medical bills, or compensation? Is that the kind of problem
you mean?"

"Oh, no. John is receiving all possible care, I'm sure of that. He
is in the company's wing of the hospital, the Loftus Clinic. And so
far as compensation, his wife will have done all that. I saw John's
lawyer at the house several times during the spring."

"Well," I began without end.

"I just want to see John."

"See him?"

"That's right. The hospital won't let me visit him."

"Not at all?"

"I've tried three times. Each time, they say he's not allowed to have any visitors, that they'll let me know when he's taken off the restricted list. But they haven't let me know. I called them again yesterday, but he's still restricted." She seemed genuinely upset.

"What do they say the reason is?"

"They say that his condition is so serious that he has to keep away from any risk of contamination."

"Just what kind of accident was this? An explosion, you said?"

"That's right. He had head injuries."

"I don't know much about these things," I said truly, "but maintaining sterile conditions doesn't sound like routine physical accident treatment."

"I didn't think it was," she said positively and with relief. "And that's why I thought that you, somebody like you, you . . ."

"Have they restricted Mrs.—?"

"My brother's name is Pighee. John Austin Pighee. His wife's name is Linn."

"Have they restricted Mrs. Pighee's visits in the same way?"

"I don't know," said Mrs. Thomas. "Linn and I don't converse. Though we do live . . ." She waved a hand in the direction of the house.

"So it's your brother's house, and his wife's."

"My brother's house, that's right. I used to keep house for them, before the accident. But now, with him not being there, I don't really bother."

"Have you had legal advice, Mrs. Thomas?"

"I did have a word once with John's lawyer. I caught him as he was leaving."

"And?"

"I don't know why John gives his business to that man," she said. "Or rather I do know why. They were in college together. They were friends. I must say I don't like him any better now than I did then."

"Then? At college?"

"Oh, yes," she said, and realized she might explain a few things. "John . . . you should know that my brother is much younger than I am, Mr. Samson. Our parents died when he was just a teen-ager and I've always had a special feeling for him. My baby brother Johnny."

"May I ask how old Mr. Pighee is now?"

"Twenty-nine."

I nodded.

"But Thomas, my husband, and I . . . went our separate ways . . . just at the time Johnny was going to college, or was supposed to go, except for Linn. . . . And I had a little money in settlement. It seemed a good idea that I make a home for them. Help him through his academic years, do whatever I could. And the arrangement continued. And here I am."

I paused, then said, "You said you'd spoken to John's lawyer."

"Walter Weston. Yes."

"What did he say?"

"That Loftus was providing more than they were legally obliged to, that Linn had been kept fully informed of John's progress, that he was satisfied that the best possible care was being provided."

"In effect, to mind your own business."

She nodded, and said harshly, "Not that Linn would mind if John didn't make progress. She's easily satisfied on that score."

"No love lost between you and your sister-in-law?"

"None. It's no secret."

"Of course the lawyer, Weston, would consider his obligation to Mrs. Pighee rather stronger than his obligation to you."

"No doubt about that."

"And you need someone to inquire about your interests."

"Yes," she said. "I want to find out why I'm not allowed to visit my own—my only brother in the hospital. After all I've done for him."

I left Mrs. Thomas after we settled the details of my fee. She'd looked up my ad in the *Star*. I didn't have the heart to put my fee up 25 percent so the 20 percent discount would bring it back to the fifty dollars a day plus expenses she would have paid if I hadn't steered her to the ad.

There were no flies on Mrs. Thomas. She wanted to know if the discount also applied to the expenses. It didn't.

Even at fifty plus, my rates were "competitive," not to say cheap. At 20 percent off, I was an anachronism.

But without any work at all, I would be extinct, so I wasn't complaining.

I got back to downtown Indianapolis a little after ten; I parked in the lot round the corner from my office where I had an arrangement: pay monthly night rates and park anytime, day or night. But all that would be gone when the developers got cracking. I climbed the wooden hill to my office/home and drank a pint of orange juice before turning on the TV. I watched a comic program and cried myself to sleep.

TWO / I woke up early. The sheer excitement of having a job.

However, life at Entropist Hospital seemed pretty well established by ten past nine, when I got there. It is one of the large general hospitals in town, neither the fanciest nor the shoddiest. It had a reputation in town as a medical research institution— whether justified or not, I didn't know.

At the reception desk a poster-pretty nurse asked me, "Is there anything I can do for you, sir?"

"Can you tell me what visiting hours are, please?"

"Is it your wife that's had a baby?" she asked.

"If she has, it's nothing to do with me."

Our relationship went downhill from there. By the end of it, all I'd got from her was a hiss and a mimeographed sheet listing the visiting hours for the various wards. Loftus Clinic wasn't listed as such, but a Loftus Pavilion was.

I hadn't asked directions and didn't feel like waiting for another hiss after the reception nurse dealt winningly with a fat woman and a little boy, so I just headed for the nearest doors that looked as if they led in rather than out.

Two rights and a left later, I found a kindly man in some sort of uniform. "You're going the wrong way, son," he said.

That's what my mother had said when I headed for the East Coast in the fifties. They were both right.

Individually named sections of a large hospital usually reflect the pocketbook rather than the personality of the donor. The opulence of Loftus Pavilion seemed to confirm what little I knew about the grand old man who founded the company, Sir Jeffrey Loftus. He was a British-noble type, of some sort, who had come to Indianapolis once upon a time and made good. Now he was in his late eighties, but still going strong. I'd never heard him called anything but Sir Jeff on television, which is the only time I'd ever heard him called anything at all. In the last twenty years he'd been one of the leaders in the big-city-style development of Indianapolis. One of the guys who were making me homeless. He was widely open-handed in construction projects that could all loosely be described as "helping the people," whatever tax or other benefits they might confer on the donors.

Not that Loftus was other than a relatively small-time kind of Carnegie, and Indianapolis-based Loftus Pharmaceuticals wasn't even the biggest drug company in town—that honor going in spades to Eli Lilly & Company.

But for whatever reason, Loftus Pavilion had a style very different from the aging institutional character of the rest of Entropist Hospital. Newer, granted, but also more evidently purpose-built. Its street-level reception area, as I walked in, gave access to the reception desk and an area with privacy, as required. It was basically a rich place, with thick carpets, as if the paternal hand of Sir Jeff had come out of the pocket with a few extra coins so that the designers could go all the way.

The Loftus Pavilion nurse wasn't thick. She had sharp eyes and realized I was an enemy as soon as she saw me. "What do you want?" she asked.

"I'd like to know when I can visit John Austin Pighee, please." I think I said please.

"Mr. Pighee is not allowed visitors," she replied without hesitation.

"Why not?"

She seemed affronted to be asked other than a time-and-place question. "Because he's not," she said. "Risk of contamination: doctor's orders."

"May I have a word with his doctor, please?"

"Who do you think you are?"

"I represent a member of Mr. Pighee's family who wants to visit him and is not satisfied with being fobbed off by someone at the front desk. It's simply not good enough. If there is a real reason why he mustn't be visited, fine. But we want to know more about it and from the doctor in charge of the case."

"Dr. Merom isn't in the hospital just now," she said.

"Well, then, I'd like to see whoever is here," I said.

She turned her head toward a man sitting in an inner office room, separated by a windowed wall from the reception desk. "Evan," she said.

The man stood up and I saw that he was wearing a para-police uniform, was clearly their security man.

"Now, look . . ." I said.

But Evan continued unhesitatingly until he was standing next to me in front of the reception desk. "You want to see a man but he isn't allowed visitors," he began, having obviously been in touch with the word exchange from the beginning. "I have every sympathy with your situation, believe me. But if I were you I think I'd just let it drop, because if you keep on trying to see this man, there's no telling what might happen. You might infect him or cause him to suffer a setback. Now, I'm painting the blackest possible picture, the blackest possible, but if you infected this man you want to see, it's possible that he could die, just because you insisted on seeing him. You could be put on a police charge, of manslaughter or even murder."

Evan wasn't armed, but he was tongued.

"I take it you will not let me see John Austin Pighee and you will not let me talk to the person on the premises who is in charge of his case. Is that correct?"

"He's not *allowed* visitors," Evan said emphatically.

"I shall return," I said. And left.

But I didn't go as far as they expected me to. Only as far as the hospital's administration offices.

"Yes?" said the man at the desk inside the room marked "Chief Administrator." "Can I do something for you?"

"The Chief Administrator wants to see me," I said.

"Do you have an appointment?" He peered into an open appointment book.

"Better to see me now than wait until my client sues the hospital."

"J . . . Just a minute," he said, and went to an inner room.

It took about a minute.

The Chief Administrator was a small, tired woman with carefully coiffed white hairs that were being gradually lost. The voice, however, was firmly rooted in Hoosierland, efficiently clipped. "I understand you want to see me urgently."

I produced my pocket identification card, which showed that I was a private detective duly licensed by the State of Indiana in accordance with the Indiana Acts of 1961, Chapter 163.

"So, a private detective," she said matter-of-factly. She'd had dealings with Us before. "And your business?"

"I have a client who wants to visit her brother and isn't being allowed to. She's not satisfied with the reasons she's been given for her exclusion."

"Mmm," she said. "A patient here?"

I nodded.

"The patient's name?"

I gave it.

"And where is he? Which ward?"

"My client says 'the Loftus Clinic' but I've only been able to find something called 'the Loftus Pavilion.' "

"Aaah," said the Chief Administrator, and she relaxed.

"And just what is 'aaah' supposed to mean?"

"Well, Loftus Clinic is a part of the Loftus Pavilion. It's an experimental section and a patient in there might well have different restrictions than patients in the rest of the Pavilion."

"Experimental?" I asked.

She didn't answer. "The administration of the Loftus Clinic has nothing to do with me."

"I thought you were the administrative head of this hospital."

"I am," she said.

I waited a moment for an explanation, but it wasn't forthcoming. "It will be your name on the suit my client files," I said.

"An action involving me would not be to the point. Loftus Pharmaceutical Company, in exchange for the construction of a fifty-two-bed addition known as Loftus Pavilion, retains control and legal possession of a ten-bed research unit known as Loftus Clinic. The ground floor of the new wing is taken up by the Clinic and technical and reception facilities. Upper floors known as Loftus Pavilion are under my supervision, but if your client's relative is in Loftus Clinic, you must go to the company."

"It's a completely independent body?"

"We provide basic staffing, maintenance, materials, and some services. They have their laundry done by our sanitation section and may draw on our kitchen facilities. They can use specialist equipment, by arrangement, can call on some of our medical and paramedical staff for consultation. But admissions, general and specific research policy, regular medical staff, and, more important for your purposes, control of access to patients, they determine for themselves and to suit themselves."

"Including having a bouncer on the premises?"

"A bouncer?"

"A guy in a uniform who gets rid of querysome people by talking their hind legs off—but making it clear that if necessary he'd pull them off with his bare hands."

"Well," she said, "for your sort of problem, it's a separate hospital."

"Who's in charge?"

"There is a department at Loftus under the Research Administration. It's called Clinical Research."

I drove, grumbling, south. But I didn't want my poor reception at Entropist Hospital's various hands to predetermine the way I went into the Loftus Pharmaceutical Company, so I stopped for a cup of coffee and took the opportunity to reconstruct, for my notebook, my morning conversations.

Red tape is red tape is red tape, and the usual way to get through is to go door to door till you find someone with a pair of scissors. The question, save a couple of details, was how long it was going to take to find the door and then what it would take to get the inmate to exercise his fingers. I had at least got the name of Pighee's doctor: Merom.

But suppose, I thought, suppose I get no joy at Loftus. What then? Pighee's lawyer, I thought. *Habeas corpus?* Or maybe a little medical help? Second opinion?

THREE / "It's a little early for lunch, isn't it?" I asked a woman about to bite into a huge sandwich. She hesitated.

"Gee, do you think so?"

"Yeah, but don't mind me. You're too thin anyway."

"Gee, do you think so?"

"Look," I said. "I was told outside that the person in charge of the Loftus Clinic at Entropist Hospital could be found here. Is that right?"

"Mr. Dundree? Yeah, I guess he's who you want. But he's not in the office right now."

"Where can I find him?"

"Well, he's over at Research Three, but you can't get in there because it's inside the security perimeter and he isn't expecting you. Hey, unless you're somebody important, then I can probably get you through. You somebody important? You don't look important."

"I'm important," I said. I get so few opportunities.

"Well, in that case I'll write you a pass that will get you through the gate, but you'll have to sign in and out."

"Tight security, is it?"

"Pretty tight. There was some trouble about ten years ago, and

people wanted Sir Jeff to have a big mop-up; search everybody
going in and out and that sort of thing, but he wouldn't do it."

"No?"

"No, Sir Jeff feels that you've got to trust the worker to get the
best out of him."

"Except you had some trouble ten years ago. . . ."

"Yes, but Sir Jeff decided that was people from the outside. Now
we have fences and guards checking who goes in and out. I.D.s and
that kind of thing."

"Must get pretty rushed when the shifts change."

"Well, a lot of them are staggered, but the workers have two
gates of their own they go through and the guards get to know the
faces. It's strangers they worry about. And you're a stranger.
You're sure you're important?"

"I'm sure."

"Well, that's O.K., then." She held out a yellow card. "Hey, wait,
I didn't put your name on it. What's your name?"

I told her.

"O.K.," she said, and handed it to me. "Of course, if any of the
workers do get caught stealing pills or anything, it's pffft."

"Just like that?"

"Yeah. But with free medical care and free prescriptions, they'd
be crazy to do it anyway, wouldn't they?"

"Yes," I said. "Crazy."

"At least that's what Sir Jeff thinks. And it seems to work."

Loftus Pharmaceutical Company occupied a large area west of
Meridian on the south side. I had turned in to the main entrance
and found a mixture of buildings, some new and some old, clearly
marked for administration and sales. A patrolling guard *cum* parking attendant had steered me to the Clinical Research section.

He acknowledged me as I left the building carrying the yellow
card. "Going inside? Down the road, show the card to the guard
in that little building, you see?"

I walked the two hundred yards to the round brick building,
with windows on all sides like a gazebo. On its right, from where

I stood, there was a high link fence; on its left, a pivoted barrier blocked vehicular access. Beyond that, more link fence. As I crossed the road to the gate, I saw a large parking lot on the left, several hundred cars. Clearly the notion of security was strict enough that "the workers" walked in and didn't drive.

At the Security Building I was challenged by a tall guard who studied my yellow card. It seemed all right to him and after he signed me in, he asked, "Do you know your way to Research Three?"

I didn't, so he gave me instructions.

"Thanks," I said.

"You sign in and out there, too. A book just inside the front door."

"Oh. O.K."

"And check out here when you leave."

"What happens if I forget? You chop me up and feed me to Sir Jeff for breakfast?"

It was a poor remark to make; taking Sir Jeff's name in vain. The guard growled and said, "Just don't forget."

I found Research Three easily enough. The building was a two-story shoe box, of recent vintage. Most of the other non-factory buildings I'd passed had been relatively old, modernized and adapted. But the temptation to sweep the area clear and build all new had clearly been resisted at various stages.

Inside the door, alone on a small wooden table, I found the book I was supposed to sign. There was nobody there to make me do it. So I did.

The corridors on my right and left were empty. Even the walls, a kind of light marine green, were bare except for four telephones, two in each direction. At the end of each corridor were what looked like showers.

I didn't feel unclean, but I walked down to have a look. A gray steel stirrup hung from a chain. Behind it a plate read "Statutory Emergency Shower. Pull handle sharply down. Stand directly under spigot. Remove affected clothing."

Not much privacy, but you can't have everything in a statutory emergency.

For the first time since I'd entered the building, I heard human voices, which seemed to come from above me. I walked back toward the stairs; as I did, a man in a white lab coat came down them. I ran the remaining distance to him.

"Excuse me, a Mr. Dundree is supposed to be here. Do you know where I can find him?"

"I am Dr. Dundree," he said.

"I'd like a few minutes of your time," I said. "I'm a private detective and I think you can help me out."

He hesitated but then led me to the privacy of a small room nearby where he had a desk and a couple of chairs. For all the people around to overhear us, we'd have been just as private under the shower. He was a smallish man, tending to overweight. He had a round face and bright brown eyes. "You say you're a private detective."

"Yes," I said. "I'm representing a member of the family of John Austin Pighee."

"Pighee?" The name had tensed him in an instant.

"That's right."

"You're not an insurance investigator, are you?"

"No."

"I didn't think you could be," he said reflectively. "Anyway, the lab was refitted within two weeks. There's not much sign left that anything happened."

"Where did it happen?" I asked.

"Upstairs."

"This building?"

"Yes." He hesitated. "But if you're not . . . What exactly is it that you want?"

"Mr. Pighee is presently a patient in the Loftus Clinic at Entropist Hospital."

"That's right."

"Well, I work for Mr. Pighee's sister. She's been repeatedly refused permission to visit her brother. I'm trying to find out why that should be, and I'm trying to get clearance for her. Which seems, I must say, only reasonable. Can you clear that up for us? Then I won't bother you further."

He seemed displeased. "Your name is?" I told him. "You must understand, Mr. Samson, that what you ask is a medical issue, not an administrative one. I'm only the administrative head of the Loftus Clinic."

"You're a doctor, aren't you?"

He smiled condescendingly. "But a Ph.D. doctor. Not an M.D."

"Where the hell does the buck stop around this place?"

He put one hand in the pocket of the lab coat. "It's not something I can help you with."

I was getting a little angry. "Now, let's get this clear. Is there some standing administrative policy at the Loftus Clinic which excludes visitors to all patients there?"

He hesitated. "No . . . Each case is judged on its merits."

"That's something. Now, someone said the Clinic is an experimental unit, is that right?"

"Yes." He seemed to be playing with something in his pocket.

"What kind of experiments have you been doing on Pighee? I wouldn't have thought that a drug company had much interest in accident victims. No disease to treat. He was in an explosion, I believe."

"Yes, a lab explosion. Part of our experimental interest in Mr. Pighee has to do with his having suffered from a violent injury. We feel that after initial stabilization of the condition of such a patient, there is not enough known about the possible uses of chemotherapy."

"So you're trying out drugs on him?"

He ignored the question. He said, "But we are also concerned to make sure Mr. Pighee has the best possible medical treatment and chance of recovery. He is one of our own employees, after all. And if his doctor has restricted visiting, I'm sure it's in Mr. Pighee's best interests."

I said, "His doctor is called Merom, I believe."

"That's right."

"At the Clinic this morning, they said he wasn't there. Do you know where I could find him?"

"Well, Dr. Merom is in this building, I believe."

"A Loftus employee?"

"We staff the Clinic from our own research personnel."

"May I talk to him?"

"Her," he said.

"To her, then."

He sighed. "We're all very busy around here, you know."

"John Pighee is very—"

"All right, all right," he interrupted me. "I'll call her and see if she can come down." He dialed a short number on the internal phone and waited while the person answering called Dr. Merom to it. "Marcia?" he said. "This is Jay. I know you're busy, but I've got a man down here who would like to talk to you about why John Pighee isn't allowed visitors at the Clinic." He paused. "Represents a member of the family. . . . No. Sister, I think." I nodded. She must have asked a question, because he looked at me and said, "I don't think there are any ramifications. I think it's pretty straightforward."

While I waited for Dr. Merom to come down, I resolved to be as circuitous as I could.

Dundree made conversation hard, while we waited, by standing in his office doorway. We seemed to wait, quietly and uncomfortably, for quite a long time.

At last he stepped back into the room and said, "Here she is."

An enormously tall man with curly flaxen hair stepped into the office. "Where is this guy?" he said belligerently to Dundree, though I was the only other person in the room. Perhaps from his height, about six ten or eleven, it was easy to overlook people.

"It's Marcia we wanted to see, Lee," Dundree said peevishly.

The tall man didn't seem impressed, and from behind him a small woman in a dirty lab coat came into the room. She was about thirty and had long brown hair.

"This is Dr. Merom," Dundree said. "And this"—the tall man—"is Lee Seafield, a colleague of John Pighee's. We are all, naturally, interested in anything to do with John."

"Can you make it quick?" Dr. Merom asked. "I'm between test tubes."

I didn't know whether she was making a joke or not. I said, "All I'm trying to find out is why John Pighee's sister isn't allowed to visit him in the hospital."

"Because the doctor says she isn't," said Seafield sharply.

"He's been very severely injured," Dr. Merom said.

"And visitors might hurt him," said Seafield.

"We are worried about infection," Dr. Merom said. "His condition is stabilized, but even some small development could tip the balance unfavorably."

"Besides," Seafield said scornfully, "who wants to visit somebody who's in a coma?"

"John Pighee is in a coma?" I said.

"Yes," Dr. Merom said. "He's been unconscious ever since he was admitted."

"Seven months?" I asked.

"He hasn't regained consciousness since the accident. Didn't you know?"

"My client didn't tell me that," I conceded.

"If it were a matter of visitors keeping his morale up," Dundree said ingratiatingly, "helping his will to live, then the case might be different. Isn't that right, Marcia?"

I said, "What about the morale of his relatives?"

"The patient comes first," said Dr. Merom.

"The patient must come first," Dundree echoed.

Seafield stood nodding.

"What would you say Pighee's chances of recovery are?" I asked.

"That's hard to say," Dr. Merom said.

"We'll do our best," said Dundree.

"Is that all?" Dr. Merom asked. "Can I go back upstairs?"

"Anything else, Mr. Samson?"

I shrugged. "Wouldn't want to delay the progress of medical science," I said.

"Hell, come on, Marcia," Seafield said, and left. She followed him.

Dundree sat down at his desk. "I hope we've been of some help."

I said, "I'll report back to Pighee's sister and see what she has to say."

"Well, that's good," he said. "That's good!" He sounded pleased with himself.

FOUR / From Loftus Pharmaceuticals I went back to my office. In case there was a long line of discount-seeking clients stretching down the stairs and onto the street.

Or maybe one.

But there wasn't, and a call to my answering servicer revealed that my phone had taken the morning off while I was out working.

"I'm sorry I called to ask," I said.

"I wish someone had called, Mr. Samson," Dorrie, the service voice, said. "I really do."

I appreciated her concern. It added to mine. I could stretch the case of my comatose salesman to last a day, maybe, but I was close to what looked to me to be a reasonable place to end it already.

I ate a can of baked beans and counted my money.

On the way out I found a letter in the basket. Special delivery. I knew who it was from. My daughter is the only person I know who can afford special delivery.

It said she was coming to visit in a week. "My God," I said to the stairwell. "My God."

I went out the door and hesitated. The question was whether I wanted to get shouted at or not. I didn't, so I went where it was quiet, the library.

I wanted the medical shelves, and found them without belying my profession's job description. A fuzzy-haired girl in a maxi-skirt and a mini-blouse stood plumb in the middle of the section and appeared to be sorting out the entire world of medicine.

"Do you think you could help me?" I asked.

"Sure," she said, turning her face to me. The rest was not far behind, though it took awhile for it to settle into its new compass bearing.

"I need some information on treatments for victims of violent accident."

"Violent accident? You mean like car crashes?"

"Yeah, explosions."

"Mmm," she said. "I don't know. Mmm." She turned back to the shelves in stages. "There are some books with bits on various kinds of physical trauma, but it sounds like you want something pretty specialized. They don't have a whole lot here. You might try some of the recent journals. There's been work recently on that kind of thing in hospitals in North Ireland. All those soldiers and civilians getting blown up! They've had so many cases that they've been able to work out some new treatments. That's all I can think of."

"That's interesting. Thanks."

"They can probably get you some journals. If you can find one of the librarians, they'll help you."

"Aren't you a librarian?"

"Me? Heck, no," she said, and smiled. "I'm still in high school."

And reading medical books in the summer vacation, at that. "Going to be a doctor?"

"Well . . . maybe. I don't know. Couple of years ago I came in here to see if I could find any books that could help me with my hair. And I kind of got interested." She fluffed her hair up, though it hardly needed encouragement. "Isn't this just the awfullest-looking mop you've ever seen?"

"Good gracious, no," I said quickly. "I've seen much worse." On the end of long wooden handles. "Besides, it's fashionable these days, isn't it?"

"Yeah. Lucky old me," she said.

I left her, but didn't go looking for librarians. I didn't feel I had the time to root through medical magazines; I'd gambled a visit against some book having it all laid out for me. I knew in laymen's terms that Pighee was in a bad way, but I wanted more detail and authority than I could provide myself. So I went from the library to see my doctor. And get shouted at. He has a bad temper.

His wife let me slip in between patients. I explained what I wanted quickly.

"Jesus fucking Christ!" he said. And I hadn't even asked what it was a picture of. "The guy's been out cold for seven months and you want me to reconstruct his entire case history!"

"Not entire," I said. "Just whatever you can."

"The guy's 99 percent likely to be a dead man. Mentally, not physically. You'd have to have some positive sign to lower those odds."

"But he might wake up?"

"It's just conceivable. In general. The specific case obviously I don't know. Presumably his medical people could tell you."

"If they would. Look, is it usual to keep a guy like that in isolation?"

"Isolation?" he asked.

"Could visitors sitting by the bed watching him not wake up hurt him?"

He spread his hands in a gesture of disgust. "How the hell do I know?" he said. Then, "I wouldn't have thought so, if there weren't other complications."

"But—" I began.

"I just don't have time now, Al," he said exasperatedly. "I'd like to help you. God knows you need help. But I've got a waiting room out there full of bunions. Come back tomorrow morning, if you must. I can't really do anything for you until then."

I couldn't press him. A guy who'd kept for seven months would keep a day. My sense of urgency was because I didn't know whether I would still be working on him in a day.

So. I sat in my van, then decided to have another shot at the medical facets. The girl in the library had mentioned soldiers being blown up in Ireland. It occurred to me a military doctor might have more explosion medicine at his fingertips than a civilian doctor. So I drove northeast to Fort Benjamin Harrison.

Not that the place exactly has a wooden stockade around it. Turning off Aultman Avenue onto Greene Road, I thought it looked more like a college campus than a military outpost and the Army's finance center. What with the old brick buildings and the sycamores.

Alongside a cemetery I hailed a soldier jogging in sweat pants and asked him where I could find some medical personnel. He sent me to Hawley Army Hospital. "That's named after Major General Hawley, Commander of Hospitals in Europe during World War Two," he said. I was fascinated.

At the admissions desk they sent me to the adjutant, who got me together with "the Doc."

He was a sizable man whose ragged hair and unshined shoes drew even my attention. And showed how fast a visitor can get used to Army norms. The Doc wasn't tall, but his size projected forward between the flaps of his unbuttoned white coat. . . . "Captain Oak says you want a little information," he said.

I told him about John Pighee.

"You understand that we don't deal much with that sort of case here," he said, and looked rather stern.

"Sure," I said, "but I assumed that if I could find a career medical officer, he'd be more likely to have had special training in physical injuries."

"That would make sense," he said, nodding. "Wouldn't know how true it was, but it would make sense." He scratched his chin. "Your man's been unconscious for seven months, you say."

"That's right."

He shook his head, raised his eyebrows, and pursed his lips.

"What I'm wondering about is whether there is likely to be a good reason to keep people from visiting him or whether it's just an administrative convenience. Is such a patient more likely than most to be vulnerable to infections brought in from the outside?"

"Resistance to infection," the Doc said, "depends on the body's production of leukocytes, a kind of white blood cell. Is there any reason to believe that your man's capability to produce leukocytes has been reduced or inhibited?"

"Well. What would it take?"

"There are some drugs that do it. And radiation treatments often do."

"I don't know the details of how he's being treated."

"Well, I can't think of any standard treatment that would involve use of any such materials."

"He is in an experimental ward."

He frowned. "Who knows what some of these people get up to? But I must say, it doesn't sound very kosher to me. Are you sure that it is the patient getting infected that they're worried about?"

"What do you mean?"

"Well, it was a drug company lab, you say. Maybe they're worried that he's infectious, that he's going to infect the visitors."

"I hadn't thought of that."

"Well." He shrugged meaningfully. "From what you say, it's worth thinking about."

FIVE / I thought about it as I drove away. Didn't even stop to watch the baseball game on the field next to the hospital. And the more I thought about it the less I liked it.

I stopped at a drugstore for coffee and brought my notes up to date. Then I extracted a dime and a name and went to the phone in the back. The name was Walter Weston, John Pighee's lawyer. His secretary seemed disinclined to commit him to seeing me if I came right over. But I gathered he was in and before I hung up I mentioned John Pighee's name. According to Mrs. Thomas, they'd been buddies from college and I hoped that might carry some weight.

For whatever reason, I got to see Weston as soon as I walked into his firm's premises, in a relatively fashionable part of the unfashionable near eastside. It was about a quarter to four.

"A private investigator," he said when I identified myself. "So?" He was a very short and slight man, with straight black hair hanging in a shock over his forehead and almost into his eyes.

"I've been asked by Mrs. Dorothea Thomas to find out why—"

He interrupted, "Why she can't visit her brother John. She's still at that, is she?" He threw his head sideways to get the hair out of his eyes. It didn't work.

"You make me feel a bit foolish," I said. "As if it's not a real problem. It's serious enough for Mrs. Thomas."

"She collared me about it once in the spring. She caught up with me as I was leaving Mrs. Pighee and she wouldn't let me go. It started to rain, but she was very insistent."

"Well?"

"I don't know what the hell she's bothered about. Poor John is in a coma; there's nothing she could do for him."

"She's entitled to be interested," I said. "I went to the Loftus Clinic this morning myself, and the reception I got was hardly reassuring."

"Really?"

"A no-help receptionist and a resident bouncer. Why can't they say 'Sorry, doctor's orders' and smile sympathetically as a consolation prize?"

"What do you want me to do about it?"

"All right," I said. "You were a friend of John Pighee's?"

"I still am."

"What exactly happened to him?"

He frowned. "What do you mean?"

"Pighee was—is—a salesman. What was he doing in a research building, getting blown up?"

"I don't know, exactly," he said carefully, but not as if it concerned him.

"You were—are—his lawyer?"

"And his wife's lawyer. And his milkman's lawyer. Yes."

"And though he's in a violent accident, you don't know exactly what happened to him?"

Weston took a deep breath and said, "You don't know John."

I couldn't argue.

"John was"—he smiled, correcting himself—"is a man with a great deal of drive. Personal ambition. He studied chemistry in college. Did you know that?"

"No."

"He had been at Loftus for five years. He took the job in the sales department because he couldn't get a job on the science side and because he was more interested in getting on in life than in science."

"But you handled the legal side of what happened?"

He hesitated, choosing careful words. "I certainly handled Mrs.

Pighee's side of the compensation arrangement."

"Compensation? All done before you know whether the guy is going to live or die?"

"Compensation for injury, with a variety of contingency clauses."

"But you negotiated for the Pighees with the insurance company?"

"No. I am very close to the limit of what I feel I can tell you without Mrs. Pighee's expressed wish that I go farther, but I said that I 'handled Mrs. Pighee's side of the compensation arrangement.' No insurance company was involved."

"No insurance? I don't understand. There must have been some kind of insurance connection."

"How Loftus deals, ultimately, with its liabilities is not my problem."

"But that will mean that there was no insurance investigation."

"As I say . . ."

"But you never saw the result of any insurance investigation?"

"Mr. Samson. The terms offered, the financial details on all contingencies have been accepted. They are certainly adequate. All things considered. But it is hardly up to me to take you through the relevant considerations. These matters are certainly none of your business."

He cooled me a little bit. I said, "O.K., but can you tell me in words of two syllables or less why his sister can't get a closer look at John Pighee if that's her pleasure?"

"Because the right of access is completely in the hands of the Loftus Pharmaceutical Company, and because, presumably, their medical people think it's better for John not to have visitors. In any case, Mrs. Pighee has agreed to leave all medical questions in their hands. So you must leave it to them. It's not a legal question." He made it clear that he was at the end of his willingness to talk to me.

"Only one more question," I said. "You say you don't know what John Pighee was doing when the accident happened. Is it possible that he became infected in the incident—presumably with something they were working on in the lab—and that he is still infectious and that is the reason he is not being allowed visitors?"

For the first time, Weston seemed to have to think slightly about something. "It's conceivable," he said coolly.

"But you're not concerned?"

"You've had your one question," he said. "But if it were so, it would be a pretty good reason not to allow visitors, wouldn't it?"

SIX / "A week!" my mother said. "What kind of warning is a week?"

"Don't ask me," I said.

"I'm asking you." Then she nodded knowingly. "You must have told them, spelled it out for them, that short notice was all right. You did that, didn't you?"

Mom runs a luncheonette called Bud's Dugout, on Virginia Avenue. Southeast Indianapolis, not too far out of the way on the trip from Walter Weston to Beech Grove and my client. It seemed only sonly to let her know that Marianne, my daughter, was due to arrive. Not her only grandchild, but the one least seen.

"How long is she coming for?"

"I don't know," I said. "She didn't say."

"Can't be for very long," Mom mused. "She must have to start school in September."

"How do we know when they start school in Switzerland? All I know is that this year they're spending the summer in some fishing village on the Connecticut coast. And that she's coming in a week."

"A fishing village," said Mom. "A child in a fishing village! Oh, dear."

"I'll give you the address and you can write them direct. For some reason they're going to let me see her, and I'm not going to put her off just because she doesn't give me a lot of notice."

Mom nodded. "You're a good son, Albert," she said, meaning to say good father. How true either was . . . But I gave her the benefit of the doubt.

"Will you stay for dinner?"

"I've got to go to Beech Grove. I'm working."

She was quiet for a moment. "I saw your ad in the paper."

"Yeah?"

"Humiliating," she said.

I let it pass.

"But at least you're in work now," she said.

"Yeah."

"Well, that's the main thing."

I didn't tell her that I was odds on to be out of work before I returned home. Mothers need to be protected from that sort of thing.

It was about 5:30 when I parked in front of the Pighees' house in Beech Grove. I got out and took one step toward the driveway and Mrs. Thomas's immobile home. But I stopped. Then turned, for the hell of it, toward the house.

I rang the bell twice. I didn't hear anything. I rang again and was about to leave when a woman inside said, "Is somebody there?"

"Yes," I called.

"I'm not expecting anybody," she said. But began to unlock the door.

Linn Pighee was a woman in her late twenties who balanced a glass with practiced ease. She had long black hair, glassy brown eyes, and she admitted strangers to her house.

"You don't mind if we don't find out what you want in the living room, do you?" she asked. "It's cooler on the screened porch."

I followed her to the porch, where she filled the hollow in the upholstery of a chaise next to a portable bar. "Make yourself comfortable," she said, but she didn't offer any means beyond a chair.

"I've had a terrible day," she said. "I've felt just so weak! I can't seem to do anything."

"I'm sorry," I said.

She laughed. She sipped from her glass but contorted her face as if what she drank didn't taste very good. "What's your day been like?"

"Like trying to pry the lid off a can of worms with my fingers,"

I said. "I can get it up high enough to see the worms are in there. But I don't have a hope without an opener."

"Gee, that's too bad." She projected surprisingly genuine concern. "Can I do anything for you?"

"You can," I said, "but probably you won't."

She laughed again, began to drink, but took an ice cube instead and chewed it up. "The ambitious, positive, confident type," she said.

"I'm rarely accused of an overweening ambition," I said.

"That's something in your favor," she said. "I don't like ambitious people." She exhaled sharply. "Well, what do you want?"

"That you could see your way clear to telling me about the arrangements you have with Loftus Pharmaceuticals concerning your husband."

She did a double take. "Interested in John, are you?" she said, and drank an inch. "I suppose I should ask what business John is of yours."

"I would, in your place."

"There's hardly room for two in my place." She twisted on the chaise to get a pack of cigarettes from behind the bottles on the bar. She took one, lit it, sucked deeply and contentedly, then stubbed it out. She got comfortable in the chaise again. "John had an accident, I suppose you know."

I nodded.

"Something serious. What happened, there was some kind of explosion or . . . something. Anyway, he probably would have died right then, but it happened on company premises and they rushed him to their fancy place at the hospital. Anyway, John is still alive and because he fits into their research or something, they foot all the medical bills, they pay me his salary, and if he dies because of the accident they give me some kind of compensation. It's all gone through the lawyer and he says it's the way John wants it and it's O.K. Nobody trying to screw me financially. So no complaint about the company, if that's what you're interested in."

"How often do you visit him?" I asked, trying to look dull.

"Oh, I don't bother. I haven't been feeling very well, and he's out cold, so what's the point?"

"It must have been a very disturbing experience for you," I said.

"I'd have thought I'd get over it by now. Got used to it. But I feel so lousy and weak. I feel I'm missing being alive. I wouldn't have thought I'd have cared that much. But I suppose I won't feel right again until John has either died or got better."

"May I ask how long you've been married?"

"Since I was seventeen. I was twenty-eight last week."

"Congratulations."

"Thanks," she said, and drank.

"I've got a birthday coming up myself," I said.

"How old? Fifty?"

"Forty-one."

"You must work too hard."

I smiled. We shared the pause. It was time for me to take what I had learned and leave or to volunteer a little something. I liked her. I volunteered.

"I'm a private detective," I said.

"Pull the other one."

"Your sister-in-law, Mrs. Thomas, hired me to find out why she's not allowed to visit her brother. Is there any reason that you know of?"

"Nope," she said. "Hired a detective, did she? Trust her."

"You're going to hurt my feelings in a minute."

"I wouldn't have said your feelings could feel pain."

"You really have hurt my feelings now," I said.

"Sorry," she said without sorrow. "And how do you like my sister-in-law?"

"I hardly know her. She seems to have a reasonable question about this visiting thing. But in her place I think I might have tried more direct methods than hiring me."

"You're going to hurt your own feelings next."

I nodded.

"She's not a very direct person, Dorothea Thomas. Not like me."

I waited.

"And she adores that damn brother of hers. Also not like me."

"And she thinks you should?"

"She thinks that because John got himself hurt I should get

myself a black veil and camp in the hospital corridor outside his door. Not my style."

"On the other hand, if you did fawn over him she'd think you were competing with her, trying to out-adore her?"

"My detective friend, you've put yourself exactly on the right wavelength. I think I'd better know your name."

"Albert Samson."

"And do you make a girl tingle when you kiss her, Albert?"

"Only one girl in ten."

"Lucky girl," she said, and mused. I mused, too. "I'm not always like this," she said. "At least I wasn't."

"And what kind of person is John Austin Pighee? Seventeen is pretty young for a girl to get swept off her feet and still be around eleven years later."

"He's the kind of man who's about to go to college and knocks up a girl with one more year of high school. He marries her and then he goes to college anyway, because he's talked his sister into helping with money and she comes to live with them."

"I didn't realize you had children," I said.

"Not the type, huh?"

"That's not what I meant. I hadn't heard about any children."

"Well, I don't have any children now, so it doesn't matter."

"Don't say it doesn't matter," I said. Trying to offer something for having turned the conversation to the subject.

"Why not?"

"Because next week I'm going to be seeing my only kid for the first time in twelve years. You don't want to put me off and make me write to tell her not to come, do you?"

"Daughter?"

"Yeah."

"How old?"

"You know," I said, "I don't know exactly without working it out. Late teens."

But she wasn't quite listening to my confessions. She said, "That's nice. Twelve years is a long time."

"I know."

"I had twin girls."

I nodded to encourage her, but didn't speak.

"Hell," she said, finishing her drink. "They were killed in a car crash five years ago."

"Both of them?"

"Yeah. Dinny outright. Simmy hung on for about two weeks before she went. She"—pointedly—"didn't regain consciousness. Just as well, I suppose. If they had to go, they went together. Exit the old life, enter the new."

"You seem to have had much more than your share of bad luck, Mrs. Pighee."

"Call me Linn," she said. "Please." Urgently.

"Linn," I said.

"Luck? What's luck? You make your own luck, John says. Said. I just wish I felt better."

A bell rang in the distance.

"I thought it was about time," she said, and rose. I followed her to the front door, stood behind her as she opened it.

Outside, holding a brown paper bag, was a tall thin teen-ager. "Hi, Linn," he said. And saw me. "Hi, you, too."

"Hi," I said.

"I brought your prescription, Linn," he said, and pushed the bag forward.

She took it. "Dougie, this is Mr. Albert. He's a private detective. Mr. Albert, this here is Dougie and he is one of Beech Grove's very best basketball players. He works at a liquor store in the summer and we have a little joke about"—she rattled the bag—"my medicine." She stepped to one side, leaning against the open door, and pushed me with her free hand. "Do come back again to talk some more. Please. Sometime soon."

I yielded to the pressure and walked out the door. It closed behind me. Dougie and I stood looking at each other.

"Gee, Mr. Albert," Dougie said, "are you really a private detective?"

I turned to the porch steps. "Are you really a basketball player?"

He caught up with me. "Don't I look like one?"

I didn't answer. He walked out to the road, then looked around as if he'd misplaced me.

But I didn't go to the road. I walked around the side of the house to call on my client.

SEVEN / Mrs. Thomas met me at the corner of the garage. "You've been to see *her*, haven't you?"

"Mrs. Pighee? Yes."

"Why?"

"I thought she might be able to help—"

"She wouldn't help *me* if—if—" Apparently there were no circumstances fantastic enough to contemplate Linn Pighee helping her sister-in-law.

"I don't know about that," I said. "But she signed an agreement giving the doctors control over decisions like visiting. I hoped she'd let me see it or at least tell me about it."

"And did she?"

"No."

"She doesn't care whether John lives or dies."

"That wasn't the impression she gave me," I said. Though I wasn't sure whether I was lying.

"Impressions! Impressions!" said Mrs. Thomas. "I *know* her."

"Much better than I do," I said. "I want to give you a rundown on what I've done today, so you can decide whether you want me to go on."

She frowned. "You're planning to stop?"

"That's up to you."

She led me into her home and we sat where we had before.

"I've asked a number of people questions, but I haven't gotten very far toward getting you in to see your brother."

"I don't expect things to happen fast," she said. "Nothing ever does."

"Most people expect results yesterday. I appreciate your attitude."

She didn't reply.

"Access to your brother's bedside is governed by the company's doctors because he's in the company's experimental section of the hospital."

"*I* told you that," she said sharply.

"You told me where he was. You didn't tell me that legal control rests with the company rather than the hospital administration."

She didn't respond.

"Nor did you tell me he'd been in a coma for seven months."

"That doesn't matter to me."

"But it means I can't go to his doctors and say he needs his morale kept up."

"But he might wake up. I can't bear to think of him waking up with nobody there. And you can be sure *she* isn't going to be."

"There is a substantial chance that he won't wake up, Mrs. Thomas."

"Yes, he will," she said simply.

"But his doctor's judgment is the one that seems to matter, and at the moment she is very negative about visitors."

"You mean . . . there's nothing you can do?"

"That's not what I mean," I said in measured tones.

"Well?" A leathery frown.

"I think there are two ways to go. If your sister-in-law would cooperate, we may be able to bring pressure through her and the legal arrangement she's made with the company. . . ."

Frown still there.

"Or we may be able to cause enough trouble for them that it would be easier to let you visit than to keep refusing."

"Trouble?" she asked. It interested her.

"Why shouldn't your brother have visitors?" I asked her rhetorically. "Either he picked up some contagious disease in the explosion or they're treating him with experimental drugs which lower his resistance to infection brought in from outside."

She looked slow but attentive.

"Either way, they haven't told you the real reason you're being kept from him. We could threaten to go to the press."

"The press? You mean call in reporters and all that?"

"I don't think we'd actually have to do it," I said. "But if we threatened to, the least it would do would be to get better reasons from them why John isn't allowed visitors."

She considered it. She liked it.

"That's the point about this whole business, isn't it, Mrs. Thomas? It seems funny that they should care whether you sat by his bedside or not. I asked a couple of doctors today, and they say it's not standard practice."

"Well," she said, "do it."

"It will stir them up. And I don't think they'd pay much attention to you without some incentive."

"You do what you think is best," she said.

"Do you mind answering some other questions for me?"

"What questions?"

"I must say, I don't understand what your brother was doing in a research laboratory."

"Oh, he worked there."

"He worked there? I thought you told me he was a salesman."

"He is. Primarily a salesman. I mean that's what he was hired to do. But a couple of years ago he started doing some extra work in the labs. That was his subject in college, chemistry. And when the chance to do some chemistry work came along he jumped at it. Even though it did mean working more hours, and a lot of nights. I know because he used to stop in and see me after he got back from work, or if he had to go in at night, before he went. He was very regular."

"I didn't know anything about this, Mrs. Thomas."

"He *is* a salesman. That's the department he works for and he does selling work, too. Very successfully. He is a very talented boy, my brother. He can do just about anything he has a mind to do."

"It sounds as if he can," I said. "So your brother did some kind of work in a lab. Do you know what kind?"

"Not exactly. Not really at all. No," she said, looking worried.

"Well," I said, and sat back. As far as the compact seating would allow.

"He's a wonderful boy," she said. "He would want me there if I could be."

I nodded.

Then she said, "I don't see any reason why I shouldn't sit by John's bedside if I want to. Do you?" And she managed a few tears.

I waited till she dried up before I left.

EIGHT / It was a few minutes short of seven when I rolled into my parking space in the lot around the corner from my office. My office of the moment. My parking place of the moment. The lot was in the same area as my building, so it was due to be built on, too.

As I climbed my stairs, I noticed my door wasn't quite closed. It's a tricky fit because it came from the last office I had that got torn down. I kept it for sentimental reasons. The writing on the glass reads "Albert Samson, Private Investigator. Walk Right In."

Someone apparently had.

Advertising pulls them in.

As I opened the door, I saw a girl sitting behind my desk. Late teens, with slightly reddish-brown hair, dark brown eyes, and freckles. She looked vaguely familiar. I took two steps inside and stumbled over a knapsack that I hadn't left in the middle of the floor.

I hadn't left it anywhere; it wasn't mine.

"This yours, Miss?"

She nodded. Then she opened the middle drawer of my desk. "Hey, there's nothing in here," she said. "Why don't you keep anything in it?"

"Because when I'm out working I leave the office open. To offer a moment's rest for strays and waifs and the occasional client. Which might you be?"

She smiled at me until she saw that I wasn't smiling. "I don't think I'm any of those categories. Do you?"

"Look here, young lady, it's hot. I've had a hard day—"

She stood up with a sense of urgency. "Don't you really recognize me?"

I frowned. She did look . . .

"Daddy!" she said.

"Oh, my God," I said. It takes a wise father to know his own child.

"I recognized *you!* And all I've had is a picture from more than twelve years ago."

"My God," I said. "My God."

After a little hugging I took her from the austerity of my office to the austerity of my living quarters. "I just got a letter today," I said. "It said—"

"I was coming in a week. But I only know you from letters and what Mummy's said about you. And I was worried that you might get all nervous about me coming. So I decided to come early because I wanted you to be relaxed about me and not worry."

"Relaxed is not quite how I'd describe myself."

"Well, sit down. You must have had a hard day to have been working until seven. Let me get you a beer. I'll have one, too."

"You're bigger than the last time I saw you," I said. Then I sat down.

She went to the refrigerator; we split the can of beer she found there.

"How—?" I began.

"Since four-forty-five. I've been waiting here for you since five-thirty. I stopped and had a hamburger in case you didn't have enough food for me."

"You're very organized," I said.

"Just like Mummy, everybody says," she said. "But I don't think that's all bad, do you?"

"No, my dear Marianne, I don't."

"And nobody calls me Marianne any more."

"They don't?"

"No. They call me Sam, from Samson, though my legal name is Meir. So you call me Sam, too, won't you?"

"My pleasure."

"Good."

"Sam?"

"Yes, Daddy?"

"How old are you?"

"Why?"

"I just wondered."

"Eighteen next birthday."

"My God," I said. "My God."

I left her reading while I took a shower. Walking carefully from shower to bedroom in order to protect her from the worst of the holes in my bathrobe. She was only a child, after all.

"It's good to have you here, Sam," I said after I got dressed. "It's terrific."

"You don't mind my coming earlier than you expected?"

"I'm not about to close my eyes and pretend you aren't here yet. Look, I'll call your grandmother so she can get a bed ready and then we'll go out to see her."

"No," she said.

"What do you mean, no?"

"I came to stay with you. I'm going to sleep here. I brought a sleeping bag and the most expensive air mattress that Trevor's money could buy. You carry on your life as usual and I'll just fit in where it's convenient. You sleep in your room, and I'll be happy right here."

"I have an instinct for tolerance," I said, "but your grandmother won't like it."

"Then she'll have to lump it. Mummy says I'm as stubborn as she is."

Poor Trevor, I thought. Having just one like that around was more than I could handle. But I remained outwardly mute.

"And I don't want you losing work or anything silly like that. Not because of me. I don't want to go sightseeing or anything. I didn't come here to see boring old Indianapolis. I came to see you. I've got books to read when there's nothing else to do. And I'm not to be a financial burden on you. I've got bags of money. Not just my own, either, because Trevor gave me a lot for this trip."

"What can I say?"

"Nothing about those things."
So I didn't.

We got back from seeing my mother at about eleven. Before we turned in, Sam said, "Are you working on a case now?"

I thought for a moment. "Yeah, I guess I am."

"Can I sort of help, maybe? Keep track of things as you work on it, or something like that."

"Sure you want to?"

"Oh, yes. You have no idea how much cachet you've given me at Madame Graumier's. The school I go to, in Bern."

"I know the school. I write letters there."

"But there isn't another girl who has one of her fathers that's a private detective. That *is* what you really are, isn't it? I mean you still are."

"I still are," I said.

"That's fantastic. Everybody else's fathers are things like Trevor —banking and business and show biz and things. I'm considered ever so lucky."

"You'll learn," I said.

"Oh, super."

"But I'll have to think about how much I can tell you about cases I work on."

Her face fell.

"I'm constrained by the law. You're not my client. You're not the police. I'll have to think about it."

"I'm very discreet."

"I'll have to think about it."

She frowned at me, but that's fatherhood for you.

NINE / Sam woke me up early by inconsiderately turning pages loudly as she read. I punished her by sending her out to get some 1″ × 1″ pictures taken.

"But what for?" she asked.

"Don't ask," I said.

I used the time she was away to wake up.

And to have some breakfast. And to dig out some dusty forms. And look over the notes I'd made from my conversation with John Austin Pighee's wife and sister. It was just as well I'd suggested more things I could do for Mrs. Thomas. For Sam's sake as much as mine. Hard to give her the false flavor of private detection that she wanted by the two of us sitting around the office.

I heard running footsteps at ten to ten. Sam threw herself at the door and bounced off. Then carefully lifted and pushed, which was what it took to open it.

"Daddy, what are they for?" she asked.

Instead of answering, I got out my ink pad and took her fingerprints.

"Why are you doing this?"

"We fingerprint all strangers in Indianapolis," I said.

"Don't be exasperating! Mummy said you were exasperating and I said you wouldn't be with me, so don't be."

"You want to be able to hear about the cases I work on?"

"Yes."

"And to help on them?"

"Of course. Yes."

"Well, I can only let you help me if you are an employee."

"An employee?"

"And for you to become an employee, I've got to send the state police photographs and a full set of your fingerprints."

"You do?"

"And they have to be identified by a code number. The number of your current Indiana driving license, if you have one. Do you have one?"

"How could I? I've never been to Indiana before."

"Well, we'll have to think of another number, then—007? Well, I'll work out something. I'll send this off this morning, marked 'urgent.' Then we'll get back a card for you. It will say 'Indiana Private Detective Identification Card' on it, and it will have the name of your employer, a picture, and the thumbprint of your right hand."

"Oh, wow!"

"There are only a few snags."

Her face showed disappointment. "Snags? Oh, I was afraid it was too good to be true. Is it that I'm not old enough?"

"No, there's no age limit. I can hire anybody I need, but if they do bad things it's me that loses my license. You'll have to have 'good conduct' while you're in my employ."

"O.K.!"

"And you won't be able to tell anybody anything you learn about people as a result of your employment. Only our client and the police, if it involves a criminal matter."

"A criminal matter?" Eyes bright.

"Agreed?"

"Oh, yes!"

"Let's get this form filled in." And there it was. I was father of the year.

I'd never had an employee before, though they send you the forms every two years when the license comes up for renewal.

"Well," I said when the form was completed, checks for fees enclosed. "I'm off."

"Off?"

"You're not an employee yet."

"But . . ."

"I've got to try to see some people before lunch. I'll stop back and try to fill you in on things when I get a chance. Bye."

End of reign for father of the year. Years get shorter all the time.

I drove to Loftus Pharmaceuticals but instead of looking for space in front of an administration building, I drove to the main gate. I was approached outside the barrier by the same guard I'd identified myself to about the same time the previous morning. He seemed to recognize me but asked me for my pass.

"I don't have one," I said. "I want to see the man in charge of the company's salesmen. I need some information about one of them."

"Sales Staff Supervisor?"

"Sounds like it."

"He isn't expecting you?"

"No." I showed him my I.D. "I want to see him about one of his salesmen, who had an accident."

"I'll call him for you," he said. "You want to park over there?"

I nodded and parked.

When I got back, the guard had cleared my way in. "Do you know where to find him?"

"I don't even know his name."

"Mr. Joseph Bartonio," he said, and gave me directions.

Bartonio was certainly a sales administrator rather than a salesman. His office was not a showy one; he was comfortingly unkempt, a middle-aged man whose face was dark, creased, and old.

"I'm investigating the accident which John Austin Pighee was involved in. I want to know what one of your salesmen was doing working in a research lab and getting himself blown up."

"Insurance people at last," he said. "You took your time." He picked up a pencil and started doodling while I decided whether to unclarify his mind. Before I decided, he said, "It shocked hell out of me to hear that John had been hurt. Awful."

This caught me by surprise; it was the first expression of sympathy for the man that I'd heard from anybody but his sister.

"It really shook me," Bartonio said, "because, see, I was responsible for him being there in the first place."

"I don't understand, Mr. Bartonio. . . ."

"Call me Joe. I get uncomfortable any more when people call me anything but Joe."

"I don't understand how you were responsible for John Pighee being in the lab."

"I been around," he said. "I know when a guy is restless. John was a good salesman. Crack. Ace. But I knew he didn't want to go all the way that route. I been here a long time. Not quite as long as Sir Jeff . . . but a guy like John who's good, you either find a slot he really likes or he moves out to somebody else. There are guys came into this company after me that make more money now and have more responsibility. But I'm good at handling people. I'm good at knowing my salesmen."

"I'm sure you are."

"Now, fifteen years ago, twenty years ago, he'd have gone straight into some kind of management. Ten, twelve years ago, he would have gone into the research labs and worked from there. But five years ago, when John came along to us, science majors were a dime a dozen. If he wanted to get his Ph.D., then maybe he'd get considered. But a guy like John doesn't have time for that kind of thing. So a couple years out of college getting the facts of life, and he walks in here, to sales. Now, a drug salesman with his kind of scientific knowledge, with his kind of go—now, there is a drug salesman."

"I can see how it would help," I said.

"Most of my guys, they got to sell to the nonscientific side of people who buy drugs. Institutions, doctors, so on. John could do that but he could also sell to their heads. You don't get them often that can go both ways. I may not be class myself, but I can tell class."

"Which doesn't tell me much about how he happened to be working in the labs."

"Part time. He was splitting his time. Part here, part there."

"Even part time."

"I saw he was getting restless. I talked to a friend of mine in the company, guy who knows about personnel, what makes guys tick. We pulled a few strings. Got him on a project."

"A friend? At the lab? Dr. Dundree?"

Bartonio raised an eyebrow. "Higher than Jay Dundree. I don't know what Dundree thought about it, but my guy has the clout to make him like it."

"But what kind of work was Pighee doing?"

"I don't know. I'm not technical, see. I can add and subtract, but ask me what I'm selling and I couldn't tell you more than what it says on the label and the guff with the instructions."

"How high up is your friend?"

He hesitated. "You ask that like I was doing something bad. I tell a guy, and he places a guy for the good of the guy and the good of the company. That can't be bad."

"I need to know what Pighee was working on. I need to know who to go to. Who is your friend?"

"Aw, hell," Joe said, "Henry Rush. P. Henry Rush."

"What exactly is P. Henry Rush?"

"Just a director, that's all."

"A good friend?"

"Just a guy on the board I know is interested in helping the company develop the potential of the people who work for it."

"Well," I said, "I appreciate your help."

"I'm just surprised it's taken you guys so long to get here."

"I don't want to leave you under a misapprehension," I said. "I'm not from an insurance company and I never said I was."

"No? Who are you, then?"

"I'm a private detective and I'm working for John Pighee's sister. She wants to know more about what happened to him."

"Yeah? Oh, well. I haven't told you anything I couldn't have told a dozen guys, one way or another."

"But you haven't?"

"Nobody's asked. I guess they already got all the answers."

TEN / I left Joe Bartonio's office and walked around the Loftus site for a few minutes. The corporate area was larger than was apparent from the main gate. Off to the south there were three large production areas, flat buildings that looked like modular units for a giant airport. Widen the connecting roads and they'd be ready to land the Concorde. Between them trucks prowled, getting loaded to disperse medicine to the waiting world. There was a lot of activity.

I worked my way to the only other Loftus building inside the perimeter that I knew, Research Three. I was looking for Dundree. I was going to threaten him.

I signed in again at the table by the entrance door. The halls were as devoid of human life as they'd been the last time I'd been there. The statutory showers at the end of each corridor were friendly by comparison.

I checked the office where I'd talked to Dundree, Dr. Merom, and Lee Seafield the day before, but no one was there. I felt free to explore. Dundree said that Pighee's accident had taken place upstairs, so up the stairs I went.

There was still nobody in the halls, but at least I heard a few voices and the hums of some engines. I was about to face up to the decision of right or left when a young woman burst from a door next to the stairwell and nearly ran into me.

"Oh, God," she said. "Sorry." She wore a white lab jacket and her hair was held close to her head by a net.

"Is this place always so empty?" I asked. "You're the first person I've run into in the corridors in days."

She seemed surprised by the question. Then said, "Well, I guess not many people actually work in the building. Most of it is routine quality testing—this side of this floor and all downstairs—and a lot of that is done with machines."

"But the place doesn't smell," I said. "Isn't it supposed to?"

"Is it?"

"Well, a research lab and all that?"

"Yeah," she said, "I know what you mean, but the ventilation here is very good."

"Oh," I said. "Do you know whether Dr. Dundree is in the building?"

"I don't think so. Mornings he's usually in the admin office, outside the gate. Did you try there?"

I shook my head. "He said that in one of these labs there was an explosion several months ago. Is that right?"

"Why, yes," she said. "In January. One of our people was hurt."

"John Pighee. Did you know him?"

"No. He was only here part time. And he kept to himself."

"You're what?"

"A technician," she said. "I've been here nearly three years, and then they brought in someone from the outside to work on Store-room."

"Storeroom?"

"Oh, that's what's on the door. The lab they had that accident in. It was converted a long time ago and they've been running some hush-hush kind of research in there for years. But we call it Operation Storeroom. That's it." She pointed to a door halfway down the hall on our left.

"Can I have a look?"

She laughed. "Lee's in there now. And he doesn't let anybody in. None of them do."

"That's Lee Seafield? The tall guy with—"

"The curly corn-silk hair, yeah. We think he bleaches it, but no one's ever spotted the roots."

"How many people work on this big project?" I asked.

"Lee, Marcia—that's Dr. Merom—and Dr. Dundree's been filling in since Mr. Pighee's accident."

"No one else? No technicians?"

"Nope. Oh, except that Lee is a technician, but he's been here for years. They say he's not very good at taking tests, or he'd have got his doctorate. He's smart enough."

"You weren't here when Mr. Pighee had his accident, were you?"

"No. But Ray was."

"Ray?"

"Ray McGonigle. He's another technician. He was the first one there."

"Is he around?"

"He was, but he's gone to lunch, I think."

"Already?"

"We're nursing some cultures and one of us has to be with them all the time. He went early. I go when he gets back. It'll be nearly an hour. He only just left."

"Do you know where he went? Is there someplace I can catch him eating lunch?"

"He went off the premises. He had a couple of records to buy, he said. He doesn't really like it here and he goes off at lunchtime a lot."

"Do you like it?"

"It's better for me, because I'm not that ambitious. Down under, Ray is. But things are just so competitive there's hardly room to turn around unless you're some kind of genius or something."

"Is Ray some kind of genius?"

"Well, he's black," she said. "And when he—"

A shout pierced our conversation: "Sonia!"

"Oh, God. My cultures!" She ran down the hall toward a doorway through which an angry Dr. Merom had put her head. I turned away discreetly, and heard the door close behind the errant technician.

I was alone in the corridors again.

I left the building and went back to the Security Building at the main entrance, where I signed out. Then I walked to the Clinical Research administration office.

Dr. Jay Dundree's secretary wasn't eating when I walked into her office. Which made a change from the day before. "You're still too thin," I said.

"What? Oh."

"Yeah, it's me again. Is Dr. Dundree here?"

"He's in there," she said, "but I don't know if he'll see you."

I gave her my card, wrote John Pighee's name on the back. "Give it to him and see."

She left me and I thought about what I'd come to do.

The secretary was smiling when she came back. "He'll see you now," she said.

"I told you I was important."

"Yeah. I'm impressed."

I went to see Dundree.

In his own office he abandoned the lab jacket in favor of a self-important three-piece item. He was standing when I came in, but not very cheerful. "I thought we'd settled this business yesterday," he said.

"I told you I'd report back to my client."

"Who is?"

"Pighee's sister." He nodded slowly and sat down. I sat and faced him. "And she's not very satisfied."

"But why not?"

"We've consulted some medical people of our own. We can find no medical reason, based on what you tell us of Pighee's condition, for the exclusion of visitors. Even if they would become bored sitting around watching him not wake up. In our opinion that means your clinic's exclusion of visitors can mean one of two things."

"Which are?"

"Either you are excluding visitors arbitrarily and for no compelling reasons . . ."

"Yes?"

"Or there is some reason for excluding visitors which you haven't told us. Either way, we're not going to let it drop."

"What exactly do you intend to do?"

"Go to the press and simultaneously file a writ of *habeas corpus.*"

"What!" The idea astounded him.

I didn't repeat it. He'd heard well enough.

"This seems," he said, at length, "to be getting blown out of all proportion."

"Like John Pighee did," I said.

"Well, an unfortunate choice of words. But you—your client seems to be getting things out of balance. It can't be an easy time or situation for her, and let me say that we at Loftus deeply regret any injury that occurs on our premises or to our personnel at any time. The more so an injury which seems to be so severe as this one."

"You'll let her visit him?"

He threw up his hands. "That," he said, "is not up to me. That's what we dealt with yesterday."

"You're not going to try to tell me that you have no influence over Dr. Merom's decision whether to allow visitors at John Pighee's bedside, are you? If you wanted to exert some influence, you perfectly well could."

"Well," he said, "I suppose I could have a word with Dr. Merom."

"If you don't want to see Loftus's name in the papers, please do."

"But the decision, the final decision, must be hers."

"See you in court," I said mildly.

"It strikes me that suggestion is rather excessive."

"From your point of view, but not necessarily from Pighee's sister's."

"I'll have a word with Dr. Merom today," he said. "And if she should reconsider her position because of the strong feeling of Mr. Pighee's sister, I'll . . ." He hesitated. "Would you give me his sister's name and address, so that on behalf of the company I could contact her direct? As a company, we like to think that we make the best decisions for our people, but when we do make a mistake, we like to admit it personally. If that's the way it works out, we will of course fully acknowledge your part in bringing the situation to our notice."

I gave him Mrs. Thomas's name and address. Since he could have got it with a phone call to Linn Pighee.

After I left Dundree's building, I hesitated before going to the lot to pick up my panel truck. Then had a look around for a building with P. Henry Rush's name on it. I ended up asking and got directed to the secretary who controlled access to directorial space. She eyed me coldly. "No appointment?"

"No. But it's about a man named Pighee, who had an accident on company premises."

She called Rush's secretary for me. "I'm sorry," she said. "Mr. Rush is out of the state at the moment and not available."

I left my card, John Pighee's name written on the back. She swore she'd pass it on to Rush's secretary at the earliest possible opportunity.

ELEVEN / "There weren't any phone calls, Daddy, and nobody came to the office. Is Friday morning usually like that? Businesswise."

"Yes," I said. "It usually is."

"I spent the morning getting settled in," Sam said, "but

I didn't really expect it to be as . . . quiet."

"Bored, were you?"

"Well, a little. But it may be bus lag."

"It's a boring business," I said.

"At least you were out. I just hung around here and cleared things up. And I found this." She pushed forward my tin money box. "Unlocked! And with nine hundred and thirty-eight dollars in it!"

"Oh." I pretended worry. "Has someone taken the picture?" I looked. My woman was still all there.

She raised her eyebrows and put it back on the desk where I'd left it.

"You don't have to stay in all the time, you know."

"You mean now I'm an employee I can come along with you?"

"Well, that's not exactly what I meant. I have an answering service. You don't have to stay in and worry about messages and that kind of thing. As long as the inner door is locked. You can go out, shopping, or whatever you want to do."

"But I can come with you?"

"Sometimes. It depends."

"What did you do this morning?"

"I gave a drug company executive a lesson in motivational technique."

"You what?"

"I had a problem, on behalf of a client, which he could solve if he wanted to. So my job stopped being to solve the problem; it became making him want to solve it."

"And did you?"

"I think so. I tried to suggest it would be more trouble for him if he didn't do what we wanted than if he made the effort and did."

"And he did?"

"He will."

"And how would you have bothered him?"

"I threatened him with a nuisance lawsuit and with going to the papers."

"That sounds great!"

"So now he has a word with somebody, and everything is all right."

"Is that what I should learn first about being a private detective? Keep after people to bother them?"

"Well," I said. "Well, it comes up pretty often."

"What should I learn first, Daddy?"

"If there was any one thing," I said, "I think it would be that you should check your facts. If you have any way of confirming things people tell you, do it. Before you draw any kind of conclusion."

"Oh," she said. "Well, now you tell me how you put it all into practice on the case you're working on."

"Doesn't your mother tell you to say 'please'?"

"Do all your employees have to say 'please'?"

"Yes." Never having had one before.

"Please."

As I looked for things to turn into lunch, I told her how I'd worked myself out of a job for Mrs. Thomas. Because there wasn't much food in, we decided to go shopping. And I explained the technique required for getting supermarket check-out people to take cents-off coupons for things you haven't bought. It's worth a buck or two each time it works.

"But I've got plenty of money, Daddy."

"Well, if you're going to be like that," I said.

The phone rang. Sam went for it immediately. "Albert Samson Detective Agency," she said. "May I help you?" Then, "It's for you, Daddy."

"Who is it?"

"Who is it, please?" Pause. "It's a Mr. Rush?"

"Rush?"

"Was that Mr. Rush?" she asked. "Yes, Mr. Rush," she said. I took it.

"Mr. Samson?" A forceful voice with a slight drawl. He sounded tall and as if he wore a white ten-gallon hat. "I understand you wanted to see me this morning about our John Pighee."

"That's right, Mr. Rush. How was your trip?"

"Trip?"

"Your secretary's secretary said you were out of the state. How are things out of the state?"

"Just fine, just fine. Got back earlier than expected. I found your message when I returned. I felt obligated to call to ask what your interest in poor John was, and what you wanted to see me about."

"I've been hired," I said, "to find out what happened to him."

"Well, he had an accident. Most unfortunate accident."

"So it would appear," I said, "but there are a number of out-standing questions."

"Are there," he said, but not quite as a question.

"I presume you are a busy man, Mr. Rush, but . . ."

"I can see you now," he said. "I can omit my lunch, if what you're concerned about is important."

"It's important to my client."

"When can you be here?"

"A few minutes. I'm in town."

"I have your address," he said coolly.

"Would you like me to bring you a sandwich?"

"That won't be necessary," he said.

"Can I come?" Sam asked when I hung up.

"Not in with me when I see the man," I said. She took it as fact. Which was just as well, because it was. For some reason, John Pighee's name on the back of my card—I couldn't believe it was mine on the front—had made a Loftus company director call me, and without much delay.

It was only polite that I should get over to him without delay, and I did. Sam stayed in the van.

I got quick escort services from both secretaries and was in P. Henry Rush's office before I caught my breath.

"Mr. Samson," he said, and came forward from his window with a hand extended. He was a well-kept sixty-year-old of medium height and build. He wore a dark blue suit, which went well with his pink complexion and white hair. He sat me down in one of a pair of chairs away from his desk. The chairs faced one another over a small table, which supported a potted philodendron. A half-size standard American flag stood beside the table, but far enough to the side that it didn't obscure our view of each other.

"John Pighee," he said. "What exactly has he got to do with you?"

"I've been hired by a party who has a humanitarian and family interest."

"I see," he said slowly.

"Let me put my questions this way," I began. "Has there ever been an insurance investigation of the circumstances of John Pighee's accident? I get the impression there hasn't."

"How do you get that impression?"

"I've been mistaken for an insurance investigator, and no one I've talked to has mentioned the existence of a real insurance report."

"There was a report, based on a thorough study of the circumstances by our Chief Research Administrator, Dr. Jay Dundree."

"I've talked to Dundree. He didn't mention a report."

"Did you ask him about it?"

"Not specifically. But he's been very cagey about just what happened to John Pighee. He had an 'accident'; he was 'in an explosion.' Those are not explanations. And now you say there was no independent investigation of what happened."

"Dr. Dundree's report was complete, thorough, and professional, I can assure you. And the insurance company accepted it without question or further concern."

"They granted your claim on the basis of it?"

"Well," he said, "there isn't exactly a question of a claim against the insurance company."

"Loftus didn't make a claim?"

"Well, it's not that we didn't make a claim, exactly."

I sat in silence for a moment.

Rush continued. "We didn't make the amount of claim we might have if circumstances had been different. If, for example, Pighee was listed on the scientific staff instead of the sales staff."

"If Pighee wasn't listed . . ." I began.

"The situation is somewhat complicated," he said.

"You're saying that if Pighee dies, the insurance company won't pay compensation?"

"Well, I'm hoping there won't be any need for compensation. We all hope that Mr. Pighee will make a full and complete recovery."

"But if he doesn't, who pays compensation?"

He took a breath. "Apart from a minimum figure due any company employee, I do," he said.

"Out of your personal fortune?"

"Out of my personal resources. Insofar as is necessary."

I frowned. "I don't understand."

"No," he said, with a wisp of a smile. "I'm not surprised. Have you, Mr. Samson, studied the legal documents covering the compensation question?"

"Not yet," I said.

"You will see, when and if you do, that John Pighee signed a waiver of a compensation damages claim in favor of a direct agreement with me on a personal services basis."

"If you say so," I said.

"I can tell you are puzzled," he said.

"You're very perceptive."

"My interest, in recent years," he said, "has focused on development of the quality of the Loftus scientific research department."

"Has it?"

"I suspect if I'd been born a decade or two later than I was, I would have gone into science myself. But as things were . . ." He spread his hands to express the uncertain nature of plans. In doing so, he touched the flag. His hand lingered on it, feeling the fabric. "The war redirected my life," he said. "As it did with many others. My work there led to my work here in security. It's only in the last several years that I've been able to concentrate again on the sort of thing that I was really interested in. Developing scientific personnel and facilities is not the same as doing it, but at least I help. And I have the satisfaction of knowing that Sir Jeff himself feels strongly that the capabilities of our employees should be encouraged, and until he gave up effective control of the company—

"I didn't realize he had."

"Yes," Rush said. "The new wave—the money men—is now in the ascendant." As a fact to be faced.

"What exactly was John Pighee's status, then?"

"He was a trained chemist, but hired as a salesman. He wanted to keep up his science on his own time and I arranged to let him."

"On his own time?"

"That's right. I've helped develop some fine talent in my years with this company. And I think this young man was very talented. Is very talented."

"People tend to talk about him as if he's dead. I do it, too."

"I never for a minute thought that it would lead to his being in a terrible accident like this."

"What was he working on?"

"I don't know."

"You don't know?"

"That would have been Dr. Dundree's decision. My part was to arrange things. Get the insurance problem overcome, that kind of thing. Let me tell you something, Samson. There are people in powerful positions in this company who would use the fact that I've found ways to get around rules to try to lever me out of my place here. But I believe in this company. And I believe in America, though there are people who don't think that's a good thing to believe in any more. But to me it means something, and opportunity means something. And if I can back my judgment with my own money, if I can guarantee a wife's future against what seemed to be the highly remote chance of an accident—why, I'm proud to do it."

"But, basically, the rest of the company doesn't realize the extent to which you were responsible for John Pighee being in the lab?"

"If you care to put it that way."

"Does the rest of the board know about Pighee's accident?"

"I don't think it was called explicitly to their attention. They will have access, if they want it, to the information that he's off work."

"And with Pighee in a company research unit, rather than a hospital, who is paying for his medical treatment?"

"Well, it's a company clinic, as you say."

"But medical insurance is not involved."

"Not directly, no."

"Nor is there any direct expense to you?"

"No, though I have personally staked a large compensation agreement against Pighee's recovery."

"In what way is the amount of this compensation guaranteed?"

"I am personally liable, if he dies as a result of any incident relating to the scientific work he was doing."

"But have securities or bonds been put forward? Has there been any confirmation on behalf of Mrs. Pighee that you have the sort of money you have agreed to provide?"

"The compensation is not all in a cash lump form. The bulk is an income arrangement, against my income."

"What income? After you die or become unemployed when the board finds out that you've been juggling staff and circumventing insurance protection to fulfill your own desire to manipulate lives, and to make up for your not becoming a scientist when you were young enough to do it?"

He didn't like the tone of my question, but he answered its content. "Mrs. Pighee's claims depend to a large extent on my retaining my position here, that's perfectly true."

"Ahh. Mrs. Pighee doesn't get compensation if somebody blows the gaff on you and you get kicked out."

"Some people might interpret the gist of the agreement John Pighee signed, concerning the eventuality of an accident, in that way."

"You're saying cooperate or Mrs. Pighee loses compensation if her husband dies."

"Things could work out that way. And as a representative of your client's interests, I can assure you that it is in Mrs. Pighee's interests that I should retain my position here."

"That may well be," I said. "But Mrs. Pighee isn't my client."

"She isn't?"

"Nope."

"But you said family."

"His sister," I said. "Mrs. Dorothea Thomas."

"Well, what the hell is her interest in the thing?"

"She hired me because the people at the Clinic are refusing to let her visit her brother's bedside."

"Is that all?"

"That's enough. She's been kept away ever since the accident. That's seven months."

"Hell," Rush said, "I can take care of that for you."

TWELVE / Two breakthroughs on the same problem in less than half a day. I went back to Sam, who'd been waiting in my van. Apparently patiently.

"I've been watching the people go by," she said. "Why are you looking unhappy like that?"

"Because I did my job. Again," I said.

"Isn't that good?"

"Things have come up."

"What?"

I explained the apparent peculiarities of the Pighees' financial situation as I made notes on my conversation with P. Henry Rush.

But Sam was less interested in the compensation situation than the notes. "Don't they take a long time if you do it for everybody you talk to?"

"Yes," I said.

When I finished them, I said, "But they help me think. If I do them soon after a conversation, I can remember almost everything that was said and sometimes when I read over them later I see things more clearly than when I was actually talking."

"Oh," Sam said. Not terribly impressed. Not many kids are impressed by long-cuts to results.

"Have we eaten yet?"

"No," she said.

"Want to go out?"

She hesitated when she wanted to ask if I could afford it, then said, "O.K."

I took her to Bud's Dugout. We played pinball while Mom worked her way through the end of the lunchtime traffic. One flipper each and when we started to get replays Sam said, "This is rather fun," in the tone of a kid who'd thought herself too good for such entertainment. A Madame Graumier's student.

"Of course it is," I said patronizingly. "And it helps support your grandmother, too. You tell your mother that I make regular contributions to your grandmother's support."

"Pay attention; you nearly lost that ball."

Then I did lose it.

"Oh, Daddy! Let me play by myself!"

After lunch I left Sam to help Mom with the dishes and I went out to Beech Grove. I got there about three-thirty.

But I thought I'd call on Mrs. Pighee before I saw my client. I rang the house bell. There was no answer, so I rang again.

"Go away, will you? I'm trying to sleep."

Before I could do anything, the lock was turned from the inside and Linn Pighee opened the door. She wore a bathrobe and a glass and said, "Oh, it's Mr. Albert come back to see poor old me again. Hello, Mr. Albert."

"Hello, Mrs. Pighee. Do you have time for a few words?"

She smiled. "It's high time for a few words," she said. "Because I'm just a little bit high." But she didn't make way for me in the doorway.

I said, "I'm glad I caught you in."

"It's the only way you'll catch me." She paused. "Say, would you like to come in?"

"Please," I said.

She led me to the screened porch and resumed her position of the day before on the chaise. I sat in my chair. I was conscious of our conversation having been interrupted last time and said, "This could become habit-forming."

"Could it?" she asked rhetorically. "What do you want, Mr. Albert?"

"Samson," I said.

"Sam," she said.

"No, Albert Samson," I said.

She waited.

"Well, I've had a rather disturbing conversation today."

"What a pity."

"Disturbing because I think it puts your financial future in some doubt."

She frowned for a long time. Then said, "I didn't think you were investigating me."

"I'm not. A man jumped to the assumption that I was working for you and told me some things that put questions in my mind."

"Such as?"

"Such as why your husband's accident compensation agreement should be with a man, P. Henry Rush, instead of with Loftus Pharmaceuticals or their insurers."

"Is it?"

"Yes."

"Is that bad?"

"It's unusual," which didn't impress her, "and it's risky because you have only the assets of the man to claim against, instead of the assets of the insurance company."

"Mmm. That doesn't sound very good." She sipped.

I waited. She didn't say anything else, so I asked, "Why did you do it?"

"I didn't. Walter did whatever there was to be done."

"But surely he acted on your instruction. Surely he outlined the alternatives to you and suggested that you pick one of them and gave you reasons for it and that sort of thing."

"Nope."

"But you signed some papers?"

She shook her head. "Walter came out a couple of times. He told me I'd keep getting John's salary and what I'd get if he died. I told him I didn't want to think about it, so he handles all the money and I just write checks when I want some cash. Not that I want much. I haven't had the energy necessary to spend money." She watched my reaction, and said, "You look puzzled."

"It's not the way things work. I don't really understand. Would you mind if I talked to your lawyer?"

"Be my guest."

"Would you authorize me to have a look at the agreements he entered into with Loftus or Henry Rush?"

"Rush," she said slowly. "I think that was the name of the man who told me about the accident."

"He did?"

"He was terribly upset. He came out here that night. He was

really very shaky. I don't think he should have been driving, he was so shaky."

"Is it O.K. for Weston to show me the relevant papers, Mrs. Pighee?"

"Huh? Oh, sure. I don't mind."

"He'll probably call you to confirm it."

She shrugged. "But what's your interest, Mr. Albert?"

I smiled. "I don't understand what's happening, and I lose sleep when I don't understand things."

"I lose sleep when I do understand things," she said. She had a drink on it. "Want a drink?"

"No, thanks."

"What's the matter, you won't drink with a drinking lady?"

"I'm not thirsty," I said.

She tried her new concoction and said, "I thought you were working for my beloved sister-in-law."

"I am. But I think I've done what she wanted me to do, so it probably won't last long."

"She wanted to visit him, right?"

"Right."

"Hell, that shouldn't be a big deal."

"I agree."

"I hope she paid you in advance."

My silence bespoke the opposite.

"Broken-hearted sister Thomas. She's the stingiest woman in Beech Grove, and if you're giving her credit you're the last of the optimists."

"Please don't say things like that," I said.

She shrugged without much sympathy.

"Who told her about John's accident?"

"I did. The day after that man came here. In the afternoon. I forgot to do it in the morning."

I didn't say anything.

She sat up suddenly.

"What's wrong?" I said.

"Your socks."

"What about them?" I looked at them. "Good God. Not matched."

She laughed. I thought for a few moments, trying to remember what had happened to the other yellow one and the other red one.

After she subsided, I said, "Do you have any notion of what your husband was doing in the research labs at Loftus? I've asked several people and they don't seem to know what he was up to."

"What he was up to in the way of work, you mean?"

"Yes."

"No idea."

"What about other than work?"

"I don't know about that, either," she said, and she drank deeply from her glass and looked unhappy. I was going to say something, when she put her glass on the side table with a bang and said, "Your socks."

"I'm—"

"You must feel pretty stupid about them. I'm going to make you feel more at ease. I'm going to go put something on to make you feel more comfortable." She got up, slightly unsteadily, and left the porch. She was gone for five minutes. It made me feel very uncomfortable.

"Are you ready?" she called at last from the doorway.

I waited.

She marched onto the porch holding her dressing gown up to display a pair of knee-length maroon-and-orange knitted stockings. "Aren't they great?" she asked. "I found them yesterday in one of the drawers. They were Simmy's, one of my daughters. She bought them in a dime store when she was six. Six! She wouldn't let me take them back because she wanted to grow into them. Aren't they just a riot! I laughed when I found them. The things that take kids' fancies. Have you ever seen anything so hysterical? I laughed and laughed until I cried." She laughed and then started crying. I stood up and held her.

"They would have been twelve next birthday. Why should I hate John?" she asked herself. "He just ruined my life and then took away its only compensation."

"I'm sorry," I said.

"What for?" She pulled away and we faced each other.

"I feel more at ease," I said.

"Well, you could be worse," she said. "Give us a hug, Mr. Albert. Every good woman needs to be hugged three times a day."

I hugged her.

"I'm so tired," she said. "So tired." I laid her down on her chaise and pulled her dressing gown round her. Then I walked back through the house and out the front door.

THIRTEEN / Mrs. Thomas was at home. Though the afternoon was clear and pleasant, and there were chairs on the grass, she was inside her aluminum home. I knocked on the door, watched her peer through a side window at me.

"Hello, Mr. Samson," she said cheerfully. "I can see that you've been at work."

"You can?" I said. Must be the socks.

"Come in," she said. "Out of the mosquitoes."

We sat.

"I have been working," I said. "But did you mean something special?"

She said proudly, "A man came to see me this afternoon."

"Ahh."

"He told me about John. About his condition, and he said how sorry he was that I hadn't been allowed to visit him."

"Sorrow now is better than sorrow never, I guess."

"He said that he was very distraught that I had had to go to the personal trouble and expense of hiring a private detective to find out what should have been available to me by right as John's sister. He said very nice things about John. I didn't realize that they appreciated his value so much."

She was basking in the attention shown her. Which seemed reasonable enough in a life that looked pretty lonely from the perspectives I'd had on it. "If they're so bothered by the expense you've gone to, they should pay you back for it."

"He did," she said.

"He gave you money? How much?"

"Well, I don't like to say how much, in case you adjust your bill to fit it."

I sighed audibly. But she didn't know how scrupulously honest I am. Fair enough.

"It wasn't very much," she added hastily. "Just a token."

I didn't believe her. I thought she'd got a lot. I hesitated. Shrugged. "Well," I said, "at least you can visit your brother now."

She didn't say anything.

"When will you be going in to see him?" I asked.

"I appreciate your work on my behalf," she said. "Don't think I don't. But you may have been a bit confused about what I wanted."

"You wanted to be allowed in to see your brother, at his bedside. Surely you can now."

"I wanted, at least, to know the reasons why I was kept from John. And the man who came was very clear and firm about why it wouldn't be best for John. I understand now. I'm not so fussed as I was. Thank you for helping me." She stood up. "If you'll send your bill," she said, "I'll deal with it as soon as I can."

"Just a minute, Mrs. Thomas," I said.

"Is something wrong, Mr. Samson?"

"I only want to get things straight. A man came out here, talked you out of wanting to visit your brother, and gave you some money for your trouble."

"Just a token," she said. "Hardly anything at all, really."

"And now you don't even want to visit your brother."

She sat again. "Of course I want to," she said sharply. "But it's not in his best interests. There's the danger of infection and he wouldn't even know I was there, so I could hardly comfort him, could I? My forcing my way in there would only make me feel better, not John. And it's hardly worth putting him at any extra risk for my sake."

"And you're completely satisfied with that?"

"I won't be needing your further services," she said.

"Can you tell me just two other things? Who the man was who came here, and about what time he talked to you."

"Well," she said, trying to think of some reason not to tell me. "Was it Henry Rush?"

"No. A Mr. Dundree, Dr. Dundree. A Ph.D. doctor, like John could have been if he wanted, but he didn't have the time. And it was a little after lunchtime."

"What? One o'clock? One-thirty?"

She nodded.

I got up. "I'm very glad that you've been satisfied about your brother, Mrs. Thomas," I said as I left. But I don't think she believed me. Perceptive of her, because I was lying.

I drove away without writing anything in my notebook. Time enough for that later. My client had been bought off by Jay Dundree, when he'd implied to me that he would give in to what she wanted. Or what she'd told me she wanted.

I felt let down. I felt angry. Even though vacillating clients with a blurred vision of what they're after are an occupational hazard in this business.

Near Bud's Dugout I stopped at a pay phone and called the Pighees' lawyer, Walter Weston. On the off chance that he would still be in his office.

And he was. I explained that I wanted to come over to have a look at the papers relating to John Pighee's financial arrangements with Loftus Pharmaceuticals.

"I can't show them to you," he said impatiently.

"I have Mrs. Pighee's permission," I said.

"In writing?"

"No. But she'll confirm it by telephone if you want to call her while I'm on my way."

"I'll have to have it in writing," he said, and I could visualize him sitting at his desk and shaking his black hair from side to side.

"Why?"

"Because I don't approve. And if John recovers and wants to know why I let a stranger go through his papers, I want to be able to show him that Linn insisted. Let them fight it out."

I called Linn Pighee's house. I'd left her virtually asleep, and I didn't like disturbing her, but it was my last day on the case. That justified the call—to me, at least.

But she seemed fully awake when she answered the phone.

"Mr. Albert! Good heavens, a girl wants to get a little shut-eye, and all of a sudden it's open house."

"It is?"

"I was sleeping and the doorbell rang and it was my medicine and then the phone rang. I must be getting popular."

I explained that I wanted to come out again to get a signed authorization to look at her husband's papers.

"You can't come to the house now," she said.

"I'll only be a minute."

"No!" she said and seemed, in a moment, to be becoming shrill. "If you come, I won't open the door."

"Why not?" I asked, my annoyance with Mrs. Thomas carrying over into my voice.

"I just don't want to see anybody else tonight. That's all. I don't have to if I don't want to. Come back tomorrow morning, why don't you."

I thought I heard a low sound behind her voice, but it didn't repeat itself. I said, "But I'm virtually in Beech Grove now. Tomorrow I won't have the time to come out in the morning."

"You can't come," she said. "I . . . I'll . . . I'll come into town if it's so important."

I sighed. "At my office. About eleven," I said, and hung up on her.

I called Weston back, saying that I didn't have time to go out to Beech Grove at the moment but that I would be seeing Mrs. Pighee in the morning and would stop by in the afternoon.

Before I drove the rest of the way from the phone to Bud's Dugout, I brought my notebook up to date. It wasn't a pleasant task. I hate unanswered questions, if I've cared enough to ask them in the first place. And I hate clients' being bought off. What good is a detective keeping incorruptible if the client is weak-willed?

And I was more than angry. Quite apart from Linn Pighee's snub in favor of her medicine, I had become suspicious. Rush hadn't acted as if keeping visitors away from John Pighee was a big deal, yet Dundree had pulled out all the stops to keep Mrs. Thomas away. It seemed legitimate to ask why. I wished someone besides me wanted to know.

Sam did. I blessed her for it.

"Bless you, Sam."

"Looks like they're covering up something, huh, Daddy?"

Put that way, I began to see the other side. "Well . . . They could have perfectly straightforward reasons."

"No," Sam said. "They'd tell you just to keep you from being a nuisance. Somebody's covering something up."

"It sounds so simple-minded the way you say it," I said uncharitably.

"I am not. I'm very complex-minded." My lack of grace was with myself, but she took it personally.

"Look, Sam," I said. "Your grandmother is busy out there now."

"I know," she said. "I have been here all afternoon. It was quiet, but not nearly as quiet as spending the afternoon in your office was."

"I thought we might go out and see somebody. Then come back when she has a bit more time."

"Somebody to do with the case?" she asked. "Really?"

"We have no client," I said, taking every opportunity to keep my grip on the facts of life. "But since I'm seeing Mrs. Pighee in the morning and her lawyer in the afternoon it can't really hurt—"

"Oh, you are working on it. Good for you, Daddy."

"Go help your grandmother while I use the phone."

There were six McGonigles in the phone book, and mine was the last one I tried. A woman who sounded like a mother said that Raymond McGonigle was expected in ten minutes, at six, but that his dinner was at six-thirty. I could talk to him till then.

Sam and I didn't find the house until ten past six. It was a small brick structure, well out east, past Brookside Park but before the Avionics.

"Now, you're here to listen, not to talk," I told Sam in the van.

"Yes, Daddy."

A large woman answered my knock. "Yes?"

"My name is Albert Samson. I called about wanting to have a few words with Raymond McGonigle. Is he home yet?"

"Raymond is here," she said, looking at us suspiciously. "Who's she?"

"My daughter," I said. "I've got her in tow today. I couldn't get a baby-sitter."

"Well, come on in, then."

Raymond McGonigle was a tall young man in his early twenties. He sat in the living room wearing a suit and tie that would have been conservative when I was his age. I got the feeling that they were his working weeds and that he bore them as a burden until after duty—me—and his dinner. Then he'd change to something a little more mainstream, not to say mainline.

"Hello, man," he said. "Welcome to my ghetto."

"Mr. McGonigle?"

"And a groovy fox, too. Hello, pretty lady."

"Hello."

"I want to ask you about an accident," I said. "Which I understand you were a witness to. At Loftus Pharmaceuticals. I understand you work there."

"A pillar of the establishment."

"Do you know a man called John Pighee?"

"Oh," he said. "That's the scene you're after."

"Were you there when it happened?"

He tilted his head and made a face of discomfort. "You put me in a difficult spot, man."

"Why's that?"

"Because I've been warned—sorry, told—that people might ask about that business and the boss man doesn't want me talking about it without . . . without direction." Under stress, his education was showing in his accent.

"He wants to clear anything you say?"

"Something like that. Not," he added, "that I've got much to say."

"Look," I said, "I'm just trying to find out what happened, so his family will feel a little better about it all. He's pretty likely to die, from what I understand. His people want to know. It's not an insurance thing. There can't be much trouble in your talking to me for his family's peace of mind."

"*I* wouldn't say so," he conceded.

"Did you see the accident?"

"No. Hell, to see a thing like that, you've got to be in it. I was working late down the hall and I was the first one there. I heard an explosion and I went to see what happened."

"So you were there, what? A minute after it happened?"

"Or less. Unless I've slowed down in my old age." He smiled at Sam.

"And what did it look like?"

"A mess. All the equipment shattered. Glass and wood and stuff all around. Mr. Pighee lying on the floor. Personally, I thought he was dead."

"Did you try to help him or call an ambulance, or what?"

"I didn't do anything. Dr. Dundree was there a few seconds after I was. He took care of all that stuff."

"Did it happen in the daytime?"

"No, about eight at night."

"How come so many people were around?"

"Research labs work strange hours. They were working on things, I suppose."

"But not in the same lab as you were?"

"No. I was going through a battery of readings on a spectrometer. We were doing a set of readings every six hours."

"What kind of work was Pighee doing?"

"I don't know. I never worked in the Storeroom. Sorry, that's what we call that lab. Whatever's cooking, they don't need technicians."

"I'd have thought that in the same company everybody knows what everybody else is doing."

"They've got something special going on in there. Still do. And they don't take the risk that industrial spies like me will go tell Lilly or the guy in the drugstore on the corner."

"Are you an industrial spy?"

"A jest, man. A joke. They don't tell me what they don't want me to know."

"I see," I said. "How long have you been working for Loftus?"

"Thirteen and a half very long months," he said.

"Don't you like it?"

"You're what?" he asked. "A detective or something?"

I nodded.

"Well, how would you like sitting around and typing up the reports of what other detectives were up to and never getting a chance to do any detectiving yourself?"

"It doesn't stretch your capabilities," I said.

"You don't really need a chemistry major to wash up your test tubes, do you?"

"I don't know," I said, trying to be good-natured. "How hard is it to wash up test tubes?"

"Shit," he said. "Oh, excuse me," he said, acknowledging Sam. "They just tell me to be patient. That I'm lucky to have a job at all."

"Are you?"

"I suppose so."

"Lot of science grads around?"

"Everyone and his cousin. I'm part of a glut. Born in a ghetto. Graduated to a glut."

"If they've got guys like you champing at the bit, how does someone like John Pighee walk in and get himself into a special lab project that even the technicians don't know anything about?"

"Dunno," he said, showing disgust.

"Raymond!" his mother called from behind the living-room door. "Time for your meal!"

"All right!" he shouted back. But didn't move into action. He saw me watching him. "No problem," he said. "Ask away."

"If you aren't happy at Loftus, why do you stay?"

"A long sad story," he said. "Even if I could get something better somewhere else, I made a deal to stick around Indy for five years. Man, long years they look like being."

"A deal?"

He nodded toward the door. "With family," he said. "And it's getting claustrophobic is what it is; I don't know if I'm going to last it."

"Problems of provincial life," I said.

"Hey, yeah," he said. "I like the way you talk. You're a funny man, man." He paused, then nodded toward Sam. "Is this little lady . . . is she your old lady?"

"My daughter."

"Is she as funny as you are?"

"Laugh a minute."

"Would you mind if, like, I took her out to a flick or something? I'm getting desperate for people who don't spend all their time talking about my future or about making Sir Jeff a little more money. Problem is all the middle-class chicks my mama tries to pair me off with, they're busy planning the kind of wallpaper they want when they're ninety-five. And the others are just so ignorant!"

"Better ask her."

"How about it, little lady?"

"Sure."

"After dinner, then."

"Hang on," I said. "She's supposed to be going to her grandmother's tonight."

"Don't worry, man. I'm no wolf."

"No, Daddy, I can go another time. I really feel like a movie."

McGonigle said, "That's terrific. Where do I find you?"

"Daddy will give you a card, won't you, Daddy?"

Daddy gave him a card. "Who," I began again, "is your boss at Loftus?"

"Guy right above me is Dr. Dundree."

"And when did he warn you not to talk to people about John Pighee? This afternoon?"

He shook his head. "Day or two after the accident. I just think he was worried about the insurance investigators."

"And have the insurance investigators talked to you about it?"

"Nope," he said. "Not yet."

The living-room door opened. "Raymond. Your supper is on the table. Come and sit down before it gets cold."

This time McGonigle stood up. "Gotta go," he said. "See you later," he said to Sam.

As we got into my panel truck, she said, "Don't worry. I'll find out everything there is to know for you."

"He didn't exactly seem to be holding a flood back now. Is that why you're going out with him?"

"Well, I thought maybe I would be doing you a favor, giving you a little time."

"What do you mean?" I asked.

"Well. When I was cleaning up this afternoon, and found that money?"

"Yeah."

"And the picture of the lady. She's your friend, isn't she? I mean you're not gay, are you? You haven't had much time to see her since I got here. I thought you'd like an evening without me around."

"And at the same time you intend to third-degree poor McGonigle. You seem to have inherited a quality we call 'organizational ability' when we're trying not to say bossiness. I wonder who from?"

She looked at me; then started to cry.

I let her. It's good for children. Builds their lungs. She whimpered half the way home. Then she said, "I don't intend to be bossy."

"Good," I said. Then, "And neither do I. You're entitled to your own life even while you're luxuriating in the accommodation I provide on the floor of my living room."

As I was parking, she said, "Anyway, it is a heaven-sent opportunity for me to pump him, don't you think?"

FOURTEEN / After McGonigle picked Sam up, I called my mother to tell her we weren't coming, after all, and then, because I lack imagination, I followed Sam's Plan and went to see my woman.

That is, I went to her house, where I found only her daughter Lucy and the news that the object of my intentions wouldn't be back till 9:30.

"She went straight from work to buy things for our summer vacation."

"Vacation? What vacation?"

"Hers and mine," Lucy said exclusively. "We've been lent a cottage. We get it on Sunday. Didn't you know?" The last, artfully.

"No," I said.

"If you'd just keep in more regular contact with her," the little girl said, "then I guess you'd know about that sort of thing."

"I guess I would," I said.

"She did think about asking you along, but since she hadn't heard from you she figured you were working and wouldn't come anyway."

By 9:30 I'd just about had my fill of people's daughters.

At 11:30 I was home in bed. Getting to sleep is not usually one of my problems, but I was restless. At first I thought it was because I didn't understand the secrecy about John Pighee's situation at Loftus Pharmaceuticals. But after I'd thrashed myself with that for an hour, I realized I was losing sleep because Sam wasn't home. I'd forgotten about father's worry. It had been a long time since I was the father of a child of whom I was the father.

I heard her bounce up the stairs at a quarter past one.

"Oh!" she said when I came into the living room. She was sitting in my dining-room chair waiting for some milk on the stove to heat up. "I was just making myself some instant coffee," she said.

"With milk?"

"Half milk and half water. What's the frown for?"

"It's just my face in repose." I hesitated, then sat down.

She put a spoon of coffee stuff in a cup, poured the pan's contents onto it, and sat down on her air mattress. "Well," she said, "where shall I begin?"

What Raymond McGonigle had expected from a date with my daughter I don't know, but from the sound of her side of things, the hours had been spent in a steady debriefing. "I started by asking him about himself," she said. "I've found that people like that."

"Have you?"

"Did you know that he has three older sisters and that he's the only boy?"

The difference—one of the differences—between a novice detective and an experienced detective lies in the ability to select from available information. Determine as you go along what's important. Sam got information, all right; but it was after two before John Pighee's name was mentioned.

"But Ray didn't know him well."

"So he told me."

"But I'm sure he didn't. They're all very stand-offish there. It sounds a horrible place to work."

"Not friendly, huh?"

"Not with lower-down people like Ray. He hates it. Not being able to work up to his capacity is bad enough, but the only people he gets along with are the other technicians. The lower technicians; there's one higher-up technician called Seafield and he sticks with the people like Dr. Dundree."

"And John Pighee."

"Yeah. Did I do well, Daddy?"

"Very well, kid."

She smiled. I noticed her eyes were bloodshot.

"Tell you what I'll do, Sam. In the morning I'll give you a notebook. I want you to write down everything you can remember from your interview with R. McGonigle. Get it on paper, and out of memory."

"I can type," she said.

"All the better."

I woke up about 9:30. I felt good, considering that I was unemployed. I knocked on the door between my bedroom and the living room.

"Hello?"

"You decent, Sam?"

"You old-fashioned?"

"Yes."

"Oh, well. I'm decent, then."

I went into the living room. She was lying on the bed with a book. Decent and dressed as well.

"Daddy? What's your philosophy of life?"

"Toast and orange juice."

"I get it. I get it."

But I got it in the end, because I knew how to brown the bread over the gas burner by holding it on a fork.

"I'll get you an electric toaster before I go," Sam said. "Mummy said I should keep my eye out for things you need but were too proud to admit."

"When are you leaving Indianapolis?"

We finished the toast in silence.

"Well, what do we do on our case today?" Sam asked brightly as she poured some coffee.

"We draw up a bill for Mrs. Thomas, put it in the mail, and sit back and wait for another client."

"What do you mean?"

"I mean we have no client, so we're off the case. That's life in a detective agency. When there's no money coming in, you don't run around spending it. You huddle in a corner and conserve your resources."

Though she was confused, Sam was about to speak when the phone rang.

I answered it. "Mr. Samson, this is Linn Pighee."

"Hello, Mrs. Pighee."

"I can see you this morning. What time can you come out?"

"Last I heard, you were coming here."

"It's not really convenient. I'd really . . . much rather you came here. It's—it's more private." Moving from a business tone of voice into neo-seductive, which was pretty good going at ten in the morning.

"Your written authorization to let me see your legal papers doesn't require privacy. I wanted to come out there last night. I

can't afford to waste time on needless trips." I was pitiless. "And
I have my crippled daughter to stay with me now and I don't like
to leave her alone."

"Please," she said.

"I'll meet you halfway, if that's any good to you. There's a luncheonette called Bud's Dugout on Virginia Avenue. I can meet you
there at eleven, if that's any better for you."

"All . . . all right," Linn Pighee said. And hung up.

Sam asked, "You're meeting Mrs. Pighee?"

"I'm not very consistent."

She shook her head.

"Look, I was joking about huddling in a corner."

"Oh."

"It's summer. It's warm. And I feel morally obliged to fulfill the
obligations I entered into yesterday. Besides, I can sponge lunch
off my mother. I'll try to get a doggy bag and bring you some when
I come back."

"Hey, I want to come."

"You have a report to type up. From last night."

"I can do that later."

"No," I said. "Business before business."

I got to Bud's Dugout a few minutes before eleven. "Mom," I said
to the lady behind the counter, "don't interrupt when this lady
comes in to see me, right?"

"Where's the girl?" she asked.

"I left her at the office typing up her report from last night's
investigation."

"What?"

"I figure she's got to earn her keep while she's here."

"She's in your office? Alone? A neighborhood like that?"

"No one ever bothers me there."

She turned away in disgust.

I played the pinball machines till twenty past eleven. I had just
got the Special Rollover lit and was on the verge of extra balls
when a cab pulled up outside.

Linn Pighee paid the driver, got out, and came in. She was

togged up to the hilt. Evening dress; make-up. The works.

She looked terrible. Mostly green.

"Mmm, may I sit down?" she asked, and lurched into a chair near the door.

"Sure," I said.

"I didn't feel like driving," she said. "Oh, God. Is there anything to drink? Could you get me a drink?"

"Two coffees, please, Miss," I said to my mother.

"Not coffee!" Linn Pighee snapped. "I mean a drink."

"Not here," I said.

"Oh, God," she said. And threw up.

FIFTEEN / Mom helped me carry Mrs. Pighee to the room in the rear. I went back to the luncheonette to clear up before the Saturday lunch crowd started filing in. I finished with an aerosol spray, giving the affected area the works. The ozone layer couldn't have protected the customers' sensibility any better than the aerosol spray did.

At a quarter to twelve I traded posts with Mom. She had eased Linn out of her clothes and laid her down on the couch covered with a sheet. The evening dress was soaking in the sink. The patient was conscious.

"I'm sorry," she said.

"How do you feel?"

"So-so."

"Are you sick? Do you want a doctor?"

"I'll be . . ." She hesitated. Then she said, "It's the first time I've been out."

"What do you mean?"

"Out. Of the house."

"Since when?"

"Since . . . the accident."

"But that was in January."

"Yes," she said, and closed her eyes.

I watched her fade into sleep and tried to imagine what it must be like to be her. Married too young, for the wrong reason. Difficult husband; difficulties with sister-in-law. Stripped of her children. And left in a personal limbo for seven months while the husband was neither alive nor dead.

All I had was superficial information and superficial empathies. But I felt sorry for her, hurt with her hurt.

Not out of the house for seven months. Mrs. Thomas would hardly credit her with the reason she hadn't tried to visit her husband: that she couldn't bear to leave the walls, which, in turn, restrained her.

At 2:15, having slept through the chaos of lunchtime in a luncheonette, Linn Pighee was awakened by a sparrow that landed on the sill of the open window and, deranged by the August heat, chirped.

"Huh? What?" She cried for a moment and then stopped.

I got her some coffee, which she seemed to take gratefully.

"When you're feeling ready," I said, "I'll drive you home."

"I'm O.K.," she said. She started to get up, but only then realized she didn't have her dress. I pointed to the sink.

"Is there something I could borrow? To wear?"

I went to ask my mother.

Mom asked, "She's awake? What are you going to do with her?"

"Take her home."

"What is she, Albert?"

"A client," I said. A moral client, if not a paying one. "Do you have some clothes she can borrow?"

We settled on a long smock thing, and before the resolve faded, I helped Linn Pighee into my panel truck.

"I look like a sack of dog food," she said as I slid into the driver's seat.

"You feel all right?"

"I feel terrible. I . . . you . . ."

I started the engine.

"Don't take me home."

"What?"

"I can't go home. I don't want to go home. I can't. Not in the light. Not . . ." And she started crying again.

I thought about it.

"Please!" She curled up on the seat and put her hands over her eyes.

"I'll take you to my place. Let my daughter look after you."

She didn't say anything.

I double-parked in front of my office door and helped Linn Pighee up to my office. It was the slowest ascent ever made; the revitalizing her sleep at Mom's had provided was all used up. Being out of doors, even in a car, destroyed her.

I got the door open and led her through the office to the living room, where we found Sam typing at the desk. "Up, Sam. Got a patient for you."

I sat Linn down, then went back downstairs to move the truck.

And found a cop writing me a ticket.

"You got to be kidding," I said. "I help a sick lady upstairs where she can lie down and it takes two minutes. You got to be kidding."

"Sorry, buster," the cop said. "I'd like to give you a break, but you see, when I get to this place on the ticket form"—he pointed his pen ambiguously—"I gotta go ahead and fill it out. Sorry for your sick friend. Hope she makes it up to you."

I stood silently while he finished his handiwork. He gave me my copy, got on his putt-putt, and went away. I watched him till he turned a corner. Then I put the ticket he'd handed me under the windshield wiper of the green Ponty parked in front of my office. It was all his fault, really, and he might even pay it without reading the ticket.

When I got back upstairs, Sam had put Linn Pighee to bed. In my bed.

"Charming," I said. "And where do I sleep? With you?"

"You're not my type, Daddy. Isn't she staying all night?"

"We didn't work it out that far ahead. I suppose she is."

"Who is she?"

"Linn Pighee. John Pighee's wife."

"Oooooo," Sam said.

I told her about Linn's visit to Bud's Dugout.

"I wondered why you were gone so long. I just thought you'd gone off to see the lawyer and were keeping me out of your hair."

"The lawyer," I said. I'd forgotten about him. No real opportunity to get a signed authorization from Linn, anyway. "I think we can kiss him goodbye."

"Daddy."

"Yeah?"

"While you were out. A man came here."

"Anybody special? Cop writing me a ticket because I don't keep a lid on my wastebasket?"

"No. A man. He was very tall. I mean, like a basketball player. And he had curly yellow hair."

She had my serious attention. It had to be Lee Seafield. "What did he want?"

"Well," Sam said slowly, making it clear that the encounter had not been a pleasant one. "He wouldn't say, but he wasn't friendly. I came out to the office when I heard someone there, but he wouldn't believe you weren't here. He pushed his way in here and he even looked in the bedroom."

"I don't like the sound of that," I said.

"He scared me," Sam said.

"He didn't leave a message?"

"No."

I frowned. "You're sure it was me he was looking for?"

"Yes."

I could see she was upset. With some cause. But I tried to distract her. "Well," I said. "Starting tomorrow, I don't expect to be too hard to find. Unemployed, and with a child and a sick lady to look after."

After a moment Sam said, "It's a disease, Daddy."

"What is?"

"Not being able to go outdoors. It's a phobia."

"Terrific. All we have to do is wait till . . ." But I stopped myself. I was going to say wait till October, when they take the building down, but there was a limit to the amount of sympathy even I was willing to trade upon.

"What? Wait till what?"

"Till the cows come home."

She shrugged. "By the way, did I mention that Ray is coming over tonight?"

"Ray? McGonigle?"

She nodded.

"No, you didn't mention it."

"You don't mind, do you?"

"Me? Mind? Me? Hell, no. Let's have a party. Linn can tell us all about the people she's known who've died. Ray can tell us about laboratory explosions. I'll give my standard lecture on bankruptcy. Should be a real gas."

"Daddy? Are you going bankrupt?"

"No more than usual. Shall I make a cup of coffee?"

"It's just that, as your daughter and heir, I have a right to know."

"Laugh a minute as advertised, aren't you, kid."

"Daddy, is it all right if I go out for a while? I've been in all day and I'd like to go out for a while."

"Go out! Go out! I'll let you know how the party goes if you don't get back in time for it."

I was getting a little tired of company. In the same way I get tired of my own company.

Sam went out.

I sat. Then made some notes. Then called my woman to invite her over. My first party since my ninth birthday. Our last visit before she went on vacation.

Sam got back at about 5:30 with two shopping bags full of foodstuffs.

"I didn't have time to take the price tags off, Daddy," she said. "So promise not to look."

"Who is your heir?" I asked. Then left her to it and turned on the TV.

My cupboards nearly buckled under the weight of food in them.

At six I was startled out of my lethargy by an inordinate pounding on the office door.

"That's not the tall nasty man, is it?" I asked Sam.

"I don't think so," she said without ruffling. "I think I know what it is."

It was the delivery of a folding bed. "Put it over there," Sam said, pointing to one of my barer office walls. "Move the bench and put it over there." To me she said, "You will want to sleep in here, won't you, Daddy? Or would you rather I did?"

"Make you your mind, Miss," the delivery man said impatiently. "I've got to get home."

"I know you do," she said, "but you were promised something to come out tonight. Could you take it out of its box, please, so we can have a look at it? I'll get my purse."

She disappeared into my living room and came back with a tightly clenched fist. The contents of which she handed to the delivery man.

He had a look, smiled, and helped pick up the cardboard shreds and wrapping tape before he left.

Sam looked pleased with herself. "The toaster didn't seem so urgent, so it will come on regular delivery. Probably on Wednesday. Cheer up, Daddy. It's only money. Have you ever heard of the redistribution of wealth?"

Linn Pighee woke up about seven. We heard her give a little cry, but before we could decide which of us should go have a look she appeared at the bedroom door. She looked firmer on her feet than she had in any previous sighting that day. "My God," she said. "Where am I? Where is this?"

"This is Daddy's apartment behind his office," Sam said, and bounced up to her. "Hi. I'm Sam. He's my dad."

Linn frowned, tilted her head. "This is your crippled daughter?"

"Any kid with me as a father must count as a cripple."

She nodded slowly. Then she gave a sign that she was feeling better. She walked into the room.

"Hungry?" Sam asked.

"A little."

"I went shopping today. There's lots of food," and Sam went to the kitchen side of the room to find some while Linn sat down.

"You wanted to see me," she said.

"You feel like it?"

"I didn't before."

"I want to look at the various legal agreements you have with Loftus Pharmaceuticals, but I need your authorization in writing."

"Why?"

"Your verbal permission wasn't good enough for your lawyer."

"Do you have a piece of paper?"

I also provided a pen. She gave me the paper after she finished with it. It read, "Walter, I order you to let Mr. Albert Samson see any of our family papers that he wants to. Mine or John's. Linn Pighee." She dated it.

"That should do it," I said. "Thanks."

"Is this the sort of thing my sister-in-law hired you to do?"

"Nope," I said. "She wanted to be allowed to visit John, and I managed to get that. Only someone from Loftus went to see her yesterday afternoon and bought her off."

"Bought her off?"

"Yeah. Talked her out of it and gave her some money for her troubles."

"That doesn't sound very good," Linn Pighee said.

"It stinks, doesn't it," Sam said. "I want to know what they're trying to cover up, don't you?"

"Cool it, Sam," I said.

Linn Pighee seemed aware of the undercurrents between father and daughter, but didn't quite understand them. "Is there anything to drink?" she asked then. "I mean like a beer."

Sam said quickly, "I forgot to buy any. *I* really feel like one, too." She looked at me pointedly. "And I did go out for food."

I scowled.

"It doesn't really matter," Linn said. "I just wondered if you had some."

"I'd *really* like some, Daddy," Sam said. "And I know Ray likes beer, too."

"Then he'll probably bring some when he comes."

"Is someone coming?" Linn asked.

"He won't. I mean he probably won't. I'd go out again, but I don't like walking the streets alone after six."

"All right," I said, "all right. Make the lady some food, then, will you?"

I went out to get some beer. It took about fifteen minutes.

When I got back, Sam was standing by the stove stirring the contents of a pan with a spoon. There were opened cans of baked beans and caviar on the counter.

"That's food?" I asked.

"She said it was O.K.," Sam said. "I think Linn has something she wants to tell you."

"Does she indeed," I said, and went to the refrigerator to put the beer away. It was hard to find room. There were three six-packs there already. I pulled one out. "And just what are these?"

"Good heavens," Sam said. "I must have bought some and forgot I did it."

"Do they teach acting at Madame Graumier's?"

I took three cans, opened them, and carried two over to where I sat down with Linn.

"Thanks," she said. "I was thinking that I'm curious, too."

"Curious is an understatement for what's going on here," I said.

"I mean I want you to find out what really happened to John."

"You mean my absurd daughter has tried to talk you into hiring me, so she can amuse herself better on her vacation, is that it?"

"I really want to know. I just hadn't thought about it before. It wouldn't have occurred to me to hire you. I appreciate her suggesting it."

I looked over at Sam, who was beaming, but turned away when I looked. "And did she ask you whether you can afford to indulge her by hiring me?"

"I have money," Linn said. "At least I think I do."

"You must have had less to live on the last couple of years," I said. "From being a full-time fast-talking salesman, your husband went to part time because of his work in the labs. And Henry Rush said he was working there 'on his own time,' so you must have had less money."

She seemed uncertain. "It didn't feel like less. He never . . . I don't think so. I . . . I don't really know about the money. I got the impression he was doing really well. That he had more money recently. But all I ever did was write checks. I never kept track."

"Since the accident, haven't you gone through his things?"

"No."

"But you have to live, to care for yourself."

"I live. I do what I always did. Except I seem to have stopped going out."

"Until today."

"Until today. And I seem to feel rotten most of the time."

"Look, Mrs. Pighee—"

"Linn," she interrupted.

"Linn. Would you mind if I went out to your house tomorrow and looked through your husband's financial records?"

"You can have the fucking place, for all I care," she said. "I've been inside for seven months and now I'm out. I feel a lot better. You can do what you like. I'll give you the keys. Where's my purse?" She got up, but quickly, and felt dizzy. I moved to help, but she said, "I'm all right," and went to the bedroom.

"So you're going to do it for her," Sam said.

"If you try to manipulate this woman, I'll send you back to your mother on the first available bicycle. I'm not going to have it, Sam, and the sooner you understand it the better."

She was distressed immediately. "All I said was that I'd pay all that it cost because I have lots of money but that I didn't think you'd do it if I asked you to. But she said she really wanted to find out what's going on. She really does, I'm sure. I just think she didn't think of hiring you."

"It hasn't occurred to you, I suppose, that it is possible she might be better off not knowing any more than she does, on the one side. And that other people's lives are not there for rich girls to play with for no better reason than because they have more money than they can use constructively."

She started to cry. "I thought I was using it constructively."

Linn appeared at the door and said, "I sat down on the bed for a minute to get my balance again." She threw me her keys. Then she noticed Sam's snuffles. "What's happened?" she asked. "What's going on?"

"Just a little fatherly lesson in minding one's own business," I said.

"Oh, don't," Linn said with passion. "I really want you to find out all there is to know about John. I really do. She only put in words what was already inside me. Please don't scold her for it. Please don't. You have so little time with her. One does. Please do this for me. I want to hire you. I do."

She sat on the edge of the desk next to the bedroom door and started crying, too. Sam went over to her and they held each other.

SIXTEEN / A few minutes before eight Raymond McGonigle appeared.

"Long time no see," I said.

He said to Sam, "Your old man is a funny old man."

Linn got up from her chair and said, "I feel very tired."

"This is Ray McGonigle," Sam said. "This is Linn Pighee."

"Pighee?" McGonigle said.

"John Pighee's wife," Sam said. "The man that was hurt."

"Oh," he said. His eyes opened wide, then narrowed. "Glad to meet you." He shook her hand.

"She's staying here," Sam said.

"I'm going to bed," Linn said, and left the room.

"After thirteen and a half months split between home and Sir Jeff," Ray said, "you two are the breath of life to me."

"Beer?" Sam asked.

"Yeah, please. Man, that is no joy spot. Her husband is well out of it."

"Is he?"

"Well, I don't know," he said. "Maybe he had it better than I do."

"I'm not clear how much work he did there," I said. "Was he part-time or full-time?"

"I don't really know, because he tended to work different hours from me—afternoons and nights—but he was there a lot for part time. I still don't know what he was doing. I asked a couple of the technicians today, and they don't know either. I don't think I'm going to be able to stick it. My only chance is to get assigned to one of the field trials somewhere. It's my only way of lasting it."

"Field trials?"

"They try out new drugs on people, like in Africa and places. When they're not suitable for trying in hospitals in this country."

"Like at their clinic at Entropist Hospital."

"Yeah, I guess."

"What do they do there?"

"That I don't know, either. Some kind of accident research, I guess."

"But do you work with Dr. Merom?"

"Yeah, sometimes. What about it?"

"Isn't she in charge of the work at the Entropist Clinic?"

"Is she? If she is, she sure doesn't spend much time there, 'cause she's running a couple of projects in Research Three."

There was a knock on the door.

I got up to answer it. Sam got Ray another beer. It was my woman and her daughter Lucy. I introduced them. Sam introduced herself and Ray, who said, "Who is this, then?"

"This is Daddy's lady friend."

"It is?" he said, and shot a look toward the bedroom door. "Wow. This is a groovy pad. You are a *funny* man, man."

"Who's got the new bed in the office, Albert?" my woman asked.

"I do," I said. "It's a long story."

I told it. Including how there happened to be a strange woman asleep in my other bed. I'd been out for a walk in the woods, see. And when I came back not only had somebody eaten all my porridge, but . . .

My woman believed me, even if Raymond McGonigle didn't.

I was up before nine. Early for a Sunday. Early for any day.

And instead of having a group breakfast, I took Linn Pighee's keys and headed for Beech Grove.

When I got out of my truck, I was surprised to see movement

on the front porch of the Pighees' house. I walked toward it and saw Mrs. Thomas closing the door. Then she turned and saw me.

"Hello, Mrs. Thomas," I said, to show there were no hard feelings.

"If you've come to see my sister-in-law, she's still asleep," Mrs. Thomas said.

"Not at church?"

"She always sleeps late," Mrs. Thomas said, in a voice half hushed and half shrill.

"Left an early call, did she?" I asked. Considering the lack of familial feeling expressed to me by both of these legal sisters, I was interested in what she was doing in the house.

"I've got to protect John's interests," Mrs. Thomas said. But she, in her turn, was surprised to see me. "What are you doing here?" she asked, not to put too fine a point on it.

I didn't really feel like telling her I'd come to look through her brother's financial records. "I've finished my work for you, that's understood," I said. "I put the bill in the mail yesterday."

"Better not be for much," she said. "You didn't do much."

"I got you permission to visit your brother, which is what you wanted. Until you decided you weren't so bothered, after all."

"It was the principle of the thing," she said.

We stood on the porch, each waiting for the other to leave.

Then she said, "You can ring the bell all you like. It's nothing to do with me."

I watched her walk around the house. She looked back only as she turned the corner.

Inside, things were neat and organized. Far more so than when I'd visited before. I'd expected disarray. Preconceptions about disturbed people predispose expectations of abnormal chaos. If anything was abnormal, it was the order.

Then I remembered Mrs. Thomas. Who used to keep house for her brother. Maybe her habits broke hard.

I found John Pighee's financial records easily, once I realized that he had had a bedroom of his own. A highly organized couple.

I went through his bank statements, but found the mass of numbers, year after year, anything but illuminating. Then I went back through them more slowly, making a list of deposits, each year, in his checking and savings accounts.

He had an electronic calculator, which I used to total the figures on the spot. Knowing that without it I would have run out of fingers.

But apart from the fact that he started life with Sir Jeff taking home about $7,500 a year and had upped it, over their five-year association, to a little under $12,000, there didn't seem to be anything dramatic. No sudden leaps up; no sudden leaps down. The surface of things proved what I already knew: everybody earns more money than I do.

I worked backward through the canceled checks but got fed up after two years. There was nothing unusual, apart from regular maintenance to Mrs. Thomas. The whole thing irritated me. There was a kind of control over the visible aspects of John Pighee's life. Many aspire to that kind of containment of life's parameters, but few are chosen. And if he was one of the few, it didn't square with the kind of activity that would lead him into a mysterious explosion. Pighee wasn't in debt, he paid his bills on time, and he had more than $3,000 in his savings account. A Never-Touch Fund, which he'd never touched.

I left Pighee's papers. I walked around the house room by room. Upstairs, apart from the two main bedrooms, there was a sparsely furnished guest room and a room with bunk beds. Neither showed conspicuous signs of use. Downstairs there were several rooms, more than minimally furnished. But it was clear where Linn Pighee's main haunts were, because only there were there the little scraps that fall from regular human usage. She used the porch where she interviewed me, she used the kitchen, and she used her bedroom. Nothing else looked lived in. Nothing else looked as if it had ever been lived in. Even John Pighee's bedroom itself. If he was an ambitious man—and everybody said he was—then he didn't surround himself with the traditional self-confidencers that most such men use to celebrate each step up the ladder. There were no fancy stereos, no expensive hobby gadgets or house improvements.

I went out to the double garage and found one car. A small '74 Ford; nothing fancy. Probably Linn's car. The hinges on the door on the empty side of the garage looked functional. But I don't know how to tell by looking whether something unused for seven months had been used regularly before then.

I got in the car that was there, tried the car key on Linn's key ring. The car started immediately. It was half full of gas, showed nearly eleven thousand miles. I found some service records and insurance documents in the glove compartment. Everything up to date. I put them back and returned to the house.

Instead of going immediately to John Pighee's room, I went to Linn's bedroom, and to the desk she had there. I packed up her checkbook and some envelopes that seemed to hold receipts and bank statements and carried them next door.

In John Pighee's bedroom doorway I paused, struck by a powerful sense of foreboding familiarity. It stopped me cold; struck me cold. The situation reminded me of two different problems I'd worked on in past days. One where I'd spent wretched, boring hours going through photographs of the financial and other records of a man who'd led a double life of sorts. A man now in jail. The other problem had been one that had led me to hunt through a house looking for a box of filing cards. I'd got tired and slept for a few hours. The house—the bed on which I'd slept—belonged to a dead man, a man killed, a man who'd been a private detective in his lifetime.

Neither memory was pleasant.

But I went in and sat at Pighee's desk. I doodled for a while. Then, one by one, I went through his drawers. I made a pile of everything financial, which was in fact almost everything. I found a gun, too. That brought back memories of years before, when I'd shot a man because he was stealing something I was supposed to guard. Another scar. I packed up all the records and left. Leaving the gun where I'd found it.

SEVENTEEN / "We thought you'd deserted us," Sam said cheerily when I came upon them in my living room.

"No such luck." I addressed Linn. "How's the patient?"

"Better," she said, without being particularly convincing.

"I was just about to go out," Sam said. "I'm glad you came back, though. Do you have the Sunday paper delivered or do you go out and get it?"

"You're not going to have time to read any Sunday paper," I said.

"I'm not?"

"You're on a case."

"I know, but . . ."

"So you've got work to do. Come on."

I took her to the office and set her to compiling detailed statistics from the pile of papers I'd taken from the Pighee house.

"Oh, Daddy!"

"Make me charts. I want charts," I said. "Income charts. Totals year by year, and individual source totals. Classify any records you can find. Then expenditure charts. Go through all the canceled checks and group them. Then through loose bills, see if they correspond to the checks. We're looking for unusual things, but we've got to know first what's usual. Complete analysis."

"Complete?" she asked, not knowing quite what was wanted.

"Yup. I'll push your meals under the door, and if you're not finished by the end of the week, you're fired."

"Oh, Daddy!"

Linn was leaning back in my dining-room chair with her eyes closed.

"Has she fed you?" I asked.

"I'm not very hungry. I don't much like eating in the mornings."

"Pregnant?"

She looked at me, but didn't say anything. Then tilted her head back again and said, "I should be so lucky."

I busied myself with toast and reheating Sam's coffee. I fought through the beer surplus and got myself some orange juice. Thus fortified, I sat down at my living-room desk. "Are you up to answering a few questions for me?"

Without opening her eyes she said, "I suppose so."

"Since he started working in the research labs, John was only on the sales staff part-time. That was—what, nearly two years ago. Why didn't his income drop? I've gone through his deposits and they rise neatly and regularly without the smallest kink to show when he changed his work pattern."

"I don't know," she said. "I don't know about his money."

"Do you know how much he was earning?"

She shook her head.

"All right," I said, "something else. Did he have a car?"

"Sure."

"Where is it?"

"Christ!" she said. Then hesitated. "Isn't it in the garage?"

"No. Only yours. The Ford is yours, isn't it?"

"Yeah. It's not in the garage? Oh, hang on. It was a company car —would that have anything to do with it? I just never thought about it. I didn't look."

"You haven't even been to the garage since it happened?"

"No," she said. "I guess they must have found the car at the company. And taken it back. Or something. Walter might know."

"The lawyer?"

"Yes. Everything addressed to John goes there now."

I nodded. "When I got to the house," I said, "your sister-in-law was just coming out of the front door."

"The bitch. She has a key. I locked it before I left, but she has a key to the front."

"Why would she have been in the house?"

"Nosing around. She wants the house. I'm sure that's what it is. She used to keep house for us. For John, anyway. Everything absolutely in place. Screwed to the shelves. The way John liked things. Since the accident, she only sneaks in in the mornings sometimes, when she thinks I'm asleep. It's not as if I can't run a house, but she thinks John is God's chosen and she's all thirteen apostles. I set a mousetrap in April. If I'd caught a mouse, I'd have left it in the front hall for her. She'd have cleared it away without a murmur."

It was the longest speech I'd ever heard her make. And hardly ambiguous. While she was being direct, I asked, "Linn, are you sure you haven't been out of the house since the accident?"

This brought her head up, and she looked at me. "You mean before yesterday?"

I nodded.

"Of course I'm sure."

"Not to buy food, or anything?"

"I phone for everything to be sent in. What are you asking, Mr. Albert? I ought to know whether I've been out or not."

"Not even as far as the garage?"

She just stared at me.

"I tried the car in the garage. Your car."

"What of it?"

"It started. Right away. If it hadn't been used in the last seven months, it wouldn't have. Who uses it? Surely not Mrs. Thomas."

"She'd run it into a phone pole just because it was mine," Linn said. Then she put her head back and closed her eyes and didn't say anything.

I waited. Then I said, "Well?"

"The car gets used sometimes."

"Who by?"

"There's a boy who brings me medicine. . . ."

"Dougie? The basketball player?"

"You know him?"

"I met him the first time I came to see you."

"Oh, yeah," she said without remembering clearly.

"And the medicine is booze and it's a regular delivery. I don't see how that ties into use of the car."

"Well, Dougie doesn't have a car, and the liquor store he works for keeps strict tabs on the mileage in the delivery truck. So I lend him my car sometimes. And he runs special errands for me. There are some things it's hard to have delivered. He does some of my special shopping. Books and stuff from the drugstore. He helps me quite a lot."

"And you lend him your car?"

"Yes," she said. "He has a girl friend and it's hard to have a girl friend around here without a car. I wish he'd use it more, really. He's a very careful type of kid. Not at all like most of them. And each time, Mrs. Nosy Thomas must think it's me going out and I really like that."

"Is lending him your car all you do for Dougie?"

"You mean money?"

"No."

She hesitated before saying, "I get very lonely. Very lonely. I'm not the type of person to live on my own. It really gets to me." She paused. "Don't think badly of me."

"I don't," I said.

She didn't say anything.

"Are you up to making a phone call for me?"

"A phone call?"

"To Walter Weston. Because of . . . your being a bit off-color yesterday, I didn't get to see him. I wondered if you might request that he drop into his office this afternoon to give me a chance to read through these papers of John's."

"He won't like that," she said. And sat up. "Where's the phone?"

She was very tough with him. Threatened to take her business elsewhere, and that was evidently enough to rouse him from the trivia of a day at home with his family. She fixed three in the afternoon as a convenient time. I gave her a round of applause after she hung up.

But she said quietly, "I don't like him much. I don't like many people. Can I go to bed now?"

"Sure."

About twelve I took Sam a cup of coffee and a set of colored pencils. She was working hard and didn't stop for my interruption. One day she would make someone a good private detective.

At 2:30 I left, but on the stairs I found a visitor on his way up. The increasingly familiar form of Raymond McGonigle.

"My ma was a little late with dinner," he said. "Otherwise I'd have been over earlier."

I presume he stood there watching me as I went out.

Weston watched me as I came in. He left me in no doubt about what he thought of the situation.

"I don't like this," he said. "You seem to have some kind of influence over Linn Pighee."

"Just because she's asking questions?"

"I thought you worked for John's sister."

"I did. I work for Mrs. Pighee now."

"I've seen some low sharpsters in my time," he said, "but you seem to work on a level new to me."

I faced him squarely. "The situation surrounding John Pighee's accident stinks," I told him. "And I don't know whether you're a source of stink or whether some of it's just rubbed off. I don't need to prove my integrity to myself. But don't be surprised if I'm not particularly tactful with you." I pulled Linn's letter of instruction out and gave it to him. "I've got the right now to look at the documents relating to your clients John and Linn Pighee. Would you produce them, please?"

He studied the paper. Then he gave in and got me a large tie-closed folder. He sat down while I opened it. "These are the basic records of my six years representing the Pighees. Tell me what you want to see, and I'll tell you whether I can show it to you."

"I'll just take the file home with me, shall I, and sort through it all without making you wait and watch."

"Like hell," he said.

I smiled. Then I asked for the compensation papers. He sorted out a five-page document. I glanced at it. A private contract. Binding neither Loftus Pharmaceuticals nor any named insurance company. "This is in addition to some basic cover from the company, is it?"

"Yes."

"Tell me about Pighee's money. Is it paid directly to you now?"

"Copies of all documents go to Linn," he said defensively, "but I handle the accounts. She writes checks on them."

"How much money is coming in?"

"John gets his full salary."

"Which is?"

"Gross about twelve hundred dollars a month," he said grudgingly.

"Hmm," I said. "And where does it come from?"

"Why, the company, of course," Weston said.

"In one check?"

"No. As I understand it, John split his time and therefore is paid by two departments."

"How much from each?"

"Well, the gross amounts, from the sales side nearly seven hundred, from the research side a little over five."

"Who writes the checks on the science side?"

"The checks?"

"Who signs them? How are they drawn?"

"John's employer. Henry Rush."

"His employer? I thought Loftus was—"

"John was under a personal service contract with Henry Rush. That is the logical basis for Rush's involvement in the compensation side. How he is secured, I don't know. But John signed the contract and presented me with Rush's compensation arrangement. He was explicit how he wanted things."

"So Pighee brought the compensation contract. You didn't negotiate it directly?"

"I never said I did."

"No," I conceded. "You didn't. How did it come about?"

He sighed, but answered. "When he started working in the lab, about two years ago . . . wait"—he checked the date on the contracts—"twenty-two months ago, he came to me and told me that he would be working with substances which were dangerous."

"He said that?"

"He did."

"What kind of substances?"

"I don't know. From what happened, obviously things that were explosive."

"He said 'substances'?"

"As far as I can remember."

"Could it have been disease substances? Like bacteria or viruses?"

"I don't know. But those things don't blow up, do they?"

"But he didn't specify?"

"No. Except that they were dangerous, potentially dangerous. And he said he'd taken steps that if anything happened to him Linn would be taken care of."

"And his sister?"

"She gets regular money as well. He brought me these papers from Henry Rush. For me to hold. When the accident happened, Rush started fulfilling his obligation immediately. We've had no cause for any complaint."

"Do you know from personal experience whether Rush paid Pighee's salary before the accident?"

"I didn't handle John's money before the accident. He did all the accounts himself."

"And the documents he presented you with included a waiver of any direct claim against Loftus Pharmaceuticals or its insurers?"

"They did." He pointed out where.

"Was this the only document he brought you? The only contingency business?"

"No."

"Well?"

"He made a will."

"Anything unusual in it?"

"He made specific bequests—the bulk of his assets to his wife, and the remainder to his sister."

"Did he say why?"

"He said he wanted his sister to have any long-term royalties as an income."

"Royalties?"

"Yes."

"Royalties from what?"

Weston smiled for the first time. "I don't know. But John had plans."

"But surely anything he invented, or discovered, while working for Loftus would belong to Loftus."

"Maybe that was part of the reason for the personal service contract."

"But surely, if he works in their labs. . ."

"Maybe he was intending to make a hit record. I wouldn't have put anything like that as beyond him.

I shrugged. "Did he leave other instructions?"

"An envelope."

"Oh?"

"An envelope," Weston said, with a sigh, "which was only to be opened if he died."

"You're joking." I laughed.

But he wasn't.

"What's in it?" I asked.

"I don't know."

"Haven't you opened it?"

"Of course not. He isn't dead."

"Is it here?"

"I can get it," he said. "But it can't be opened."

"I just want to see it," I said. "I want to feel it and hold it up to the light. Like a Christmas present. There's no law against that, is there?"

He got the envelope, which was kept in the firm's safe.

It was a thick brown envelope, sealed with impressed wax. As Weston had said, it read, "Not to be opened before I am dead." Signed and dated. It was fat with its contents. I couldn't resist. I ripped it open.

"Hey!" Weston was outraged.

"I never was very good at waiting till Christmas," I said.

"You've committed an offense," he said.

"As far as I'm concerned, it was open when you brought it to me," I said. "And you got huffy when I told you you shouldn't have peeked."

I poured the contents of the envelope on the table.

It was another envelope. On the outside it read, "To be delivered immediately to Marcia Merom, 4901 Washington Boulevard."

That was interesting, but I was in no mood for half measures. I ripped the second envelope open.

It was full of money. Twenty-two thousand dollars. In used hundred-dollar bills.

EIGHTEEN   /   I let Weston put the money back in the envelope, and I signed a paper saying that he had given me a pile of documents, as per Linn's instruction, and that I had opened the envelope before either of us realized it was prohibited territory.

He agreed to let it go at that because he was as suspicious of used hundred-dollar bills as I was. Quite apart from any other considerations. And I agreed to let him go, back to his day off. We parted on better terms than we had met on.

The existence of the envelope wouldn't leave my mind as I drove back to my office. "Not to be opened before I am dead."

It added to my worries. John Pighee had seemed able to anticipate the need for various contingencies that, from what I knew of his situation, most people just wouldn't have thought likely enough to allow for. Which meant only that there was a lot about his situation that I didn't know.

As I walked up the stairs to my office, I could tell something wasn't right. I had no door.

"What the hell is going on here?" I asked as I walked in. But I could see what was going on. I had left my daughter working at my desk. But now, in her place, I found my door and a sweat-soaked Raymond McGonigle.

"Hi, man," he said.

Sam appeared at the living-room door. "Ray's fixing your door," she said. "You knew it stuck in the doorframe, didn't you? Well, Ray's going to fix it. We found some tools in a box in the other room. Isn't that great?"

"Yeah, great," I said, and walked through to the other room. Why don't people leave things alone? Especially my things.

Sam followed me. "Isn't it great?" she asked. "I knew you'd be pleased."

"Linn's asleep?"

"Yes. Is something wrong?"

"Doors are hard to hang. Has your friend ever 'fixed' a door before?"

"I don't know," she said.

"Go find out. Then bring me your charts."

She left without question. I called the only "Bartonio, Jos." listed in the phone book. John Pighee's sales supervisor.

I reminded him who I was. He was still concerned about John Pighee. I told him there'd been no change in his medical condition.

"Gee, that's a shame," he said.

"There was a question I missed asking on Friday."

"Shoot."

"John Pighee was on your staff part-time?"

"Right."

"Was he being paid part-time? What was the arrangement about his money?"

"Ahh," Bartonio said. "Well, he was still on nine-sixteenths time with my department, though to tell you the truth he wasn't really pulling that much weight. He was only getting about a third to half of the orders he had before he shifted, so his commissions were down. But we have an income-leveling plan for salesmen, and he was drawing on the basis of nine-sixteenths of his last two years' commissions, plus nine-sixteenths of his base salary. So he hadn't quite felt the full impact of his change."

"If he was only doing a third to half of the work, why was he on nine-sixteenths rates?"

"Because that was the original arrangement about his time. We got four mornings and two afternoons a week. But really because the rest of his money was on research rate and those guys don't come close to making the kind of money a good salesman can touch."

"Let me get this right," I said. "Pighee was also pulling seven-sixteenths research salary?"

"A technician's salary, I think," he said. "I didn't handle that side of it but that was my understanding."

"But he'd have been on the official payroll with two departments?"

"That's right. So that he came under the full-employment terms for insurance and pension and that sort of stuff."

"And you're also sure that Pighee would have taken a cut in pay to go into this arrangement?"

"Oh, yeah. No question. But John had interests which overrode money. That's a sign of a guy who knows where he's going."

Sam was waiting for me when I hung up.

"What was that about, Daddy?"

"I was taking the opportunity to check some facts. To confirm what I thought was pretty clear."

"And did they check?"

"I don't know. Let's see your handiwork."

She had analyzed the Pighee financial situation in detail. On the surface it showed what my superficial figures had. No cut in money. The opposite. And no unusual expenditures. Except about $1,500 a year to Mrs. Thomas. I wondered if she got some used hundred-dollar bills to supplement her monthly check.

But a look at the deposit records showed when Pighee's rearrangement had come. November of 1975, there were two credit entries adding up to what had been deposited in October, 1975. Payment suddenly by Loftus and Rush, instead of by Loftus alone.

Sam had laid the figures out well, made me pretty charts, and I told her so.

"What does it all mean, Daddy? What has happened? Aren't you going to tell me?"

"It means we may have a police matter on our hands," I said.

"Police!" she said. "What's it got to do with the fuzz?"

"They can find out quickly what I could only find out slowly, if at all."

"But the police . . ." she said, as if involving them were somehow not within the scope of fair play.

"Go remind Ray which end of the door goes at the top," I said. She left without saying anything. Which surprised me.

Then I followed her to my office. "Are you an insured builder?"
I asked Ray. Then I remembered that the building was coming
down in two and a half months. With luck he would still be inside
it.

"Aw, come on, man," Ray said. "I'm only trying to help."

"Take a breather," I said. "Answer a question for me."

He stopped mutilating my door for the moment.

I asked, "How much work did John Pighee do around the labs?
How much time did he put in?"

"I don't really know," McGonigle said. "My hours are so funny."

"Try and remember. Was he usually there? Sometimes there?
Always there?"

"Usually," he said.

"Usually in the morning? Afternoon?"

"I don't remember him in the morning much. Except maybe
weekends sometimes. But he was there most afternoons and he
seemed to do a lot of night work."

I nodded. "Is there any record made of the hours he worked?"

"There's no punch clock, if that's what you mean. If he stayed
late, he'd have had to sign out, but that's all."

"Signed out?"

"If you go in or out after six, you have to use the main gate and
sign the log."

"Even if you're a regular employee?"

"Yeah."

"Thanks," I said, and walked back to the phone in my living
room. I called my friend at the police department, a graying lieutenant named Jerry Miller.

"Who's there?"

I told him.

He said, "What's the occasion? Trying to sell tickets to the detectives' ball?"

"Sorry to bother you, Jerry."

"I'm sure you are," he said. "Tell you what. Why don't you cut
the stuff about how sorry you are, how's Janie, when am I going
to make captain, and get down to what you want from me. The
answer is no."

"I want to come in tomorrow and tell you about some things I've come across."

"Like what?"

"Like a quantity of used hundred-dollar bills."

"A quantity? How many?"

"Two hundred and twenty."

He was silent. I knew I had his attention. "That must have been some poker game, Albert," he said.

"They're not mine," I said.

"Whose are they?"

"Tomorrow," I said. "First I wondered if you—"

"Oh," he interrupted. "Just a little something else first." But he didn't say no.

"All I wanted to know was whether you have any connection with the security people at Loftus Pharmaceuticals."

I could practically hear him raise his eyebrows.

"I want access to some logbooks they keep. I'm trying to reconstruct the movements of a man who worked there—works there. Sometimes he stayed late and when he did that he had to sign out. I want to go through the books and find out how often it happened. That's all. I can go now, I can go tonight, I can go tomorrow, but the sooner I have it the sooner I come to talk to you."

"Loftus Pharmaceuticals, huh?" he asked.

"Yeah."

"I don't know. I'll see if I can turn someone up."

We hung up. I waited by the phone, listening to Ray scraping my door to sawdust in the other room. Nothing else happened for twenty minutes. So I made myself something to eat. Baked beans and caviar, which seemed to be the only thing in the house, besides beer.

At twenty past six Sam came in and announced, "The door is back up." At the same time the phone rang.

"Yeah?" I said. Into the phone.

"I've got a contact with one of the main-gate guards. He's on duty now. His friend says that he'll call him, but that you'll have to go down and do whatever work you want to do on the premises. You can't take logbooks away. That O.K.?"

"I'll go down now," I said.

"Guy's name is Russell Fincastle. He'll know your name."

"O.K. Thanks, Jerry."

"Tomorrow," he said sternly. "Tomorrow."

I gathered my notebook and headed for the outer world.

"How do you like it, Daddy?" Sam asked, but not confidently. The door was back in place. With a two-inch gap at the bottom. I looked at her scientific friend. Then I tried the door. It opened easily. Just by turning the handle and pulling.

"At least it doesn't stick now," I said. And left. I pulled the door closed behind me. It hit the frame and flew open again.

"You can close it, Daddy," Sam rushed forward to assure me. "If you lift it and pull it gently."

Russell Fincastle was short and lean, and young. I introduced myself and he shook hands with me left-handed. He showed me two heavily taped fingers on his right hand.

"Rough job here, then?" I asked.

He laughed modestly. "Broke them playing ball," he said.

"Ball?"

"Basketball. Thought I'd just stunned them the way you do, hit them on the ends, but both bastards were fractured."

"That's bad luck. Where do you play?"

"Summers in the park. Winter the Industrial League. Semipro. And a little cash from it hurts me not a bit." He looked at me coolly.

"Ah," I said. "A little cash. What's the rate for looking through your logbooks, then? Five do it?"

"Ten would do it better," he said.

"I'm sure it would, and twenty better still, but five's my limit."

He just nodded. I pulled out my wallet. Found four ones. Fished through my pockets and turned up ninety-eight cents.

He laughed, which was just as well. "Bargain day," he said. And he showed me the current log.

"I'm interested in January, this year."

"January?"

"Yeah. You keep them that long, don't you?"

"Well, yeah. Hell, that's O.K., I suppose." He pulled out a big book from below the counter level of the guard's window.

"Who exactly has to sign these things?"

"Everybody who goes in or out after six, or anytime on weekends and holidays."

"Everybody? There are no other points on the premises where people go in and out?"

"Not after six."

"Would Sir Jeff have to sign out?" I asked.

"If I was on duty," he said.

I started on the first of January, since I didn't know the exact day of John Pighee's accident. Everyone said it was seven months ago and that meant January.

I found John Pighee's name, signed in at 1:15 and out at 6:30 on January 1st. There were eight other names in the book for January 1st. Which seemed pretty busy going for New Year's Day. Which is the day after New Year's Eve. But on the second of January there were thirty-one names. Not including Pighee's.

"A lot of people come in and out out of hours," I said to Fincastle.

"That's what I'm in business for," he said.

"Is there any way of telling where inside the perimeter they are?"

He showed me the column of squiggles that indicated where people said they were going or said they had been. "R 3" for Research Three. Which made a certain amount of sense.

In the first three weeks of January, Pighee's name was in the book twelve times, half of them signing out after midnight. He was there each of the three Thursdays and never on Monday, with each of the other nights being represented at least once. His timings were not regular; he had signed out as early as 6:15 p.m. and as late as 3:30 a.m.

The first day of the fourth week was Thursday, January 27th. He had signed in at 7 p.m. but had not signed out. I managed to hypothesize that that was the night of the accident.

I called Fincastle's attention to the entry. "What do you do when somebody signs in but doesn't sign out?"

He squinted over it. "Let's see. That one's been checked out and approved. That's what that check is about." He pointed to a red tick.

"But what happens?"

"Well, about eleven-thirty we go through the book and make a call from here to everybody who's still in, reminding them they're supposed to be out by twelve."

"They're supposed to be out by twelve?"

"Mostly, yes. But it wouldn't apply to your fella there. He was in a research building and they work some weird hours."

"So you'd just let him stay."

"We'd let our patrol people know which building he was in. They'd usually have a look before 1 a.m. And even the scientists don't stay much after that, usually. But we keep tabs on them."

I went back to the books. Confirmed that John Pighee's name didn't appear after the twenty-seventh of January, then went back to the accident night, to see who else was in Research Three.

I found Ray McGonigle's name, signed out at 10:15. And Dr. Marcia Merom's for 7:39, which was before the accident. Ray had timed it about eight. But those were the only signatories for Research Three.

"This is funny," I said.

"What is?"

"I know of at least one person who was in Research Three on the twenty-seventh who isn't signed in or out."

"How do you know that?"

"The guy I'm tracing had an accident. People have told me he was there." Ray had said Dundree was quickly on the scene.

"Accident?"

"A guy blew himself up in Research Three. January 27th."

"I remember something about it, vaguely," he said vaguely. "I suppose sometimes people get in or out without signing. And if they stay there all night, they wouldn't sign out."

"You don't seem all that worried."

"I wasn't on that night," he said.

I thought for a minute.

"You wouldn't want to do me a favor, would you?" I asked.

"Shouldn't think so," he said, with a smile.

"For maybe ten bucks?"

"What kind of favor?"

"I'd like a list of all the people who signed out or in and out of Research Three over the year or so before this guy's accident."

"You're talking about a long list," he said.

"I thought maybe something you could do easily enough in your slow times tonight."

"You gave me four dollars and ninety-eight cents just to look in the books yourself. At that rate, what you're asking me to do would be worth forty-nine ninety-five."

"Twenty's the limit."

"Done," he said without hesitating.

NINETEEN / When I got back to the office, Ray McGonigle, finished with my door, was working on my doorframe. I just walked through to my living room. It was a quarter to eight and Linn Pighee was awake, talking with Sam.

"Hello," I said. "Sam, I think your friend wants some help on his carpentry lesson."

"What?"

"Go help your friend."

"But—"

"This is your employer speaking."

"Oh. I . . ." She went.

"How do you feel?" I asked Linn.

"Better, for the moment," she said. "Sam said you've been out working. Do you work seven days a week?"

"Only when I'm employed," I said. "Linn, we've come to the time to try to find some things out. All I've got for my efforts, so far, is more questions and none of the answers."

"What do you want to do?" she asked uncertainly.

"I want to go to the hospital tomorrow," I said. "And I want you to come, too."

"Me?"

"Yeah."

"But why?"

"Because I need someone who can identify your husband."

"Identify him? What do you mean?"

"The Loftus people—or the Rush people, at least—have gone to a lot of trouble to keep John's family from seeing him. Just seeing him. That's suspicious behavior in my book. But it's more suspect because John was involved in a setup which not only took a lot of shortcuts about his salary and getting him into the labs despite a shortage of lab space for more qualified people, but provided him with a lot of cash."

"Cash?"

"He left an envelope with twenty-two thousand dollars in used hundred-dollar bills with Walter Weston. So far, I don't have any idea where he'd have come across money like that. Have you?"

She shook her head.

"Linn," I said quietly, "he left it in an envelope saying it should go to someone named Marcia Merom."

"It's his money."

"Do you know Marcia Merom?"

"No."

"Have you heard the name? Do you know who she is?"

"No."

"She works at Loftus. In the lab he worked in, and she's his doctor at the Loftus Clinic."

"Cozy," she said.

"It doesn't bother you?"

"You obviously think it should."

"It seems to imply the sort of thing that does bother a lot of people."

"Albert," she said warmly, "I was missing my huggings a lot longer ago than seven months." Then she said, "Walter never mentioned an envelope of money."

"He didn't know until today. The point is there's nothing on paper in your husband's records to show where that kind of money came from. It opens a whole group of questions, which tend to imply some criminal activities."

"Criminal? Oh, no," she said. "John wouldn't be involved in anything criminal."

"That is something we'll have to confirm," I said.

"Oh, dear."

"But I have to ask questions about why they don't want people seeing him in the hospital. Hard questions."

"Like?"

"Like, is it John Pighee who *is* in the hospital?"

She sat quiet for a moment. Then said, "My God."

"Has anyone seen him there that you know of? Has anyone seen anybody?"

She sat silently. She hadn't. She didn't know.

"I need someone who knows him. Someone I can trust."

"But . . ." she began. "But . . ."

"He might be alive somewhere. He might have cooperated in this whole business to leave and start a new life."

She shivered. Whether because she thought that impossible or just because she didn't like the idea, I didn't know.

"Or they might have someone else in there for some other reason."

"What?"

"The range of possibilities *could* be very wide. He might be off doing something for somebody . . . and not want to answer questions."

She shook again.

"It's also perfectly possible that something about the work he was doing needs covering up."

"But which . . . ?" she asked, a little frantically.

"I don't know," I said. "But it's time, tomorrow, that we stopped asking people to tell us. And started making them."

TWENTY / At 9 a.m. I called Loftus Pharmaceuticals and asked for P. Henry Rush's office.

His secretary told me that he wasn't in and might not be coming in today; who was calling?

"Don't tell me," I said. "He might be going out of the state today."

"Yes," she said.

"My name is Albert Samson," I said. "I'm calling about John Austin Pighee. I want him to call me back before ten, because that's when I'm going to the police."

With no apparent emotion she read the message back to me, and we severed our connections.

"That sounded pretty tough, Daddy," Sam said with her eyes wide. "Are you really going to the police? If he doesn't call back, I mean?"

"I don't expect to have that condition met," I said.

And I didn't. At 9:50 the phone rang. P. Henry Rush.

"I just came in and my secretary gave me your strange message, Samson. I don't know what it's about but it sounds a rather thinly veiled threat to me. Perhaps I should be the one talking about going to the police."

"We'll go together, shall we?"

"What's all this about?" he said, firming up.

"It's about access to John Pighee," I said.

"I thought we'd been through all that. Last . . . Friday. Lunchtime, wasn't it? I contacted the Clinic and left them instructions to allow family visitors. Has your client been turned away again?"

"No," I said.

"Well?"

"My client as of Friday was Pighee's sister. An hour after I talked to you, Dr. Jay Dundree called on the lady and bought her off."

"Bought her off?" Said as if such a phrase tasted bad on his lips.

"Talked her out of her expressed and strong wish to visit her brother and gave her money."

"So you're without a client," he said. "I see."

"I have a new client," I said. "Mrs. Pighee. And she wants to see her husband."

"Do you?" he said. "Does she?"

"That's right. Today."

"I can see that you might well feel disgruntled if Dr. Dundree convinced your client that she didn't need your services. But you sound as if you've taken it all personally. Are you implying that I had some hand in Dr. Dundree's action?"

"Tinker to Evers to Chance," I said. "Yes, it crossed my mind."

"Well, I didn't. While Dr. Dundree was taking time out from his duties to visit an injured colleague's sister, I was arranging that she be allowed to visit if she wanted. I only found out afterwards that he had obviated the need. But we certainly acted separately. I believe you saw him Friday morning and told him of the sister's worries. He acted in response to that visit. He didn't know that you had seen me in connection with the same matter."

He sounded convincing. "You won't be offended," I said, "if I don't necessarily believe you."

"What I say is true, Samson. But it's also past. You say you have a new client who wants to see John Pighee?"

"His wife, yes. She wants to see him today."

"Out of the blue? After seven months."

"Today," I said.

"I don't know what satisfaction she hopes to get from visiting a man in a coma."

"I'm sure you don't," I said.

"Does she know the medical risks she may be putting her husband to?"

"Here we go again," I said. "We'll be at the hospital at four o'clock and we'll expect to see John Pighee. If we're prevented, you can expect, at the least, legal action and newspaper reports. And in all likelihood criminal investigation."

"You said something about the police in your message," Rush said. "I thought it was just a cheap device to impose on my attention."

"I'm not expensive," I said, "but I'm not cheap."

"Are you seriously suggesting some police involvement in this business? Because wasting police time and money is not something to be done lightly."

"Thanks for your concern," I said. "See you at four."

"You're requiring my presence now, are you?" he said with growing exasperation. He was giving a good performance of someone dealing with a madman of ever-increasing dementia.

"No," I said. "All we want is to see John Pighee."

Well, nearly all.

Sam sat in silence while I made notes of this conversation in my notebook.

"I don't know whether Linn's up to seeing her husband," she said as I poured myself a cup of coffee.

"I asked her last night," I said.

Sam shrugged. "Is there anything for me to do?" she asked.

"I'm going out now," I said. "Mind the shop and take care of the customers, will you?"

"I guess so," she said. Without enthusiasm.

"Look, I'm going to see my friend at the police department. I don't think you'd much like that."

"No," she said, and wrinkled her nose.

I realized she hadn't smiled at me all morning. "Is something wrong?"

"I just wondered if you were sure you are doing the right thing."

"Going to the police?"

"Pushing things."

"I'm stirring the pot, at least," I said.

"Linn seemed so sad last night."

"Did she?"

"Didn't you notice?"

"She was tired. But she's always tired. I thought she was getting a little better, though."

"She doesn't eat anything," Sam said.

"She doesn't?"

"Almost nothing."

"Well," I said, picking up my notebook, "feed her." I left.

I caught up with Miller at about twenty past ten. He looked surprised to see me.

"I said I'd be in today," I said.

"You must want something. I thought I was going to have to put out a pickup on you to get you in."

"But I said . . ."

"So what is this business about John Pighee?" he asked.

I showed my surprise. I hadn't given him the name.

"I had a little talk with Russ Fincastle, yeah. I put you on to him. I thought I was entitled. So you're working on a guy who had an accident in January. So a guy got himself seriously injured. Big deal. It happens in the best of companies."

"They don't usually know it's going to happen before it does," I said.

"He knew it was going to happen?"

"He made some unusual contingency plans," I said, and told him about the agreement and the envelope marked "Not to be opened before I am dead." "The used hundreds were in the envelope."

"Has he been declared dead?" Miller asked solemnly.

"No."

He rubbed his face as if that was the answer he'd expected. "How is the guy?"

I told him.

He said, "I was thinking about those used hundreds. They don't have to have been obtained illegally. They might just be a crude way of getting around inheritance taxes."

"The guy wasn't blatantly crude," I said, "and his financial records give no indication where he'd come across a lump sum like that. I've been through them. He's got three thousand or so in savings, which came from his earnings over the last five years. He couldn't really have saved a lot more than that from the incomes he declared on his tax returns without living a lot more austerely than he did. So he had some other income, and it came in cash and without records. You've got superficial tax evasion if nothing else."

"But you think it's something else?" Miller asked.

I went through the history of the exclusion of family from Pighee's bedside and why it seemed suspicious to me.

"I don't know," Miller said.

"I'm taking Linn Pighee over there this afternoon at four. I want you to come."

"Me?"

"As a sort of unofficial official witness."

"It's not a police matter, Al," he said.

"I didn't say it was, but we're less likely to get fobbed off if you're there sort of on your own time."

"You want me to come on my own time, on police time, to be an unofficial official witness?"

"I couldn't have put it better myself."

I left without his promise, but I knew the situation interested him. That was almost as good as a promise.

I enjoyed the idea of pulling a string and having people jump a little. Having jumped to many a string myself. So after I left Miller I phoned Walter Weston. He was one of the world's unlucky people. Whenever I called him he was in.

I said, "Linn Pighee is going to Loftus Clinic this afternoon, to visit her husband. At four o'clock. She would like you to be present."

"Me?" he said. "Why?"

"There may be legal complications, and she'd like her own and her husband's interests protected."

"What kind of complications?"

"Identification, for one."

"Identification? Of what?"

"Of John Pighee. It's not entirely certain that the man in Loftus Clinic is John Pighee."

"You're kidding!" he said.

I wasn't. "Can you be there?"

"What reason do you—"

"Can you be there?" I repeated.

"I guess so," he said.

I was having a party and the guest list was complete.

TWENTY-ONE / I went back to the office, where I found Sam looking sternly at Linn Pighee.

"What's up?" I asked them.

"She won't eat breakfast," Sam said.

"I'm not hungry." Linn's voice was very weak.

"You've got to keep your strength up," I said. "And we've got a big afternoon today."

"I don't really feel very well," Linn said.

"She doesn't want to go, Daddy," Sam said.

"She doesn't?" I asked sharply. "You don't?"

"I never said that," Linn said.

"But you don't want to, do you?" Sam asked.

"None of us *want* to," I said.

"I'll go," Linn said, "if you think it's best."

"If we want to find out what's happening about your husband, I think we have to."

"Do you really think John is somewhere else?" Linn asked.

"I don't know what to think. But after today we'll know a lot better."

"You shouldn't get her hopes up, Daddy," Sam said.

"And you shouldn't go around telling everybody what they want and what they think," I snapped.

"Well, she's not well! She shouldn't go out. And you complained when *I* tried to push her around."

"Don't argue," Linn said plaintively. "I'll be all right. I just didn't sleep so well last night. I'll take a nap now so I'll be ready this afternoon."

"Won't you have something to eat?" I asked.

"I'll try later," she said.

Sam and I watched her go to the bedroom.

"I don't understand you, Daddy," Sam said as soon as Linn had closed the bedroom door.

"What's that supposed to mean?"

"She doesn't want to go out. Anybody can see that."

"But she wants to know about her husband. People often have wants which conflict with each other. It's up to her to choose."

"I understand that," Sam said sharply. "I'm not stupid. But what I don't understand is you pushing so hard for her to go. *You* are the one who's pushing her into decisions."

I started to defend myself. But stopped. She had a point. I shrugged.

"Why does she have to go today? Why not tomorrow?"

Not that she'd be more likely to want to go out tomorrow, either. But I said, "I feel it's the right time."

Sam still didn't understand.

"I feel it, Sam. I feel there's a momentum and a correctness to the timing. I don't want to lose it."

"The feeling?"

"And the concentration. I hate to let something I've worked on go. I've built up an understanding of what I don't understand. Another day and I might confuse myself. I don't like to toss away the pieces easily."

She was quiet for a while.

It gave me a moment to reassure myself that if Linn really didn't want to go out, I wasn't threatening to tie her up and roll her down the stairs. If her problem was mostly mental, concentrating on clearing a small obstacle might help build confidence for clearing larger ones.

Sam said, "You and Mummy must have had a lot of trouble when you lived together."

"What?"

"You must have had some feeling for her once. You wouldn't have wanted to throw all that away easily."

"I didn't," I said, after a moment's catching up with the long gone. "And it wasn't exactly me that threw it away."

"Mummy says it was."

"You talk about me?"

"Of course!" She burst with it. "You're my father. She's my mother. Of course I want to know about you. I've got curiosity, too, you know."

And I finally understood why an active kid could cut a few weeks out of a summer to hang around Indianapolis with an old man she'd hardly ever met. It was because it was her old man, and, thrust into other people's lives, she had little enough that was hers, all hers.

"We . . . your mother and I . . . we sort of met each other when we were both thinking about being things that we weren't, that we aren't."

"She thinks you're stupid to waste your time being a detective."

For all the years, it hurt.

"And I think she's stupid contenting herself with being a rich man's wife. She did all that while she was still just her rich father's daughter. She had a lot going for her, underneath all the silk."

"It still hurts?"

I didn't want to admit to her what I'd already admitted to myself. "Once stung," I said. Trying to be ambiguous. I didn't fool her a bit.

"I thought it might," she said. Then, for no logical reason, "You wrote me super letters when I was young."

"That's 'cause we were pen playmates. You've outgrown me now."

"Daddy, why are you a private detective?"

"It just seemed like a good idea at the time. And now—well, I know a lot more than I did about how to do it, and it seems a shame to throw all that good knowledge away. And I like those odd times, every year or two, when someone tells me something interesting."

"But why without really trying at it? Why without working hard at it?"

"There's no reward for working hard except more money and less time to enjoy it."

"But . . ."

"And I don't like to waste my concern, my feeling, on things that aren't really interesting. I'd rather save them for situations like this one, so I can pull out my best, even if it isn't good enough."

It seemed to satisfy her. Even if it didn't satisfy me.

At least she didn't ask another question. I said, "So I don't want to make Linn go out this afternoon. But if she will, then I'll encourage her."

Quietly, Sam accepted the return to work. "Isn't there something else you could do?"

"Any suggestions?"

"I don't know," she said. "I don't know all that much about it, do I?"

I spent the rest of the morning going through my notes on the case with her.

When it was ten minutes past the time I thought Linn should be up, I said, "Is Linn awake?"

"No," Sam said. "If she is, she hasn't made any noise."

"I'll go look."

I went to the bedroom and opened the door very quietly. Linn Pighee was still and facing the wall so I couldn't see her face.

I said, "Linn?"

She didn't move.

I said her name again.

She turned over. Her eyes were still closed, but she clawed at the space next to her. She made sounds, breathing at first and then some crying. She slurred the word "John," said it again. Turned back to the wall and became still again.

I left her, wondering how much stress she could take. And decided to make some coffee before waking her up for real.

But as I was pouring it into three cups, the bedroom door opened and Linn walked out smiling. "I'm getting used to your mother's smock, Mr. Albert," she said. "Do you think she'd let me buy it from her?"

"I doubt it. But she'd give it to you. Want some coffee?"

"Lovely," she said, and took it. "When do we leave?"

"A little less than an hour."

"You know," she said, "I don't have anything suitable to wear."

She decided to dress from Sam's wardrobe, rather than mine, and when we descended the stairs at 3:40 they looked more like sisters than I would have thought possible. Out for a walk with Pop. Linn remained cheerful. Only at the outside door did she shudder and ask, "How far is the car?"

"It's a panel truck and it's around the corner."

"Couldn't you go bring it up to the curb, Daddy?"

I did.

Sam sat in the back on the cushions I keep there. "I don't often have two passengers at the same time," I said.

"You should go out and get my car," Linn said. "I'd be very happy for you to use it. It ought to be used."

We were quiet for a while as I made progress toward the hospital. Then Linn said, "I'll bet Dougie is worried about me. He's very responsible that way, you know."

"Who's Dougie?" Sam asked.

"He's a boy who used to bring me medicine, when I was in Beech Grove."

"That was nice of him," Sam said.

"I'm sure Mrs. Thomas is aware by now that you're not at home," I said. "If he asks, she'll tell him that."

"I suppose so," Linn said.

I saw Sam's face wrinkling in the rear-view mirror. She said, "He'll probably stop by in a few days, and you'll be able to tell him yourself."

Linn didn't say anything.

Neither did I.

"You're bound to be feeling better by then," Sam said.

"I'm not going back to that house," Linn said. "Not now I'm out. Not ever."

TWENTY-TWO / Walter Weston was sitting in the Loftus Clinic waiting area. He didn't see us when we walked in; he seemed to be brooding.

"Hello, Walter," Linn said when we arrived in front of him.

He literally jumped up. "Linn! Hello."

"Hello, Walter," she said again.

"You don't look very well. Sit down."

She did.

He acknowledged me and then looked at Sam. "Who is the young lady?"

"My daughter," I said. "But she's also a trainee detective. It's a family business."

Weston didn't say anything, but he brushed at the hair that hung over his forehead.

Sam asked Linn if she felt all right. She said she did, but her voice lacked conviction, even to me.

"Let's get going," Weston said. "If we must go through with this bizarre episode."

"We're not all here yet," I said.

"No?"

"A friend of mine from the police department is supposed to meet us here at four."

"Police?" he said. But didn't press it, because the envelope of used hundreds had been bothering him, too.

I looked at my watch. It was five past four. I said, "We might as well go ahead with preliminaries." I walked to the reception desk and said, "We are a party with Mrs. Linn Pighee. We want to see her husband, John Pighee."

The nurse was the same one I'd dealt with four days before. She didn't say anything to me but turned to the room behind her and called "Evan!"

The bouncer. I thought she was calling him out to dribble with me again. But he came to the door and walked away from us through the swinging doors to the Clinic proper.

I went back to my party. It was seven past four. "Things are rolling," I said. Linn looked seasick.

"Exactly what is this friend of yours in the police department?" Weston asked.

"A detective lieutenant," I said. But I was more interested in where he was. He hadn't promised he'd come. "He said he would try to make it," I said.

Behind me doors swung and I turned to face Evan and Jay Dundree.

"I didn't expect so many people," Dundree said. He was frowning and making no effort to put on a braver face. "Henry Rush said Mrs. Pighee would be here."

"This is Mrs. Pighee," I said, and introduced Linn. Then Weston and Sam.

Dundree said, "Dr. Merom is ready. Shall we go in?"

Linn said, "I'd like to sit here for a while."

Dundree looked at me; I looked at Linn.

Sam interceded. "I'll stay here with her, Daddy. You and Mr. Weston go ahead. He knows Mr. Pighee, doesn't he?"

Evan accompanied us through the swinging doors into the Clinic. At the second door on the left, Dundree knocked once and then led us into a comfortable medical office where Marcia Merom was waiting. Dundree said, "I've asked Dr. Merom to describe Mr. Pighee's condition and history and to summarize the treatment he's received to date. Then we will go to see him."

"O.K.," I said.

"The patient," she began, "arrived at the Clinic with severe head injuries on the night of January 27th." She described the injuries in some detail, but I found my mind wandering to the $22,000 that Pighee had apparently left for her. I looked at Weston and realized that he had picked up her name in the introductions. I was urgently curious what Pighee's involvement with her was. With hair rolled tight and eyes bright with precise recounting of the medical history, she certainly didn't do anything for me.

"In our opinion," she continued, "had the patient come to any other emergency clinic within four hundred miles, he would have died that night. Fortunately for him, and his family, the company had recently begun a research project related to the development and testing of possible chemotherapeutic aids to treatment of severe physical trauma. The initial problem in such cases, as you may know, is the very short time available to stabilize the patient's critical body functions. Without these, the body's natural repair mechanisms have no time to operate, because the patient is already dead."

"Of course," I said.

"Do you want me to go into more detail?"

"We want to see the patient."

"So I understand," she said. She got up from her chair.

We were led to another room, where we were dressed: masks, hairnets, and gowns. Part of making a convincing performance, if nothing else.

Merom led us into Pighee's room

At first I couldn't see him. There was a committee of machines surrounding what turned out to be his bed. His body was encased up to the neck in a plastic bag. Electrical and physical connectrodes grew off him like hair. There was a machine positioned over his chest.

His head down to his nose was covered in a brown material, like a bandage impregnated with some chemical. His eyes and the rest of the left side of his face were covered.

"My God!" Weston said. It was not a pretty sight.

"I will ask you all not to move too close," Dr. Merom said. Dundree nodded slowly behind her. "I won't go into detail about the apparatus you see before you. Just a few of the more obvious things."

Which included the monitors of his heart, breathing, kidney function, nutrient input, waste production, temperature, salt balance, various blood factors, liver function.

"Are you satisfied?" Dundree asked us.

"Yes," Weston said sharply.

"No," I said. Then to Weston, "Get a good look at him."

"What's to look at?"

"Is he John Pighee?"

"How could anyone tell?"

Dundree frowned. "Are you suggesting that he might not be John Pighee?"

"Yes," I said.

"Ridiculous."

We talked about it more in the dressing room. "I don't think it's ridiculous," I said. "When you people won't let anybody near him, how are we supposed to know?"

"Your imagination must be running away with you, or you're ill. That is most certainly John Pighee."

"I'd like a set of his fingerprints," I said. Just to take my popularity ratings to a new Olympic and world record.

Merom was impassive, but Dundree was furious. "Who do you think you are!" he shouted. "What kind of madman?"

"I think I'm the authorized representative of Mrs. Linn Pighee, and I have a right to ask for positive identification."

Dundree turned to Weston. "You're the lawyer. Do you concur in this . . . this insulting request?"

Weston looked very uncomfortable. But he came down on the side of the angels. "If it can be done without undue risk, I don't see why you should object."

They got the patient's fingerprints on a sterile glass, and ten minutes later Weston and I were on our way out.

But before I left Dr. Merom, I said, "I hope you won't take this all personally. I am trying to act in the best interests of my client as you, presumably, are acting in the best interests of your patient as you see them."

She didn't seem very charmable.

"What is Pighee's prognosis?" I continued.

"That is impossible to say."

"So he might just die, after all this?"

"It's certainly possible, although his condition has been stable for some time now."

"What about brain damage?" It was the one organ she hadn't made a point of drawing our attention to.

"We monitor his cerebral activity, of course," she said. "It's about all we can do. We would be more hopeful if he were conscious, but he may yet be."

"Well, there will be at least one good side, if he should die," I said with artificial jauntiness.

"What's that?" asked Dr. Merom.

"I'll be able to open an envelope I've got in my office. John Pighee left it. It's only to be opened in case of his death."

Merom and Dundree exchanged glances that were momentarily worried, shocked, puzzled. Then Dr. Merom said, "Well, I certainly hope that it won't come to that."

They hadn't given me much joy, but at least they'd given me a reaction. We came to the swinging doors, and Weston and I were back in the Clinic waiting area.

Sam and Linn weren't there.

The nurse behind the desk pre-empted my question. She said, "The older woman became ill while she was waiting. The young lady took her to the emergency ward for examination."

"Not here!" I said, without thinking.

The nurse got my meaning all too quickly. "This is an experimental clinic," she said. "We don't take just anybody."

Weston said to me, "This hasn't been a very successful venture, Mr. Samson."

I cradled the fingerprint glass uneasily. I knew in my core that the fingerprints were Pighee's, that Linn was not well.

.

We found Sam in the emergency ward waiting area. She was sitting with her head on her hands. I sat down next to her and put my arm around her shoulders.

"She's been admitted," Sam said. "I couldn't think of anything else to do. She was very sad, Daddy."

So were we all.

TWENTY-THREE / Weston didn't have much to say to me before he went on his way. He was sympathetic with my suspicions, but he was glad that he hadn't been responsible for this particular effort at elucidation. I could understand his point. I didn't feel very elucidated.

Sam and I didn't talk much all the way home.

Sam and I didn't talk much during the rest of the evening.

I woke up in the middle of the night and talked to myself. I asked me what I'd thought I was doing. Forcing my way into a desperately ill man's sickroom. Insisting that his unwell wife go out when she didn't want to.

More deeply I asked what reason I had for thinking I was a private detective when I couldn't keep myself together, when my enthusiasm for suspicion could outweigh my better judgment.

I asked what I was doing sleeping in the bed Linn should have been sleeping in.

At twenty past ten Sam woke me up. "Daddy. Daddy! There's a lady to see you."

There are worse reasons to wake up. I stretched, scratched, covered up, and walked through to my office.

Where I found Mrs. Thomas. "It would be nice if we could all sleep past seven-thirty," she said. I got the feeling that she was not all that pleased with me. But she'd have to take her place at the back of the line.

"What can I do for you, Mrs. Thomas?"

"You can explain this," she said, and handed me a piece of paper.

"It looks like a bill," I said. "From me."

"That's right. For eighty-two dollars! That's ridiculous."

I skimmed through the accounting of time and expenses. "No, it's not. It's very reasonable."

"Reasonable? Who do you think you are—Sherlock Holmes?"

"We agreed on the rate before I started the job," I said. "And if anything, it's an underestimate."

"Well," she said stiffly, "I didn't expect that attitude."

"What attitude did you expect?"

"I expected you to be more apologetic."

"If you feel dissatisfied, I suggest you go to another agency or the Better Business people and ask whether they feel the rate is unreasonable for the job."

"You seem to be willing to make pretty free with my time," she said. "No doubt as free as you made with the time total on this bill."

"A lot of people would bill you for 20 percent of what Jay Dundree gave you. A kind of finder's fee, as a direct result of their work."

"It's a good thing you didn't try," she said. But she didn't deny the implication that the 20 percent would have come to more than the eighty-two dollars I'd billed her for.

"I am untypically scrupulous about my accounting of client's time," I said. "I'm sorry if you were surprised at the size of the bill, but the only way you would have had it done for less is by realizing before you started you weren't as eager as you thought to visit your brother."

"Don't think I'm going to let this pass," Mrs. Thomas said. But at least she passed from my office.

How long did she think eighty-two dollars kept a private detective going? With an office to hire. With a daughter to feed.

After feeding my daughter I got dressed.

"Where are you going, Daddy?"

"Out."

"Hey, don't I get to come with you?"

"You've got another job."

"I do?"

"You're to go visit our client in the hospital."

"Gosh," she said. "I sort of forgot."

"A private detective," I told her, "never forgets. Because he writes everything down in his notebook."

"You said you'd give me one," she said, "but you forgot. I didn't want to ask."

"A private detective always asks, whether he wants to or not," I said stuffily. I gave her a notebook, and left.

I went to the police station.

After waiting forty-five minutes, I got in to talk to Miller.

"The bad penny," he said. Then frowned. "Sorry I couldn't make it yesterday. But I couldn't."

I put the glass with its fingerprints on his desk. "I wouldn't lie to you," I said. "You didn't miss much."

"It didn't go well?"

"I think the fingerprints on this glass will prove that the guy in the hospital is John Pighee."

"Isn't he supposed to be?"

"Yeah."

He shook his head. "You're a mess, Albert. You even look a mess."

"Something's wrong about this, Jerry," I said with surprising passion. "But I don't know what to do, where to look."

"Is it just that money?"

"No," I said. "Why did he seem to know that something was going to happen to him? Why doesn't anybody know what he was working on? Why has there been such a big deal about no visitors?"

"It could be O.K.," he said.

I just shook my head. "And now my client's sick and in the hospital. My last client is bitching about her bill. And they're going to pull my building down."

"I think you're just in a bad patch," Miller said. "If the rest of your life was going better, this Pighee business wouldn't bother you so much. Is your lady friend around?"

"She left on vacation a couple of days ago."

"See, nothing's right in the world."

I shrugged. I pushed the glass toward him.

"What am I supposed to do with it?"

"Take the prints."

"Where am I supposed to get a set of Pighee's for comparison?"

I pursed my lips. "Hadn't thought of that," I said.

"Take a vacation, Albert."

"No," I said forcefully. "Run them through, Jerry. You may have Pighee's prints. Or if they're someone else's maybe you have his. It's a small enough thing to do."

He sighed.

"The situation just doesn't make sense to me," I said.

"Does the whole world have to make sense to you?" he asked sharply.

I thought about that question for quite a while. Then I answered him truly. "Yes," I said. "It does. It's what keeps me going."

"It's why you're a failure."

"I don't think I'm a failure," I said. "I'm just broke, stupid, and on a bad streak of luck."

Miller shrugged.

I thought about things as I was waiting for the elevator. Realized that rationalizing the strange facts I had about John Pighee was important to me, that I couldn't worry about other things until I'd eased my mind about it. So I was being evicted; I've been evicted before. So I was broke; there are worse things in life than having to stop being a private detective. I was lucky to have the luxury of having only myself to worry about. Decisions affected me alone. I had no money, but I had the greatest luxury of all: the freedom to decide how I wanted to go to hell and when.

I went to the Loftus Pharmaceuticals Security Building. It wasn't until I saw Russell Fincastle there that it occurred to me that he might have been on a different shift. Maybe it was my lucky day, after all.

"Mr. Samson," he said cheerfully as he let me in. "Come for your list."

"Yes."

"I worked for my money, I'll tell you that. There's a lot of people work late in Research Three." He pulled out several sheets of paper covered with large loose handwriting.

I smiled and nodded and pulled out my wallet. And remembered an awful truth. The last money I'd spent had been $4.98. "Oh, Christ," I said. "It's not my day."

"What's the matter?"

"I didn't bring any money. I'm trying to figure out how I could be that stupid."

"I don't like being messed around," Fincastle said, making it clear he'd already spent the twenty.

"I'll go home and get it," I said.

Fincastle folded the list ostentatiously and put it in his pocket.

I walked back to my van shaking my head. I drove home.

The office was in chaos.

I couldn't believe it. Paper scattered everywhere; drawers out. I hadn't realized I'd had that much paper in the office in the first place. I don't keep much of value there. Because it's open to the public.

I sat for a few minutes in my swivel chair. It was a shock. Though any thief who robbed me must be pretty hard up.

Hard up reminded me of what I'd come home to do.

I went into the living room. It was strewn with everything I owned.

I didn't run, only walked, to the box my Never-Touch money was in. It had been touched.

I sat in my dining-room chair, and rested. They even took my woman's picture.

"Daddy!" Twenty minutes later Sam burst in, followed closely by Ray McGonigle. "Daddy, what happened!"

I was about to tell her I'd decided on some spring cleaning, but the words were hardly in my mouth when I sighed instead. "We've been robbed," I said.

"Wow," McGonigle said.

TWENTY-FOUR / I borrowed fifteen dollars from Sam and five dollars from McGonigle and a couple of dimes from the pocket of my other pants. I drove back to Russell Fincastle.

His list covered six sheets of paper. After I bought it, I went straight back home, where I dropped into my chair, a clapped-out yo-yo.

Sam and Ray had piled my disturbed belongings against spare walls without attempting to sort them out or put them back where they had come from. Sam was making us lunch. I surveyed my kingdom. Decided to leave it in untidy piles. I was moving soon anyway.

Lunch was goose pâté on hot crumpet.

Ray asked, "You always eat this kind of funny food here, man?"

"I only buy the kinds with a joke on the wrapper," I said. "Hey, why aren't you at work?"

"I got a call this morning from the boss. He said he found some mistakes in my time records and that they owed me some vacation time and could I take it this week."

"Isn't that lucky, Daddy?"

"So I called up your lady daughter and she said she needed some wheels so I came over."

"Wheels?"

"I needed some way to get to the hospital, Daddy."

"Did you get in to see her?"

Sam's face saddened. "No. She was asleep. We waited nearly an hour, but she was still asleep."

"Did you find out what's wrong with her?"

"They're still doing tests. But they said she's got malnutrition. She hardly ate anything while she was here. I really feel bad about it."

"It takes longer than a couple of days to get into that kind of condition," I said. "No one's been looking after her for a long time and she hasn't had much of an urge to look after herself."

"But we're looking after her now, aren't we, Daddy?"

"Yes, love," I said. "We're looking after her now. If we get half a chance."

I put Sam to work on the list from Fincastle. Making a tally of each of the people who signed out of Research Three in the calendar year before Pighee's accident. I wanted patterns.

Myself, I went to find Lieutenant Miller again.

"But they robbed me!"

"Somebody robbed you," he said. "You don't know who."

"I don't believe in coincidences," I said.

"What coincidences?"

"Yesterday at the Loftus Clinic I mentioned that Pighee left an envelope to be opened after he died. They reacted surprised, or worried, or something. I said that I had it in my office."

"Was it in your office?"

"Of course not. The Pighees' lawyer has it. But the next day my office is turned over, and out of frustration they rob me of nine hundred and thirty-eight dollars."

"That's a lot of bread to have lying around."

"I like to keep a little change on hand. In case I don't feel up to going to the bank."

"But whoever it was took the money. So you don't know they were after anything else."

"Except that all my files were turfed out. The whole place was turned over. I don't believe in coincidences. The simplest explanation is that the Loftus people had a guy break in to look for the envelope that wasn't there. Other things are possible, but that's the simplest, so I accept it as a working hypothesis. Occam's razor."

He thought about it and said, "It doesn't sound so simple to me."

"The implications are complicated."

"Even so," Miller said. "What I don't see is what you want me to do about it all."

"You agree the situation stinks?"

Not the technical description for the condition, but he nodded.

"Well, what do you suggest we do next?"

"I'm not opening it as a case, Albert. What's the crime I'd be supposed to be solving? There is some unexplained money. There's a break-in at your office that you leave open to the public. There's been reluctance by medical people to let relatives visit a man who would be dead if they hadn't been taking such good care of him. There's a bit of mystery about what he was working on that was so dangerous." He spread his hands in a large shrug. "But where's the handle that I'm supposed to grab on to? I'm here in Homicide and Robbery with Violence. It's hard to see where I can fit in."

"Even unofficially?"

"But what? What am I supposed to do? As it stands, I can pass the money question to the tax people, who will say he must have had some source of income unknown to them. They'll take the cash and wait for an explanation till he wakes up."

"Except he's unlikely to wake up."

"I can ask the safety people to check out the record of accidents in the Loftus labs. I mean, hell's bells, Albert. What do you want me to do? You haven't got *anything* I can work from."

So I resolved to try to get him something.

As I rode down in the elevator, I started drawing simple conclusions from what facts I had. Like the money in the envelope. Suppose it came from the unknown but dangerous work Pighee was doing in Research Three. Work that had exploded? What sort of things explode?

And leaving money for Marcia Merom. Conclusion: he liked her. . . .

And Merom, Dundree, and Rush's reluctance to let people see Pighee? People might ask questions, which might lead to unsecreting their secret work.

Which was . . .

Which was exactly what I determined to find out.

Even if it meant taking chances that were bigger than I usually allowed myself. Chances that might cost me my license. I laughed to myself. The way things had been going, my license wasn't worth much anyway.

Dr. Marcia Merom was listed only as "Merom, M." in the phone book. Modesty, no doubt. I dialed her number. While it rang, I worked over how I was going to get her to invite me over for a cup of tea.

But after twenty-five rings I hung up. That was all right, too: I wasn't that thirsty.

Plan B. I went to the address on North Washington Boulevard and, as I expected, found it was a block of apartments. But not a shiny new building. It was a forties brick collection, three floors high. Well taken care of, with air conditioners sticking out of windows like infections of a rectangular type of parasite. More windows were affected than were unaffected.

I parked across the street and watched for a while. I was gratified by the lack of conspicuous activity, the implication that it was a largely empty building during the working day. Then I walked into the lobby, found Merom's apartment number and bell, and rang it.

Four times, with feeling.

After no response in either the intercom or the door buzzer, I settled to the problem of getting in. I rang all the first- and second-floor apartments, then waited. I rang them again. Finally the intercom crackled. A male voice came through: "Who's there, for Chrissake?"

In my own crackly falsetto I said, "I arr oiga electric rhumn squargiarra urgent singalyally farumshia fleemickality official."

The intercom said, "Shit." The door buzzer went. I was in.

I sprinted up the stairs to the third floor, in case my intercom converser opened his door to see what he'd let in.

I caught my breath. Then rang 3C's doorbell. I didn't expect an answer. I only tried twice.

I got to work with a couple of picks and a plastic ruler.

It took me seven minutes to convince myself that Marcia Merom had a better than average lock on her door. Most people secure their doors with locks that look good but lock bad. I can get past those.

But I was left with Plan C.

I went outside again, got in the van, and went round the block to the alley behind the building. I pulled in at the base of the building and worked out which of the sets of stairs up led to Marcia Merom's back door. Having a panel truck is an advantage when you're trying to break into an apartment in the middle of the afternoon. You look more like a repairman.

I got out a few tools and walked slowly up the stairs. At the door, I decided to forget the lock and go to Plan C sub-plan b immediately. I chipped all the putty away from a pane of glass in the door, pulled the glazing pins with a pair of pliers, and eased the glass out.

I felt something on the back of my leg. It startled me. I nearly dropped the glass.

It was a gray-and-white cat, giving my leg a desultory rub in hopes of a presentation mouse. It rubbed my other leg, but without conviction.

"Go away. Shoo," I whispered.

It looked at me and made up its own mind. It walked half a dozen steps and sat down next to the porch railings. It watched me. Made me nervous. When I'm being naughty, I don't like witnesses.

"Shoo," I repeated. "Go on."

It ignored me. Didn't even yawn and lie down. It watched the variegated spectacle of life passing before its tiger-tawny eyes.

I've been some pretty demeaning things in my life, but between-meals entertainment for a cat was a new low. "Shoo," I said again, but no longer hopeful.

I put the glass down on the porch next to the doorway and reached inside the window to open the door.

I got hold of the lock latch.

At the same moment a hand took a powerful grip on my wrist and pulled. My arm had little option but to follow inside. Where a body pressed it against the inside of the door.

An angry voice said, "Don't struggle, Lee. I've got a gun pointed at your stomach and I know how to use it."

"Use what?" I asked instinctively. "My stomach?"

TWENTY-FIVE / I'm just not the adventurous lucky-type detective. I get caught when I try to do things. It's not fair.

I heard a click from inside the door. I don't know much about guns but I know when a revolver hammer is being cocked.

"Don't do anything I might regret!" I shouted. "I'll do anything you say!" Hearing my squeaks, the cat cocked its ears.

The pressure eased from my arm, though the grip remained on the wrist. I didn't struggle. I've never liked the idea of running for it in a situation like this: with bullets coming from behind, you can't see to dodge them.

Besides, I was curious. The voice the other side of the door was a woman's, and I had a question or two to ask her.

"We've got to stop meeting like this," I said as I entered Marcia Merom's kitchen through the back door. She stood well away from me and with two hands held a long-barreled revolver pointed at my chest. Without a wobble. "It would help if you would answer your phone or your doorbell."

She was intensely serious but without any fear, because she hadn't expected me to be me. It was Lee that she really hadn't been expecting. "Don't make any fast moves," she said.

"Why should I? Oh, I see. You think I've got a gun, too. But I don't."

"Go into the living room," she said.

"Your wish," I said.

I preceded her into a pale blue room filled with tables, chairs, bookshelves, and ornaments. Also a desk, which would have been a prime candidate for my interest if I had entered the room unescorted. There were pictures on the walls of horses and mournful dogs. They weren't prints, but genuine pictures, like with paint on them. There were many signs of significant means and a certain, if not congenial taste. Over the desk there was a certificate from the University of Minnesota, awarding a Ph.D. in biochemistry to Marcia Janet Merom. The date was 1972.

Merom directed me to the front door. I started to complain that we'd hardly got acquainted. But she said, "Shut up!"

"You're the one with the gun," I said.

"Don't forget it," she said.

I reached the door.

"Now take the position," she said.

"Excuse me?"

"Against the door. You must know how to do it."

"You mean lean against it? Like they do on television?"

"Stop stalling."

I took the position. Gingerly but thoroughly, she assured herself that there were no lumpy objects of metal concealed beneath my clothing. She didn't seem embarrassed. I was.

"Any happier?" I asked.

"All right, get up," she said. "Turn around. Now sit down."

I moved toward a chair.

"No! At the foot of the door!"

I didn't understand, but sat on the floor with my back against her front door. I began to think about my story. But she began to smile. "You know I could kill you right now if I wanted to?"

I was surprised, shocked. It wasn't the story I'd been thinking of.

"Breaking into my apartment," she said. "A big strong man against a poor defenseless woman."

"Why ever should you want to shoot me?" I said.

"I didn't say I wanted to," Marcia Merom said pedantically. "I said I could if I wanted to. You're at my mercy." A certain intense pleasure passed through her eyes, and then seemed to fade.

I followed the impulse to counterattack. "Is this what you had in mind for Lee if it had been him instead of me?"

But she seemed not to hear. "Is there any reason why I shouldn't call the police and have you arrested?"

"Yes," I said.

"What is it?" She seemed curious to know. She lowered her gun.

"Do you want to pretend that you don't know as well as I do?" A counter-counterattack counterattack.

She was remembering me. The episode we'd gone through at the Loftus Clinic. With and around John Pighee. She didn't move toward the phone.

I feigned unconcern. "You heard the phone ring twenty-five times. You heard the buzzer downstairs, the doorbell here. Why didn't you answer them?"

"Why should I?"

"I only came here wanting to talk to you. They show that I wanted to talk to you."

"And," she said positively, "what I did shows that I didn't want to talk to you. Or anyone. Why didn't you just go away and try again another time?"

"Well, I live on the other side of town. While I was in the neighborhood, I thought I'd leave you a note."

"A note?" She didn't seem particularly quick.

"Yeah," I said. "So I said to myself, a busy scientist like Dr. Merom, she might not have time to look in her mailbox. So it would be better to put it where she won't miss it. So I was going to leave the note on your kitchen table, so when you ate your Soggy Pops you'd be sure to see it."

She paused to think. Then said, "I am not amused by facetiae."

At least now she was reacting to what I was saying. Instead of the other way around. "You had the gun out because you thought I was Lee. What's the matter, aren't you getting along with him?"

"You might say that."

"You expected him to force his way in here?"

"When he gets an idea—about anything—it's very hard to get him to . . ." She tailed away. Then: "I don't want to talk about Lee."

"Must be a strain on your business relationship if there's problems like these," I said. "Members of a gang should get along. They should work like a well-oiled machine."

"What do you know about business?" she asked.

I tried to look inscrutable. "Isn't it enough for me to know that there is a business? And a gang."

"Gang?" she said. As if it was a strange word to use for whatever was going on.

"The strain of the Pighee situation beginning to catch up with people? Must be hardest on you." I paused, but she didn't say anything. "Considering your intimate relationship with Pighee." No reaction. "Did you know he'd left you quite a lot of money? If he dies, I mean. Maybe I shouldn't have told you that, if you like to kill people so much. You might pull the plug on him just to get your money."

"Not . . . I wouldn't do something like that for money. I mean . . ."

"No, no," I said, and looked around the room. "You seem to have plenty. Of course, doctors make a fortune these days, don't they. No, you don't need any more money." I hesitated, then said, "But what I don't understand is if Pighee's been out of the way for so long, why is Seafield only horning in now?"

She lowered her head. "Lee's all right," she said.

"Oh, yes?" I said. And I stood up. She did nothing to react. Her hands rested limply on the gun, but didn't move. She seemed to have forgotten it was there. Even if I hadn't.

"I can't say that I understand things precisely," I said. "But what

I wanted to tell you and your people is this: I'm not going to quit poking around in this John Pighee business until I understand what's going on. And the police are going to be interested, too."

"Police," she said, shaking her head. "No."

"Yes," I said, but she didn't seem to hear it. She seemed to hold most of our conversation with herself.

Then she said, "Wait a few days. Wait, will you? You . . . you don't understand, I'm sure. But you might hurt people, things. Things you would not want to hurt, I'm sure. Give it a few days. Please." She stood up and left the gun on her chair. "Please! I'll call you then and we'll talk about it. Do you have a card? With your phone number on it? I'll call you, I promise."

I gave her a card. And, having done more than I could ever have expected, I left. By the front door.

TWENTY-SIX /   I was about to start on the stairs from the second floor to the first when a big hand grabbed my shoulder.

"Hey!"

The hand spun me around.

"What do you think you're doing?" I asked.

"That's what I want to ask you." The hand was connected to a man who was about six by six by sixty. And he was strong with it.

"What's the problem?"

"You're the guy what rang my bell, ain't you?"

"Don't be absurd," I said carelessly.

"You are," he said. "I saw you. Through the peephole. You fucking well woke me up and talked to me over the intercom and then didn't come to my door. I saw you go by through the peephole. I saw you come down again. And now I seen you come down again. Why you doing all that?"

It was a difficult question to answer. The hand on my shoulder didn't relax. I had a card in my wallet that said I was a swimming-pool salesman. But I didn't think he'd be interested.

"I work all night," he said. "And if I'm gonna get woked up in the day, then I'm gonna know why."

"I'm a private detective," I said. "I rang a lot of bells because I was trying to get in the front door. There is someone who lives upstairs that I'm investigating and I needed to get in the front door to get into the apartment."

He looked up the stairs I'd just come down. "Love nest, huh? Who is it?" He released my shoulder. "No shit," he said musingly.

"I can't tell you who it is," I said piously.

He nodded.

"Only I couldn't get into the apartment when I got up there. So I came down again and went around to work on the back door."

He kept nodding. "A lot of these people here, they put pretty good locks on their doors. Ever since about four years ago this guy got killed by a burglar."

"Yeah?"

"No shit. Right here in this very building. Cripple lived in 3C. Got his neck broke falling off that back porch. Made people very nervous, you know. So a lot of them got better locks than they had before."

"I can understand that," I said.

"People here, they're mostly single or people without kids. They all work. Means they have some money, you know. And they got pretty valuable stuff. Me, I'm not afraid."

"I believe that," I said.

"I'm what they call a fatalist, you know what I mean? If it's going to happen to me, it's going to happen. You really a private detective?"

"You want to see my I.D.?"

He did. I showed it to him.

"I'll be goddamned," he said. "I didn't think people were, you know, that sort of thing any more."

"It's a dying art," I said. We became friends. He let me leave.

I sat for several minutes in my van trying to make notes on the conversation with Marcia Merom. It was more confusing than usual. What with being at her mercy, having my arm twisted, and the damn cat.

Finally I started the engine and pulled back into Washington Boulevard. There I noticed a red Thunderbird in front of the building. I saw Lee Seafield get out. I idled while I saw him go into the lobby. I didn't need to follow him. I had a good idea of what he had in store.

An idea but not much understanding. The story of my life.

"You've been gone a long time, Daddy," Sam said as I came throught the office door. She was sitting behind my desk with a pencil in hand and another behind her ear.

"Picked any winners?"

She didn't understand. But said, "I've been working on your list. If you go and make some coffee, I'll be finished in a few minutes."

"Where's your scientific friend?"

"He'll be back later. He got tired of watching me."

"When you have a minute," I said, "I picked up a letter for you on the way up." I spun an envelope onto the desk.

"For me?" She looked at it. "But it's addressed to you!"

I went to make the coffee.

As it was perking, she came in with her final list and a look on her face that was all girl. The opened envelope was on top. "It's my I.D. card," she said. "I am a real detective now?"

"When you sign it. Next to the thumbprint."

I lent her a pen.

"I'm a detective *now*," she said.

"You retain that card until you get fired, convicted of a crime, or until I lose my license."

But she just sighed. "A real detective." What nicer thing could a father do for a daughter?

While we drank our coffee, I looked over the summaries that Sam had extracted from the Fincastle list.

It proved that whatever Sir Jeff paid people, he got his money's worth. John Pighee had stayed late in the labs every single Thursday the calendar year before he went to pieces.

He'd also been in the lab either Saturday or Sunday each week and on 42 of the available 52 Tuesdays. A total of 147 entries.

It represented a colossal amount of work, considering no one seemed to know what he was doing with his time there.

Or, rather, no one would tell *me* what he was doing.

Sam had also analyzed the after-hours attendance of other late workers in Research Three. There were nine names that appeared 12 times or fewer. Then three between 29 and 48 times, headed by Raymond McGonigle, technician. It included an S. Grace: I presumed the technician Sonia I'd run into in the lab.

And three names appeared more often. M. Merom, 93; L. Seafield, 118; and J. Dundree, 140. But more curious than the totals, Merom was in the lab every Wednesday night; and every Sunday that Pighee was in the lab, Seafield was there, though not the other Sundays. As a rule, Seafield was in on Tuesday night—though, unlike Merom and Pighee, he missed some. And Dundree's night was Friday, though his late appearances were more evenly distributed over the nights of the week than any of the others.

Henry Rush's name appeared, too, but only seven times during the year.

I was excited when I digested the information. Not because I knew what the pattern meant, but because it meant there was a pattern. Something was being done on a regular schedule.

"You're smiling, Daddy."

"You're very observant," I said.

"You're happy, aren't you? Did I do good work?"

"Very good," I said. "You'll make a terrific detective. Good thing I didn't lose my license today."

"What do you mean?"

"I broke into an apartment and got caught. Detectives lose licenses for that sort of thing."

I got my notes and told her about how I'd carried on about the gang and its business.

"You don't know anything about their business," she said.

"But they know. So the problem becomes motivating them to tell me, instead of finding out directly. Do you see what I mean?"

"More or less."

"Sometimes it pays to make people believe you know things you don't. It changes their assumptions about you. It changes the way they act to you, and the changes depend on just what they think your knowledge is. By seeing what they do that's different from what they did when they thought you were ignorant, you learn things."

"O.K."

"I told Marcia Merom I knew she and the other people at Loftus were in some business. And I threatened to go to the police. Instead of treating me as if I was crazy, she took me seriously. So now I know something."

"Are you going to the police?"

"What for? To confess I broke into her apartment?"

Later, Ray came to take Sam out. To avoid getting lonely, I went to visit Linn Pighee.

I found she had been moved to the Loftus Pavilion wing of the hospital. But upstairs in the hospital part. Not in the Clinic.

"It's something to do with the insurance," she said, in a fragile echo of a voice. "Because John is a Loftus employee."

"How are you?"

"How do I look?"

"Terrific," I said. Terrible.

"Well, I feel as good as I look."

"Are you eating well?" I asked. "For a change. Sam is unhappy that she let you get away with not eating while you were with us."

"She told me. She shouldn't feel bad. I just haven't been hungry. It's hard for me to eat when I'm not hungry. It makes me sick."

"You're in a bad spot," I said. "Sick if you eat and sick if you don't."

She nodded acquiescence.

"When do you get out?" I asked. "Have they told you?"

"They say they're still doing tests."

"I hope they pass," I said. But it passed over her. Her eyes fluttered.

"I'm going to go to sleep now," she said.

I sat and watched her do it.

TWENTY-SEVEN / Sam and Ray weren't back when I got home.

I spent five minutes making a list of some things I wanted to know. Then I waited for my legwoman to finish her fun and games for the week.

They wandered in about a quarter past eleven.

"Hey, funny man, how you doing?"

"Hi, Daddy. We've had a super time."

"Your little girl is a terrific athlete."

"We went to visit Grandma," Sam said, "and then we played miniature golf."

"She had three holes in one and she'd never played before," Ray said.

"I'd never even touched a golf club before, Daddy!" Sam shone.

"You'll be the next Babe," I suggested.

"Who?"

"Hell," McGonigle said. "Babe Ruth didn't play golf. She said you liked sports."

"I am a sport," I said.

"Maybe he was just being funny," Sam said.

"Didrikson," I said. But decided not to try to cap their energy. Or turn it off. I stood up. "Sam, you've got work in the morning."

"I do?" she said. "What, Daddy? Oh, what?"

I went to bed.

"But how do I find out those things, Daddy?"

"You're a private detective now. You're supposed to know how. Is there any orange juice left?"

"But—!"

"Work out what you know. Then what you want to know. Think about who knows it. Then move. Pass the margarine, will you?"

"Well, there was this man who died four years ago. He was killed or died when there was a burglar, right?"

"Yes. Is there any more guava jelly in that jar?"

"So the police would know all about it."

"Bound to. Do you know anyone at the I.P.D. who would help you?"

"No. But . . . but . . ."

"Can I have that knife, please?"

"But I could go in and pretend to be his daughter. They'd tell me all about it then, wouldn't they?"

"Do you know his name?"

"Ahh. Well."

"You know more or less when it happened. Something about what happened. Where it happened."

"You mean I could go to the building and ask there."

"Isn't there some sort of place that might have done most of the work for you? At the time. Something you could just go and consult."

"What do you mean?"

"Pass the newspaper, please, will you? The *newspaper.*"

"Ahh."

I sent her off to the library to look up old paper reports on the incident. A good place to start, and also cool in a hot summer.

I retired to the office with the last of the orange juice to consult my own filed paper, my notebook. My researches lasted as long as the juice. I decided to follow Sam's good example and get out into the field. To try to find out something about Seafield.

There was only one in the phone book. Which made it look as if it was going to be easy to find. But when I got to the right place on the right street, the address listed in the phone book didn't seem to be there. Until I found it behind a house that was there. It was a converted carriage house from days long gone everywhere, but particularly distant in that part of north central Indianapolis. You could just make the building out from the sidewalk when you knew where to look for it.

I walked away. Until I found a telephone box.

"Loftus Pharmaceuticals."

"Lee Seafield in Research Three, please."

It took a full minute to ring the right bell, but when the call was answered, the answerer said, "Seafield." A deep, quick voice.

"Who?" I asked.

"Seafield. What do you want?"

"I didn't ask for Seafield. I asked for Sealy."

"You haven't got him," Seafield said, and hung up.

I was able to stride up the path to his door with a calm heart.

The building was substantial. Closer inspection showed it was not all used for accommodation. The entire ground-floor area was garages, space for four cars. Above it was a full second story. There was an attic above that, with large windows flush with the sloping roof on the southwestern side. It suggested the sort of studio required by an artist or an indoor naturist. As far as I knew, Seafield wasn't artistic.

The garages opened on an alleyway, and at one end of the façade of doors an electric bell glowed next to a residence entrance.

Though I knew Seafield to be at work, I rang. And knocked loudly. And rang again. He might share with his mother.

Nobody answered from within. I examined the lock on the door.

"Looking for Mr. Seafield, are you?"

"What?" The voice came from behind me, where I saw an old man, stooped to the shape of a gibbet. He could only look at me by facing sideways. He stood at the corner of the path I had used, but behind him I saw an open door at the back of the main house.

"Looking for Mr. Seafield?"

"That's right," I said. "He doesn't seem to be at home." I held my notebook in clear sight. To make me look a bit official.

"He's to work," the man said. "Don't rightly know what time he'll be back. Keeps unlikely hours, you know. Sometimes here and sometimes not. Sometimes comes late. Three, four, five in the morning."

"Wakes you up as he comes in, does he?"

The old man smiled and nodded. "Light sleeper. Say, care for a cup of coffee, stranger? I got some on the boil."

"I'd appreciate it," I said, and followed him through the open door to his first-floor room.

The boil turned out not to be an exaggeration.

"You get to be a light sleeper as you get on," said my host. I put him at seventy-five. "It kind of balances the heavy sleep coming later."

"Too true," I said. "My name's Samson."

"Walker," he said. "Thomas Jefferson Walker."

"Pleased to meet you, Mr. Walker. Do you know Mr. Seafield well?"

"Not that way, no. But I can't but help keep track on his comings and goings. I do the maintenance around here. For my son, which owns the property."

"Well," I said, "I'm trying to get a little background on Mr. Seafield."

"Are you, now? Which side do you work for?"

"Which side?"

"The federal or what?"

I didn't get his drift, but continued on the line I had planned. "I'm a personnel investigator. Mr. Seafield has applied to us and we're trying to fill in our picture. Life-style, that sort of thing."

"I see," Walker said. But didn't volunteer.

"So. He rents the place, does he?"

"That's right. From my son Tommy, Jr. Tall fella."

"Your son?"

"Naw, Mr. Seafield. Real tall and thin. My boy's only about six foot, despite my height. I'm six foot four and one half inches," he said. "That is . . . I was. Seafield has inches on me."

"Does he have a lot of friends?"

"Friends? I don't know. He seems to draw the womenfolk and there's a lot of beer cans in the trash."

"Easygoing kind of guy?"

"He treats me like a piece of dung," Thomas Jefferson Walker, Sr., said. "Course my age, and I'm only caretaking for the place." He indicated the rest of the big house. "He don't have to treat me human, so he don't. No, he don't strike me as an easy guy. Flashy clothes."

"Dresser, is he?"

"Seems like they make them out of what they used to make little girls' dresses out of in my day." Which took inches off Lee Seafield in Walker's eyes.

"What kind of car does he run?"

"T-Bird. I s'pose it's from the company. My boy used to get one."

"Your son worked at Loftus Pharmaceuticals?"

"That's right."

"He's not a scientist, is he?"

"No. He's an executive. Had big plans when he joined up with them fifteen years gone, but he got stuck, dead end. In part of the quality-control section."

"That sounds pretty important," I said.

"May sound that way, but he says it was really fancified pot-washing. Killed his ambition. So he up and quit. Puts his energy into other things. Works with some people in Detroit a lot, and he's got him half a dozen properties around town. This is the littlest."

"Tycoon, your boy," I said.

"Yeah," the old man said. He wasn't very interested.

"Don't you get on with your son, Mr. Walker?"

"Comes right down to it, Tommy, Jr., treats me like a piece of shit, too. Probably because he got treated like that where he worked. Sir Jeff couldn't look after everyone." Walker continued, "But it's not right a boy shouldn't reckon his father."

TWENTY-EIGHT / Sam wasn't home when I got back. With the amount I'd given her to do, she could take a week.

I sat and brooded. Reviewed my notes. A lot of things troubled me. Then the phone rang.

"Al?"

"Albert Samson, Private Investigator. Debts collected. Divorces sought. Discounts for minority groups. Like policemen." It was Miller.

"You finished?"

"Not finished, but the count has just reached nine."

"Can you come over? I want to talk to you."

"When?"

"Now," he said. His tone was serious. More serious than usual.

"What's up?"

"I'd prefer to talk to you in person."

"I don't like surprises, Jerry."

"It's about your case. Pighee, the guy that had the accident."

"What about him?"

"Come over, Albert," he said quietly. Then, "Don't make me make a federal case out of it."

I left a note for Sam and walked to the City-County Building.

Miller sat at his desk waiting for me. Not even pretending to do anything else. That made it the most important business conversation we'd ever had.

"So what gives?" I asked. I sat down.

Instead of answering right away, he folded his hands.

"I'll come back later when you've learned English," I said. Surprises are bad enough, but long-drawn-out surprises are intolerable.

"This is hard," he said.

My turn to wait quiet.

"You were right about the Pighee case," he said, at last.

"What? You mean the fingerprints show it isn't Pighee?"

"No, it's Pighee, all right. You were right that something bigger was going on than seemed to be going on."

"You've found something out," I said. You sometimes need a divining rod to locate what people are getting at.

"I've been in conference with Captain Gartland about it twice today. I just want you to know that your nose is unerring."

"They're giving me a police medal or what?"

"Did you know that Pighee was . . . is . . . that he is a federal agent?"

"A what?"

"A federal agent."

"I wouldn't swear in court that I know now," I said.

"Well, he is."

"Who says?"

"Gartland says," Miller said in such a way as to leave no room for doubt.

"You mean F.B.I.?"

"I mean F.B.I."

It gave me something to think about. I talked instead. "Even if it's true, it doesn't explain the things I wanted explained. Unless you're going to tell me that Loftus Pharmaceuticals is a subversive front and the F.B.I. infiltrated it with Kamikaze chemists."

"I don't know what he was doing there or why he got blown up."

"What do you know, Jerry?"

"Gartland called me in this morning. He said he'd been filled in about your interest in Pighee, and in particular about your visit to the hospital. He said he's looked up your file and—"

"My file!" I interrupted.

"Yeah."

"What file?"

"Well," he said uneasily. "The file we have on you. We picked you up a few years ago on breaking and entering."

"And the charges were dropped and that isn't what you were talking about."

"Well," he said. Then bit the bullet. "We keep records on local private detectives."

"Bull. The state police are the licensing body. You might keep lists, but—"

"Honest, Al. Files."

"On people in suspicious professions, then, is it? An unofficial file? Or maybe just on all suspicious people."

"Well," he said. "Kind of."

"Maoists, Minutemen, and Albert Samson?"

"You're making too much of it. In our shoes you'd want access to information about—well, interesting people around town. It's really files on people who might know things, or who have helped us in the past, or—"

"Nixon had his hate list. I shouldn't be surprised that you have yours. From what I read about in the *Star.*"

He let me have that without response. Compensation. A couple of years ago, the *Star* had spent months having to fight hard for the simple truth that the Indianapolis police had gone over their quota for graft. For a while it looked as if the pair of reporters involved might end up in jail on bum raps. But justice outed. Part of justice, anyway. The police were cut back to size and the rest of the graft infrastructure had due warning to be careful despite times of economic hardship. Judges, people like that.

"I'm caught in the middle, Al."

"You're breaking my heart. Get on with it. Pighee the G-man."

"Why are you giving me a hard time? I thought we were supposed to be friends."

"Where did you read that?"

"All right! That's it. Gartland says you're to get off the Pighee case. Pighee and some of the people involved are F.B.I., and you're to give them peace."

"And if I don't?"

"You don't seem to understand the situation, Al."

"Damn right I don't."

"Gartland wanted to act direct, but I said it would be better to talk to you, that you were a reasonable guy. That if there was a good reason not to stick your nose in somewhere, you could be convinced. You concede there are things in the world you don't have a right to know about, don't you?"

"I guess so."

"Well, this is one of them. But don't take it from me. You see Gartland."

I thought about it for a minute. Then asked, "What do you mean, Gartland wanted to act 'direct'? What's 'direct'?"

"You ask him. Come on."

"Now?"

"Now." He got up and led. I could but follow.

———

From the detective dayroom, the Homicide captain's office is the first past reception. Gartland, a career officer in his late fifties, was enjoying his fourth-floor view over the roof of the City Market when Miller led me in.

"Shall I stay?" Miller asked.

Gartland turned and waved me to a seat. He said, "In the building, Miller, but not in the room." Miller closed the door behind himself.

"Well, what's the story, then?" Gartland asked.

He was trying to put me off balance. Having had me brought in, he acted as if I was the one who sought him. I didn't say anything, just sat.

After a few moments, he smirked and turned to a top desk drawer. "Smoke?"

"No."

He took a single cigarette out of the drawer, lit it deliberately with a pocket lighter, inhaled deeply, and leaned back in his chair. "Lieutenant Miller has filled you in?"

"He says you want me to stop a perfectly legal investigation I've been hired to make."

"You're old friends, I understand."

"Out of business hours."

"Which means, I would have thought, that you have some trust in his judgment?"

"Up to a point."

"Miller is a good officer, I think," Gartland said.

"He isn't any better than anybody else at making decisions without good information. My impression is that all he knows is that you want something and that you are his superior officer."

"There is more to the situation than that."

I sat silent again.

"For some time now," Gartland said, "the Federal Bureau of Investigation has been engaged in a special project centered in the Loftus Pharmaceutical Company."

"For 'some time'?"

"For about seven years. Slightly more."

"And when did you first hear about it—today?"

"We," he said, "were informed at the beginning. The two agents leading the case came in to inform us in rough detail of the nature of the work they were doing and—"

"Two? F.B.I. agents?"

"One Washington-based. One local man specially recruited for this project. A man whom, I must say, I know well. Whom I worked with in the war, and whose personal credentials are of the very highest rank."

"You say they informed you. Does that mean the police haven't been asked to participate?"

"You may conclude that, yes."

"And I take it these guys produced I.D.s."

He inhaled, then said, "You may take it."

"Who is the specially recruited agent?"

"That, Mr. Samson, is not properly your business. But," he said with directness that was emphatic, "you may also take it that the subject of your investigation, John A. Pighee, was involved, and that your further inquiries about his functions at the Loftus Pharmaceutical Company would endanger the lives of other people working on the project. Your continued investigation would, in all respects, be contrary to general public interest." He stared at me with his lower lip pushed out, to push the point home.

"What," I asked, "is the nature of the project?"

"Negative."

"But how am I supposed—?"

He interrupted. "I am obliged, in the public interest, to ask you to terminate your investigation and to satisfy your client as best you can without revealing even as much as you know already."

"That's not going to be easy," I said.

"I sympathize," he said.

"Look, you're telling me Pighee was involved in an F.B.I. project."

"I am."

"He was working for the F.B.I.?"

"He was. Is. Naturally, we share everybody's hopes that he will make a complete recovery."

"And he knew it was dangerous work?"

"One presumes so."

"All right," I said. "Just tell me the general area of the project and I'll do my best for you."

Gartland nearly jumped out of his chair, reversing his previous success at self-control. "Samson, you don't seem to understand your situation. I'm not asking you to do anything. I'm telling you."

"I hear you trying to give orders to a civilian proceeding lawfully about his business. But what I do is my decision."

"You have no choice," he said.

"I don't?"

"The only decision is mine. Whether I trust your sacred promise to cooperate enough to let you out of the building."

"You can't arrest me."

"I wasn't planning to," he said darkly. "But if you are likely to be a danger to the public, I can take you out of circulation. Make no mistake about that. I can and I will."

"I want a lawyer," I said. I got up.

"Sit down, Samson!"

"Am I under arrest?"

"Sit down," he said again, but more quietly. I took the "please" as meant but unuttered. I sat down.

"The reason," he said, "that you are here at all is because you are not entirely unknown to us."

There was a lot I could have said to that, but I was worrying less about making my points than about getting back home to take care of my crippled daughter.

"You have assisted us, I understand, a number of times over the last few years. And Lieutenant Miller vouches for what he calls your scrupulous honesty, as well as for your basic intelligence."

I gave Miller silent thanks for that.

"Set against that, studying the records of the cases brought by you and against you—"

"Now, just a minute—"

"Set against the good things," Gartland insisted, waving some papers, "there is in this file clear evidence of a tendency to irresponsibility. Honest irresponsibility, but irresponsibility nonetheless."

I stopped protesting. He had the ball.

"You have an unwillingness to consult with people, to listen to their judgment. You seem to draw your own conclusions and then take rash actions on them."

"If something holds water, I drink out of it."

"This sortie of yours to Entropist Hospital is a recent case in point. Endangering the life of a patient while trying to prove he wasn't who he is."

"That is what I appeared to be doing," I said sharply. "But the basic intention was to get people to stop ignoring the unanswered questions surrounding the situation, and my presence here seems to prove that I've done just that."

"But at the risk of a man's life?"

I began to elucidate further, but he held up a hand to stop me. I stopped. The Entropist escapade wasn't one of my finer moments, whatever the justifications and results.

"No," he said. "But I have to decide whether, knowing or surmising things which could endanger a number of lives, you are the sort of person who can be trusted to act responsibly."

"Am I likely to go and tip off people who might not like the idea that the Loftus people are working for the F.B.I.?"

"Basically, yes."

"Well, I'm not likely to tip anybody off. Even if I knew who they were."

"Well, then," Gartland said, "if I have your promise to wind up your investigation forthwith . . ." He waited.

"Within reason," I said.

"Now, look, Samson . . ."

"I have no desire or intention of interfering with an important F.B.I. project. But I can't give a blanket assurance without thinking about it. That," I noted, "would be rash of me. I've got some peripheral inquiries in hand, and I will also have to work up a convincing way to sign my client off if I'm not to tell her the truth. But whatever I do from here on, I will certainly consult Miller, if something bothers me, before I do anything, rash or otherwise."

Gartland thought about it for a moment. He'd got basically what he wanted. He said, "I will personally be following what you do about this. And if there is the slightest hint that you might be putting the people involved to unnecessary risk in these final stages of their work, you'll be back here faster than you can blink."

Miller walked me to the elevator. "How'd it go?"

"Tough boy, your Gartland. He said if I didn't play it his way, he'd take me out of the game. Rights or no rights."

"He's got fucking blinkers on," Miller said. It didn't make much sense to me, but it was the closest thing to an expression of disloyalty to any part of the police system that I'd ever heard from him.

"Could he do it?"

"Probably," Miller said. He didn't want to think about it. It wasn't his kind of copping. "Don't make him prove it one way or the other."

"On the other hand, he seems to have a pretty good case."

"You're going to ease off, then?"

"Yeah, I think so."

"I'm glad. You're such a cantankerous son of a bitch, I was afraid you'd go against him just for the hell of it."

"Cantankerous? Me?"

"Is it going to put you in financial trouble?"

"I'll just starve to death. Those swines took all my emergency money when they turned my office over. I suppose your Captain Gartland isn't going to do anything about that."

"Is it Sunday every day this month?"

"You don't want a divorce, do you?"

"I don't. Janie might. She thinks I ought to go harder for captain." He looked positively despondent about life.

"Want to come out for a cup of coffee?"

"I can't," he said. "But I appreciate your asking. In the circumstances."

I was on the street before I realized that the circumstance he was particularly referring to was Gartland's threat to limit my liberty. And if Miller was that worried about it, I recognized that I should be, too.

TWENTY-NINE / Images and snatches of conversation came to mind as I walked home. Marcia Merom handling a gun with assurance. Old stooped Thomas Jefferson Walker asking me who I worked for, was it federal. As details, they fit. The mood of conspiracy fit. It made me curiously happy.

Though I couldn't quite believe that I—*I*—had stumbled across a big federal operation, of whatever nature. But it seemed to be a fact. I wondered what the nature might be. In a drug company . . . But as far as I knew, drugs didn't involve explosive chemical processes. So maybe the work was on explosives. And explosives could well mean terrorists. No wonder people could be in danger.

Sam was in the office when I stumbled up my stairs.

"There you are, Daddy! I was afraid you'd be away for ages!"

"Been here long?"

"About twenty minutes. Where have you been? I didn't know that you had anything to do."

Cruel from one's kid. "Found anything out?"

She positively glowed. "Yes," she said. "First I went and rented a car, because I thought I might travel around quite a lot. So," she said, "now I have wheels."

"I'm surprised you get shoes to fit," I said. "Is there any coffee?"

"Daddy!"

"You make us some coffee while I get my own work up to date in my notebook. Then I'll debrief you properly."

"Oh," she said. But she went before I had time to make explicit that I was assigning her to the coffeepot as an employee, and not as a female.

I did my notes on the conversations with Miller and Gartland. I wondered if I could legally say in a newspaper ad, "Scrupulously honest, as advertised in Indianapolis police files."

When I rejoined my highly trained staff, I asked if she'd had time to see Linn, as part of the day's flurry of activity. She hadn't.

I poured the coffee. "Right, Sam, short and sweet."

"As it turned out," she began promisingly, "I did most of the work in the library. I found a boy there who helped me go through the microfilm of the past issues of the *Star*. I never realized microfilm was so big."

"What did you find out, Sam? Details only when they qualify the facts."

If we were playing detectives, we might as well play by the rules.

"Oh. Well. Let's see. Anyway, we found it. In June, 1973, on the seventh, a man named Simon Rackey died while 'repelling an intruder,' it said. He was twenty-six years old, he lived alone at 4901 Washington Boulevard, and he was a technician at the Loftus Pharmaceutical Company, Incorporated. He had had polio when he was young, and went around on a metal crutch. He slipped on the back porch of the apartment and went through the rails. It was from the third floor." She paused.

"Were there any other names in the story? Police spokesman, Loftus representative, relatives?"

"There was a neighbor. I looked her up in the phone book and tried her on the phone, and she was there!"

"Good. What did you ask her?"

"Oh," Sam said. "I didn't ask about the man who died. I asked her about who owned the building. I told her I was looking for an apartment." I nodded. "She said that the building was owned by a man named Walker, but that there weren't any vacancies at the moment. But she looked up his phone number for me, and his address. She said he has some other buildings around town."

"That's good work," I said. "You didn't happen to ask if Walker owned the building four years ago when Rackey died, did you?"

"No, Daddy, I didn't."

"That's all right. Don't worry," I said.

Instead of worrying, she said, "What do we do now, Daddy?"

I hesitated. "You're not going to like my answer to that," I said finally.

"I'm not? Why not? What is it, Daddy? Tell me!"

"For the moment, we don't do anything much."

She thought. She said, "What do you mean?"

"I mean we ease off for a while."

"But that doesn't make any sense, Daddy. We've only just started finding things out."

"You mean you've only just started finding things out."

"But—"

"Look, who's head gumshoe around here?"

She thought again, and asked the right question. "Who were you out with this morning?"

I began, "When I say ease off . . ." But I was stopped by her stony face. "Hang on a minute."

I picked up the phone and called Miller.

"Al?"

"Yes, Lieutenant Miller. I realize I forgot to ask you about one other detail concerning the subject we had our discussions about this morning."

"And what would that be?"

"It's the matter of a suspicious death a little over four years ago. One Simon Rackey, who died on June 7, 1973, at 4901 Washington Boulevard, while the occupant of the apartment Marcia Merom lives in now. I'd like the details you have on file concerning that misfortune."

"You're supposed to be off this. Don't mess with Gartland, Albert."

"As I explained to your superior officer this morning," I said, "I must develop a convincing story for my client if you want this business wrapped up tight. I also told him that I would liaise with you at every opportunity. Please don't waste everybody's time by delaying and asking obtuse questions."

I hung up. To Sam I said, "We ease off by request of the Indianapolis police. But that doesn't mean quit—not exactly."

Sam was half pleased and half puzzled. "Why slow down at all?"

"Because, my dear employee and beloved offspring, I say so. And if you don't like it, then go get a job with some other detective agency, O.K.?"

She studied me without speaking for an uncomfortably long time. I felt she was trying to unriddle the me behind my sphinxlike face. Innocent, obvious, topside me. She said, "So what do you want me to do?"

"This afternoon I want you to use your new wheels and give your grandmother a few hours of your company. Then report back here."

She picked up her notebook and left, with no goodbye. I suppose no goodbye is better than a long goodbye.

I went to Entropist Hospital to see Linn Pighee.

"I thought you'd forgotten me," she said, with a reassuring smile. She was pink-cheeked and spoke crisply.

"It's been my day for remembering important people," I said. "How's the patient, then?"

"I'm O.K. I've been sleeping and sleeping and sleeping."

"Do they drug you or do you do it all by yourself?"

"They help. It's nice to be looked after. I sleep so much, but I don't rest much with it. I suppose it will work out."

"No doubt," I said. It was good to talk to her again. "It's good to talk to you again," I said. I took her hand.

"You're a nice man," she said. "It's nice to see you again." For a moment she closed her eyes. She turned in her bed to face me better, then opened her windows on the world again. "Albert, I've been wondering," she said.

"Wondering what?"

"Something you can tell me, maybe. I don't quite know whether I should already know, from the things you've told me. My head, it isn't quite right."

"What is it, Linn?"

"What happened to John? I mean was it an accident or what?"

The question sliced through me like I was soft margarine. I had to say, "I don't know. Honestly, I wish I did."

"But . . ." she began. Then blinked and changed direction. "How is he? Is there any change?"

"No," I said, not wanting to tell her I hadn't checked. "He's just the same."

"I wish I knew," she said. "I wish I knew what had happened."

After five minutes of talking, she could hardly keep her eyes open.

She seemed to have the energy of a morning-glory, open, dramatic, strong, but short-lived. I waited until her breathing was regular. Then pulled the covers up to her chin and left her.

I sought a nurse and found one stacking linen four doors down the corridor. I asked for medical information about Linn.

The nurse was a patient woman. "Are you a member of the family?" she asked.

"No. I . . ." Friend? "I'm an employee. I work for her."

"She's not a well woman. I hope you didn't talk business with her."

"We talked about the flowers and the trees and how much wetter it would be in the Sahara if it rained there occasionally."

The nurse nodded. "We're still not exactly certain what is wrong with her. We're running tests, but slowly. She's not very strong at all. She's totally run down and seems to have been undernourished for a long time. There are a number of vitamin and mineral deficiencies. It's a miracle she hasn't become a battlefield for every infection known to man."

"Good heavens," I said.

"We don't see this sort of thing very often in someone so young."

"She lived alone for several months," I said.

"She's such a pleasant woman, I don't understand it. She's hardly had any visitors. Just yourself and a young girl."

"My daughter," I said.

"It's very unusual," the nurse said. She was referring both to the visitors *manqués* and the medical situation. "She must have neglected herself dreadfully."

And been neglected.

THIRTY / Before going back into the glare of Indianapolis in August, I brooded for a while in a corner of the Loftus Clinic waiting room. I deeply wanted to find out what had happened to John Pighee. And, in honesty, not only for Linn Pighee but for myself. I hate investing in questions without getting the dividend of answers.

But if my guts' guidance was unequivocal, my mind was full of conflict. It wasn't merely that I was afraid of Captain Gartland: I thought he had a reasonable point of view. I conceded that there were things that I didn't have a moral right to go poking in.

But seeing the other guy's point of view is confusing. There was no real decision to be made about the direction of my actions. I would go ahead.

Carefully, if it meant possible danger to legitimate participants in a legitimate operation. But I had a right to pursue my own legitimate questions.

And if it meant personal consequences, then that's what it meant. If I went out of business, then I was out of business.

It was a good time to go out of business. As I was about to have no further premises. An excellent time to have my license revoked, to seek a new life. Maybe in some new city. It could be the best thing that had ever happened to me. It depended on whether one looked at the future positively or negatively, and those of us with a propensity to martyrdom tend to see other people drinking at our cup as leaving the cup 10 percent full.

I walked up to the reception desk for yet another encounter with the stern guardian of the Loftus portals. But all I asked was how I could get to the emergency ward, and since it meant I would leave her domain, she told me clearly and succinctly.

The emergency ward had a hotel-style entrance bay around the corner from the Loftus Clinic. As I watched, a white ambulance screamed past me and screeched into the bay. For a few steps, like an ambulance-chasing lawyer, I trotted. But I slowed again to a heart-easing walk before I made the turn.

In the minute before I had arrived, the ambulance had been disgorged of its contents. I saw no trace of stress or urgent activity. I walked to the desk and said, "I'd like to talk to someone."

A man looked at me momentarily, pushed a piece of paper my direction, and said, "Fill in your name, address, occupation, here, here, and here. The emergency treatment fee is thirty dollars, payable in advance. You can claim it back off your insurance, if you have any. Then wait over there." He pointed to a row of chairs half filled with people looking ill or clutching parts of their bodies.

"I don't want emergency treatment."

"This is the emergency ward," he said. "The general entrance is left out the door, left around the corner, and the second entrance on your left."

"I want to see a doctor," I began.

He was only thirty but spoke as if he had only one year to his pension and didn't know whether he would last it. Then, "Fill in the form. Pay the cashier. Wait with the people over there."

I looked again at the waiting people. None of them were dripping blood. I took the form he had pushed at me again, held it up, and wadded it into a ball. "If you don't shut up and listen to me for a minute, I'll blow this place up with a bomb I've got in this." I held up my notebook; he studied it with wide-eyed awe.

"What?"

"I want to talk to the doctors who were on duty here on the night of January 27th," I said. "I need to know their names."

"January 27th?" he asked stupidly. I lowered my notebook and he leaned forward, trying to keep it in sight. "How the hell am I supposed to know who was on duty that night?"

"Keep your voice down. I'm very unstable."

He looked me in the eyes for the first time. "Sorry," he said.

"Where are the records of duty assignments?"

"I . . . I'll tell you how to get to the office."

"Office office office!" I said, and opened my eyes wide to make the red lines in the white of my eyeballs visible. "I'm sick to death of offices."

"I'm sorry," he said lamely. And looked again over the desk.
"It's all right," I told him. "I realize it's not your fault."
"Thanks."

"You call them and find out for me—O.K.? And no one will get hurt."

He called them and found out. Drs. Norman Kewanna and Fowler Boone. "O.K.?"

I did the eyeball thing again. "Where can I find them?"

"I . . ." he began. Then phoned back to whoever he'd phoned first. He got me their home addresses.

I raised my notebook to the level of his counter, slowly opened it. His eyes bugged out. I wrote the names and addresses down. "Thanks," I said.

As I left, I passed close to a woman who sat holding her jaw, which was swollen. I gave her the thumbs-up as I said, "Good doctor, that one. Top drawer. Your mouth will be in good hands."

I parked the car and made my way back to the office. The only exciting thing that happened was that I walked over a chalked message on the sidewalk: "I love Paul Millard."

After calming down, I went up the stairs to the balmy calm of an empty office. I sat in my swivel chair and tried to relax. Instead I fell asleep.

Sam woke me up at about four. "Daddy!"

It pulled me out of a world where I understood everything that was going on. "Hi," I said.

But before we could pursue the subject further, we both heard heavy steps on my stairs.

Lieutenant Miller walked into the office to find us both looking directly at him. He growled threateningly. "What's going on?"

"We don't know," I told him.

He shrugged. Then, indicating Sam, he said, "Can we talk alone?"

"Feel free to talk in front of her, Lieutenant. She's my new employee."

"Employee? You?" He looked at her again.

"Show the officer your I.D., Sam."

She obliged. He studied it with a brief flicker of interest.

"She's apprenticed to me. Under bond for seven years to learn the detective business."

"Seven years," Miller said. "That's too pitiful to be funny."

"Come, come, Lieutenant," I said.

"Because at the rate you're pushing your luck you'll be lucky to be in business seven days."

"A poor joke," I said. "But you didn't come over here just to show me that you haven't got any sense of Yuma."

"Any what?"

"Just an Arizonan quip."

The mood grew serious.

"You wanted information about the death of Simon Rackey in June '73."

"True."

"Well, I've looked it up. But you're going to misinterpret it, if I know you."

"And why is that?"

"Because the first patrolman on the scene—a rookie—thought that the circumstances were suspicious and he filed a report to that effect."

"Did he?" I said. Sam smiled.

"But he was wrong," Miller said. "He was overruled and it was wrapped up as accidental. Look, Al, you'd be amazed how many rookies come across suspicious cases in their first couple of weeks that no one comes across again except maybe once or twice in a lifetime."

"Tell me about it, will you?"

"The rookie thought it was very unlikely that an educated man, a polio victim fully conscious of his need to maintain his balance, would have lost his cool so badly that he fell off the back porch. Even chasing a burglar."

"Was that all?"

"Yeah. He just thought it was suspicious, and rated further investigation."

"Which it didn't get?"

"No."

"So we'll never really know."

"They're bound to have looked into it, Al. If they overruled it, then they had good reason. I don't think you should follow this up."

"Why not?"

"Because you're not easing off on the case," Miller said explosively, "and you said you would." He acted as if the worst thing about it was that I wasn't playing fair.

For all my sympathy with him and for him, I'd still cast my die. "I undertook not to jeopardize anybody," I said sharply. "But if your captain thinks that he can give me orders, without even saying please, then he's not in touch with reality."

Miller sighed and shook his head. "I'm going to have to go from here and tell Gartland. You realize that, don't you?"

"What you do with the information that I'm not spending my days watching TV soap operas is your business. I suggest you trust my good sense, but you can also tell your hifalutin friend that if he tries to strong-arm me out of circulation, a full account of everything I know and guess will go to four newspapers. And let him try to bottle them up."

"You're going to have me pounding a beat, you know that," he said despairingly.

"If the worst comes to the worst," I said, "I can always find a place for you here."

He left to see his doctor for some antidepressants on his way to Gartland.

"Have you really written out what you know for the papers, Daddy?"

"No," I said. "They wouldn't print it anyway. They might go after the local police for corruption, but around these parts they have strong feelings of support for the enforcement arms of the government."

"Are we going off now?"

"I'd rather eat. Are you in some kind of hurry?"

"I was going out with Ray tonight," she said.

"Well, that's just as well," I said. "I've got some soap operas to catch up on."

Ray and Sam left at seven and I made some phone calls. I wanted to talk to one of Drs. Norman Kewanna or Fowler Boone, but I didn't know which. Fowler Boone, I found, was on duty that night, but Kewanna was due home. His wife said I could come over. Rather than go again to the hospital, I plumped for Kewanna.

His house was in west Indianapolis; a sizable frame building, with a screened porch and the yard full of odds and ends. Not just children's toys, adult toys, too: old wheels, bits of building material, bags, a pile of logs. It was refreshingly ordinary, compared to the stereotype of the ambitious young doctor.

A miniature Phyllis Diller answered the door. I asked if its father was home. It turned its back on me and shouted, "Mom!"

Mom was a thin woman in new jeans and a very large man's shirt. "Hi," she said brightly, projecting an enthusiasm for life that I thought had been lost in the modern world. "What can I do for you?"

I reminded her of my phone call and asked if her husband was home yet.

"He was here," she said, "but he's just gone out for some beer. Should be back in a few minutes. You come on in and wait for him, hear?"

She led me to the kitchen, where she was baking cookies. Three children of assorted sizes were making contributions to the project.

"This here is Allison," their mother said, "and this is Corinne, and the little'n's Marina, but you already met her."

"How do you do," I said to the girls. "My name is Albert."

"Albert!" said Marina. "What a funny name. Isn't that a funny name, Mommy?"

"Hush, child," she said. "You want a funny name, you try mine. I'm called Fayette."

"I know that," Marina said.

Corinne said, "I don't think that's a funny name, Mamma."

"That's just you're used to it," she said. And then, to me, "I was born in Fayette County and my mother must have liked the sound of it."

"Lucky it wasn't Tippecanoe County."

"I sure am," she said. We both heard a car turn in to the driveway and then stop on the gravel. "There's Norm now."

Kewanna came in through the back door carrying a crate of beer. He was a big man but more wide than tall. He and his burden seemed to fill the doorway nicely. He paused as he saw me, then remembered. "The guy who wanted to see me," he said. "Hang on a sec." He set the crate next to the refrigerator and went back outside. In a moment there was a second crate on top of the first.

He opened the refrigerator and began transferring bottles to empty shelves at the bottom. The last four in the bottom crate he took to the work-top next to the sink, where an opener was screwed into the wall. The four bottle tops bounced to the surface and Kewanna handed me a bottle. One for Fayette, one for himself, and the last one he held up. "This is for you girls to *share*," he said. "I don't want one of you hogging it, now." To me, he said, "Shall we go out on the porch? Bit cooler there."

I followed. It was cooler there.

"I hope I'm not wasting your time," I said.

"So do I. I don't have much to spare."

"You were on duty in the emergency ward at Entropist Hospital last January 27th," I said.

He smiled slightly. "I was?"

"So I am told. You and a Dr. Boone. It was a Thursday."

"If you say so."

"According to wherever records are kept of such things . . ."

He shrugged.

"Anyway, a case came in that night. If you dealt with it, you might remember it."

"Possible."

"It was a man who'd been seriously injured in an explosion, in a lab accident at Loftus Pharmaceuticals."

"Yeah?" He was trying to remember.

"A man named John Pighee. Was working in a research lab when something happened."

"Head injuries," he said slowly.

"That's it." I nearly tipped forward out of my chair.

"I remember a guy who was rushed to us with some administrator in the ambulance with him. I started to examine him, but the administrator insisted—that's right, Loftus, because of the Clinic —this guy insisted that they take him straight up to the experimental section. He said they'd been alerted and were expecting them. And he wheeled him off himself. Yeah, I remember."

"So you didn't examine him?"

"Not thoroughly. But from what I could see, I told the guy it wasn't worth the effort. He took him through anyway."

"Wasn't worth the effort? Why not? Don't they have fancier equipment in there and that sort of thing?"

Kewanna pulled hard on his beer. "The guy was D.O.A."

"Dead?"

"You've heard of the condition?" he said.

"Look, don't mess around. Are you sure he was dead?"

"It's one of the first things they teach us, how to tell when you've killed a patient. Or someone else has. No heartbeat, no breathing, smashed head. Dead."

"How would you react if I told you that John Pighee has been in the Loftus Clinic for seven months. Unconscious, but alive."

"Are you telling me?"

"I am."

He was surprised.

"How do you explain that?" I asked.

"I don't."

"Try."

"Well, I never got a chance to try and resuscitate him, and I don't know how long his heart had been stopped for. Loftus Pharmaceuticals? That's a few miles. Got to be ten, fifteen minutes at the very least between the time it happened and when I saw him."

"Or half an hour."

"Could easily have been half an hour," he said. "I don't know. They rushed him right past me; I only had a minute. But . . ." He shook his head. "The virgin birth and now this . . ."

"You say this administrator said the Clinic was expecting them?"

"He said they'd been alerted and were expecting them."

"Does that often happen?"

"Only once to me," he said.

"You don't remember the administrator's name, do you?"

"Didn't have time to get his autograph," he said. Then, somewhat apologetically, "I didn't ask. He said he was head of something, though."

"Do you remember what he looked like?"

Speculatively. "Chubby little fella. Bright weasel eyes. Nothing else."

It had to be Jay Dundree. "Do you know any of the medical staff in the experimental section?"

"We don't mix," he said, "though I understand that it's controlled by a woman called Merom. Don't know anything about her, though. And I don't know whether there are any others. Probably some on part time. Depends on what they've got cooking there."

"What would you say this man's chances of surviving and coming out of the coma would be?"

"Look, pal," he said to me, "as far as my professional judgment goes, this guy was dead in January, and there aren't many of us survive that."

THIRTY-ONE / I called Merom's apartment from a phone box, but there was no answer. Then I called the Loftus Clinic and, after waiting two minutes, was told Merom wasn't there. I would have called Miller, but I didn't have another dime.

On the way to Loftus Pharmaceuticals, I realized I could have used the dime to call Miller, if I'd thought about it. Because Wednesday was Merom's night at the lab, according to Fincastle's list. But then I wouldn't have known whether to call Miller at home or at the police department. I probably would have lost the dime anyway.

Fincastle himself was on the job in the Security Building. I told

him Dr. Merom was expecting me in Research Three. He just
pushed the logbook toward me. It was a quarter past eight.

I walked quickly to the building. There was only one light visible
in it. The Storeroom lab. I didn't bother to sign in at the table
logbook next to the door in Research Three.

Marcia Merom was singing to herself. I heard her at the top of
the stairs and paused momentarily to listen. She had a clear and
rather pretty voice and she sang with feeling enough to make me
think she sang often. Only the words jarred with the surprising
pleasantness of discovering her new talent. It was one of the rock
dirges from the late fifties, unfulfilled love leading to violent and
anticipated death. "Curly Shirley sure woke early on the day-ay
she died."

I scuffled my feet as I walked down the hall toward the open
door.

Merom stopped singing. She listened. She said, "Lee?" She
sounded cool and businesslike and expectant. "Lee?"

I stepped into the doorway. "No," I said. "Not Lee."

She whirled toward me, and her hands shook. She dropped a
pen. "My God!" she said. She steadied herself. "You gave me the
most terrible fright. Don't ever do that. Ever!" It was a formula
of speech rather than a reaction to the actual situation.

"Sorry," I said. But I concentrated more on the lab. It was
packed from floor to ceiling with machinery. There was virtually
no surface space for miscellaneous work. The first things to catch
my eye were several clock-face gauges, a stack of packing material
in a rack underneath the window, and an open box containing
little metal vials marked on top with the three-leaf-clover design
used to identify radioactive materials.

The dials seemed to cover several kinds of measurement: the
packing material included both small unerected cardboard boxes
and a pile of clear plastic bags; the box of vials had spaces for a
couple of dozen containers but was only half full.

Merom saw me looking around the room. She immediately
marched forward. "You're not allowed in here. Get out. Go on."

"I want a word," I said.

"Outside."

We went out into the corridor. She closed the door to the lab, but that left us standing in the dark. Uncertainly, she opened the lab door a crack, so we could at least see where the other was.

"It's been nearly a day and a half," I said to her. "You were going to talk to your people. I left you my card with my phone number."

Her voice became sly. "Haven't you seen the police since then, Mr. Samson?"

"Yes," I said. "Your people went to the police, and the police came to me, and now I've come back to you, because certain things still need explaining."

I'd taken the offensive. She had considered me to be a solved problem, and all of a sudden my solution was uncertain again. "What do you mean?" she asked.

"Why, for instance, have you kept John Pighee's heart beating for seven months since he died?"

"What—? How—?"

"And after you stutter through that one you can tell me how you come to be practicing medicine without a medical degree." It was an attacking gamble. I'd seen the Ph.D. certificate on her wall. I was guessing that if she'd had an M.D. it would have been there, too.

She opened her mouth, but didn't speak.

"Let's have some answers. I'll settle for them now."

"I'll . . ." she said. Then decisively, "We can't talk here."

I shook my head, but before I could find words exact and emphatic enough to show the end of my patience with these people who'd been playing with the cadaver of John Pighee for more than half a year, she said, "Lee is due here any minute, and if he finds you here . . . We've got to go to my place. Give me a minute, just a minute to hold things together in there. Then we'll talk."

She ducked into the Storeroom lab. I stood in the dark, but before I became anxious she was out again and locking the door. We made our way down the stairs and out of the building. At the Security Building she studied the log as we signed out. Seafield hadn't signed in yet. She relaxed visibly. Our vehicles were in the same lot. I followed her to her apartment building and parked behind her.

While she was opening her front door, she said, "Yesterday afternoon I had the glass put back in the kitchen door."

"Oh?"

"But it worries me that there was only that pane of glass between me and the outside. I may have a new door fitted." I wondered if I should recommend the work of Ray McGonigle.

She led me in. I remembered she had been afraid of Seafield, not the outside world in general. The thought of Seafield didn't, in itself, inspire me with fear. But she knew him better than I did.

While she locked the door behind us, I sat down on her couch. She sat in a matching chair and said, "Please tell me what you know, Mr. Samson."

"No," I said. "That's not the idea. The idea is for you to tell me what the hell you've been doing with John Pighee's body."

"Maybe," she said, "maybe I should have killed you yesterday while I had the chance." It was said speculatively and without apparent malice. I ignored it. Then she said, "John was dead when he came into the Clinic. We hitched him up to some excellent machines and we've kept his heart pumping and his lungs breathing, all that sort of thing. But he was dead from a few minutes after his accident."

There it was. "But what I don't understand is why."

"Because accidents on company premises which result in death or permanent injury are thoroughly investigated by the insurance company," she said. "Whether there is a claim or not. This way, with no death or injury reported, they haven't gone through their investigation procedure. Our situation—well, it would have been highly detrimental to have an insurance investigator asking questions. You've been bad enough. But those guys are good, and they're given free run of the place."

"Are you trying to tell me Pighee doesn't count as 'permanently injured'?"

"In a coma, unconscious, a firm diagnosis can't be made. And with no claim . . ."

I found it all a bit difficult to take. "And you were going to keep him wired up forever?"

"No," she said. "Just a year and a day."

"A year and a day?" I shook my head in wonderment.

"After a year and a day," she said, "his death would no longer be the result of the accident."

"What?"

"It's the law. Not only in Indiana. In most states. And besides, we hope to have the operation wrapped up by then."

"On January 28th or 29th you were going to pull the plug on him?"

"On it," she said. "He is dead, after all. Yes, we will."

"This is a bit much to take in," I said. "Just how was it you were going to get around practicing medicine without a license?"

"I haven't been," she said. "You can't practice medicine on someone who's dead. I've never done anything on someone who was alive."

"But he's not certified as dead."

"Well, no."

"My God. What a crew."

She said, "Now, look, Mr. Samson—"

But I interrupted. "All right. As far as you're concerned, that's just an adjunct to the operation you're supposed to be working on."

"It's very important," she said piously.

"The police, in the form of Captain Gartland, seem to think that you and your colleagues are working for the F.B.I."

"We are," she said.

"Are you an agent?"

"Not in the full-time sense. We were recruited for a special project. It required specialists, scientists. We are doing work that requires a good deal of scientific sophistication."

"Like what?"

"I'm not going to tell you that."

"Pighee was in an explosion. Is it something to do with explosives?"

"No comment."

"You've got radioactive material of some sort in there. What kind of work requires radioactive materials?"

"Look, Mr. Samson—"

"Was there radioactive material in the lab when Pighee was

blown up? Is he contaminated with it? Does that have something
to do with whatever is happening?"

"I . . . I don't know," she said. "I never thought about whether
he might . . ."

But whatever had been overlooked, radioactive contamination
didn't play a part in what was being covered up. Her surprise was
genuine, as I read it.

"How much of the lab was destroyed when Pighee blew up?"

"Quite a bit," she said.

"But it looks all right now, and full of toys that look expensive."

"They are."

"No expenses spared for the F.B.I., is that it?"

"Something like that."

"And this place," I said, waving a hand at the fittings in the
room. "No expenses spared here. The F.B.I. pays pretty well, does
it?"

"Well . . ." It meant yes. I already knew it paid well, because of
the extra money floating around John Pighee.

"How were you recruited?"

"I don't know if I should tell you—"

"Who was it? Dundree? Rush? How long have you been involved?"

"Several years. It . . . Lee was the one who sounded me out about
it. We worked together and then he talked to me about it."

"He courted you when you first came to work at Loftus, did he?"

"Courted me?" she said, with a pained smile. "You use a funny
old word."

"I'm a funny old man," I said.

"There was nothing like that with him then," she said. "We just
worked together. . . . They made contact through him."

"How did you know they were real?" I asked.

"Real?"

"If someone comes up in the street and says they work with the
F.B.I., you don't just take their word for it, do you?"

"They didn't come up in the street."

"But they must have corroborated it somehow. Do you get paid
from Washington? Or get Christmas cards from the Chief?"

"I . . . I don't get paid from Washington. I'm undercover. There were letters and identification. And besides, they are respectable people."

"Like Lee Seafield?"

"Lee's all right. He's respectable. But the others are—"

She was going to say something like "above reproach," but instead the doorbell rang.

She went rigid. Listened hard, as if she hadn't heard it the first time. There was a pause. Then it rang again. She jumped up out of her chair. "Who can that be?" she asked.

"It's your apartment," I said.

The bell rang again. "How did he get up here without ringing the downstairs buzzer? God. Oh, God. Don't leave me. He knows I'm here, because the car's parked out front. He should be at the lab. So should I. My God. Don't leave." She ran into the bedroom.

THIRTY-TWO / By the time the doorbell rang insistently for the fourth time, Marcia Merom, Ph.D., had returned from the bedroom carrying her gun. She seemed much calmer, as if the weight of the oversized thing itself steadied her.

As the would-be visitor banged on the door, she slipped the weapon under a cushion on the couch. I had become extremely uncomfortable. Not just because of the gun, but because of the roller-coaster changes in Merom's apparent personality.

From outside, a syrupy and suggestive voice called, "Marcia Janet Merom. I know you're in there. You're going to let me in, Marcia Janet Merom."

Merom fluffed up her hair, a reflex that made me pity her. Then she opened the door wide, and stood out of the line of sight.

Seafield saw me first. He wasn't pleased. He paused. He thought. Then he marched into the room, and virtually without looking at Merom he closed the door and locked it.

He pointed a finger at me. He nodded and said, "The fart private detective."

Merom sat down on the couch and slipped her hand under the cushion that covered her revolver. If it comforted her, she was the only one.

Seafield stood in front of where I sat and looked like Paul Bunyan. "You don't know when to keep your nose out of other people's business," he said. Then to Merom, "What's he doing here, Marcy?"

"I can see who I want to," she said, mistakenly responding as if the question had been from the jealous lover, when it had been from the suspicious covert conspirator. Whatever the details, he obviously had her twisted into knots emotionally.

"You're supposed to be at the lab," he said, as a matter of fact. "What have you been telling him?"

"He knows most of it already," she said more stoutly.

"And what he didn't know you've been filling in, I suppose," Seafield said. "Including what happened to the treacherous John Pighee."

"No," Merom said suddenly. And more leisurely, "But he knows about John's . . . condition."

"If you've told him anything, anything at all—"

"He already knew!" she pleaded, and began to cry.

"If you've told him anything," Seafield insisted, "I'm not answerable. It's not up to you to take on that kind of responsibility."

"I didn't tell him anything," she whined. "He already knew it. I didn't say anything."

Seafield said to me, "You'd better go now." He had nearly a foot on me when I was standing; when I was sitting, he seemed to be suspended from the ceiling.

"I'm not going anywhere," I said. "Dr. Merom and I were talking when you intruded. I don't know what kind of personal hold you have over her, but she seems to fear you. I'm not leaving until you do."

Seafield just smiled at first. "You like to play rough, do you?" he asked. "She likes that. You like playing rough, don't you, Marcy?"

"No!"

"I ought to know," Seafield intoned. "I ought to know."

I stood up.

"You're still too little," Seafield said. I felt like a bear being baited. Fortunately I have a small mental advantage over a bear. I stepped behind the couch to the telephone. While I dialed, I made small talk. "You know your way around this apartment pretty well," I said. "You'd been here even before Dr. Merom moved in, yes?"

Seafield grew dark, instead of merely casually threatening. "What's that supposed to mean?"

I heard the phone being answered and held the earpiece away so they would have a chance to hear as the reception officer said, "Homicide and Robbery with Violence. May I help you?"

"Lieutenant Miller, please," I said.

But it was a brief conversation. Seafield ripped the phone wire out of the wall.

"Well, well," I said. He was the bear now. I stared hard at him, and grinned like Davy Crockett.

He thought, balancing wisdom against preference in deciding how to deal with me. Wisdom won. He said, "I'll wait outside. I'll give you ten minutes." He went to the door, unlocked it, and turned back to us with an ugly leer. "She doesn't like it to take any longer than that anyway," he said. He closed the door behind him.

Merom sighed. I turned to face her. She was only partly expressing relief. The other part seemed to be an unmistakably sexual kind of admiration. I realized she had been watching, not crying, as Seafield and I had held our little showdown.

I didn't really understand what had happened in either of them, why he had backed down for ten minutes, and why she was now stepping up. But I'd won a victory, however temporary, and I wanted to make sure it wasn't Pyrrhic.

"Come on," I said to Merom. I had another question or two.

"What?" Words had broken the initial spell.

"He's out there." I pointed to the front door. "So we're going out there." Through the kitchen.

She hesitated, uncertain again.

I tried to be reasonable. "You can't live under his constant threat. You can't come back here until the phone is fixed. It's your only protection."

But reason didn't impress her, Ph.D. or no Ph.D. She looked one way, then the other.

Her dithering only made me angry. I shouted, "Move!"

The volume startled her, but made her act. She walked smartly toward the kitchen door, and as she passed me she took my hand.

THIRTY-THREE / We went down the back stairs and around the side of the apartment building to my van. It wasn't a long time for me to work out how it was I came to be walking hand in hand with Marcia Merom in the dark August night.

But long enough. What had happened to me must have happened to a lot of people who knew her. Seafield said she liked playing rough, and he had been telling a form of the truth. Merom seemed to be missing something when it came to dealing with people. A missing synapse that meant she couldn't respond to civilized and gentle urgings. But let someone shout, or insist, let someone treat her roughly, then the gap was jumped, and what was asked of her she gave. Either to Seafield, who was a ruffian by style. Or to me, insistent because I lacked other options. I'd won a tiny battle with Seafield: then, to hurry her along, I'd shown anger. She was mine.

She got in the passenger's seat.

I started the engine and tried to sort out how unnice I had to be to get the answers to the questions I wanted to ask. And where to go to ask them. We couldn't stay put. Seafield's time would be up before long, and his patience not long after that. The man wasn't stupid; he'd realize that we'd ducked out the back.

At first I headed for home. But by the time I had gone through Monument Circle and was about to turn off Meridian onto West Maryland, I realized that when Seafield figured out that we'd left the back way, he would probably head straight for my office. He'd been there before while I was away, at least once.

I turned onto Maryland anyway. There was no Thunderbird

parked on Maryland in the vicinity of my office. But it was only a matter of time.

I pulled to the side of the road to think. In the process, I patted all my pockets and got an idea. It's a good thing I don't automatically change to a clean pair of pants each week. I still had the keys to Linn Pighee's house.

I pulled out again and turned south, to find Madison, then southwest to aim at Beech Grove. Questioning Merom hard in the Pighees' house appealed to me.

It was in Garfield Park that I realized what was wrong with that idea. We'd just crossed Pleasant Run, one of the city's little White River tributaries, and were coming up to a bridge over Bean Creek, a tributary to Pleasant Run. I pulled over to the side of the road again.

Merom squirmed in her seat, seeing us parked in a park in the dark. "What's happening?" she asked.

I should have told her to shut up. Instead I said, "I'm thinking." Not nearly so impressive to her.

What I was thinking was about Sam and Ray McGonigle. I didn't know when they would be coming back to my office. It would do Ray no good at all if Seafield found him at my place and connected him with me.

The only thing to do was to go back to the office.

Merom said, "I really should get back to the lab. I've got work unfinished there."

"Quiet," I said, but without adequate conviction. My ascendancy had slipped. I made a U-turn on the park road. "We're going to my office," I said. I was trying to be forceful, but it came out explanatory and therefore weak in the terms I had decided Merom worked in.

While I drove, I wondered if I was right about her. Certainty gave way to fuzziness. I'm not a natural bully.

I tried to rebuild my resolve. There were things I needed to know. Seafield had accused her of telling me what had "happened to the treacherous John Pighee." I wanted to make his accusation justified. I also needed to know, accurately and in detail, the nature of this F.B.I. project. And I needed to know how people had become involved in it.

"Are you from Indianapolis?" I asked Merom.

"No."

"Where are you from?"

"Originally, Lewisburg. Pennsylvania."

"How do you happen to be here?"

"It's not easy to get research jobs. There are too many doctorates around. Even too many women. For the jobs. It was the best I was offered."

"How long have you been with Loftus?"

"A little over four and a half years."

"Did you go straight into the apartment you have now?"

"No," she said.

"When did you get it?"

"About . . ." But she decided not to answer. "Are you going to take me back to the lab or not?"

"We haven't finished our business," I said.

"I don't think I've got anything to say to you. I don't think we've got any business."

"Oh, yes, we do," I said, and felt the blood rising again.

"I don't think so." She slouched in her seat and looked out the window. "I want to go to the lab."

"Do you know what happened to the last Loftus scientist who lived in your apartment?"

"No," she said without interest.

"He accidentally fell off the back porch and broke his neck."

Her head turned toward me. I had her attention again. She didn't speak.

"What," I asked, "did John Pighee do to make you people decide to kill him?"

"*We* didn't decide," she said. And then tensed.

"Your friend Lee took it on himself, did he?"

"He's . . . It wasn't like that." She seemed about to speak again, didn't, then did. "You're in pretty bad trouble, you know. The things you are poking around in could—will—put a lot of other people at risk."

"Is that what John Pighee did? Put the rest of you at risk?"

"John was selling out," she said.

It was food for thought. I thought for a while. We were getting close to my downtown home. "So Lee killed him."

"He had to be stopped somehow. But what happened wasn't what we had in mind."

"I see," I said. "Lee jumped the gun and did it on his own."

"Something like that."

"And he's going to do the same to me, is he?"

"You are a terrible danger to us," she said. "And it doesn't look as if the police are able to keep you under control."

"Look," I said. "I'm no threat to you if you're what you say you are."

"And just what does that mean?" she asked.

"If you're really F.B.I. on a real project."

"Of course we are," she snapped. "Don't be stupid."

"All I need is some corroboration, whatever they used to convince you."

"Ask the police," she said.

"Whatever they used to convince the police will do," I said. "I'm interested in checking the truth. That's all. Pass the message on to the people in charge. Not Seafield, but Jay Dundree. Henry Rush. Or someone else."

She didn't say anything.

We pulled up near my office behind a new Plymouth. I looked around for a Thunderbird but didn't see one.

"Where's this?" Merom asked.

I was about to answer when I saw Sam and Ray get out of the Plymouth. Instead of words, I said, "Ah uh uh mmm." Then, "Is that Seafield's car over there?" I pointed to the other side of the road. There was only an old pickup truck.

"Where?" she asked.

"Over there, near the corner."

"I don't see anything."

I started the van.

"Where are we going?"

"You wanted to go to the lab," I said. "I'm going to take you to a cab."

"A cab?"

"You don't want to walk, do you?"

We found a cabstand near the bus station. I pulled up near the first taxi and walked her to it. I held the door for her and told the driver, "Loftus Pharmaceuticals."

"And how am I supposed to get home?" Merom asked me.

"Get Lee to put you up for the night," I said.

She seemed to consider it a positive suggestion.

When I walked into my living room, Sam and Ray were playing cribbage and sharing a cup of hot chocolate.

"Oh, Daddy!" Sam said.

"Hi, man," Ray said.

"Hello," I said. "Goodbye."

"Goodbye?" they asked.

"Are . . . are you going somewhere?" Sam asked.

"No," I said. "You are."

"I am?"

"Both of you," I said.

"But where?" Sam asked.

"It doesn't much matter. I feel like being alone tonight, so you're off. Maybe Ray will put you up."

"Mama would love that," he said. But he was thinking about it.

Sam wasn't. "Daddy, what's the matter? Is something happening?"

"Yes," I said. "You're both going out and you're starting on your way now. Immediately. *Tout de suite. Instantemente.* If Ray won't take you home to meet his mother, then you can go and sponge off my mother. Or go to a hotel. Why should I put you up when your rich stepfather has nothing better to do than earn money to give you?"

"He doesn't earn it," she said. "He inherited it."

"A non-issue," I said. "Go on. On your way."

"Not until you tell me what's going on," Sam said, bluffing recalcitrance.

"If you're not out of that door in thirty seconds flat, I'll have your detective card back. And if you spend any more time anywhere near this office tonight, I'll call your mother and tell her to come and take you home."

"You're serious," she said.

"I'm serious." She was hurt, which was too bad. "Someone is coming to call on me tonight," I said. "And I don't want any company."

"Ahh," Ray said.

"That's right," I said. "And she won't wait outside much longer."

Reluctantly, Sam conceded. "You'll tell me about it in the morning?" she said.

"You too young," Ray said.

"I'll tell you about it in the morning," I promised. And added, as I carefully closed the door behind them, "If there is a morning."

The outer door to my office had no lock. Since Ray had worked on it, it barely closed. For the first time I regretted it.

I locked my inner door and spent twenty minutes summarizing the things I knew, had found out, and guessed. Then I hid the notes in Sam's knapsack, and felt that justice was now slightly protected, even if I wasn't.

I considered leaving the office myself, but opted against it. If I wasn't there, my visitor would at least be likely to return until he caught up with me. I wanted that to happen when Sam wasn't present.

But I wasn't going to wait for him lying in bed holding a lily.

I started with a little furniture arrangement, moving my comfortable chair behind the door. I put my baseball bat next to it and then ran a remote-control cable to my cassette tape recorder.

It didn't take long.

I didn't think I had very long.

Seafield would have had only three options when he established, finally, that I had absconded with Marcia Merom. And I didn't think waiting for her in her apartment would be one of them.

He could have come straight to my place. He could go to the Loftus lab. He could go talk to people like Rush and Dundree.

And I was pretty sure that even the second and third options led to me eventually.

But I made him a rash fellow. I expected him to come straight to me.

I went and looked down my stairs.

When I came back into the office, I had a flash of inspiration and went to my darkroom closet for my flashgun and a camera.

These I set up on the stove in my back room, which was against the wall on the side a visitor would have to turn to to see me behind the door. The idea was that if he turned toward me and I needed to delay him, I would trigger the flash, which would blind him momentarily and give me time to get to my bat rack. The flashgun is the only gun I own.

It took about twenty minutes to set it all up. I put film in the camera. I didn't think a picture would be of any use, but it couldn't hurt, and lining the lens up to catch the face of a six-foot-ten-inch assailant gave me something to do.

Still he didn't come.

I sat in the chair and drew pictures for a while.

I got out of the chair and rifled Sam's knapsack for money. I found some loose change.

I tried to read.

I tried to write a letter to Sam like I used to, about animals and objects that acted like people and people that acted like . . .

But it wasn't any good.

I fell asleep in the chair. I dreamed about hitting a man hard on the jaw, but it was my jaw that hurt. I woke up. I dozed. I slept.

THIRTY-FOUR / There was an enormous crashing sound, somewhere near me. I was on an endless conveyor belt. No, I wasn't; I was on a bed of hot coals. No, I wasn't; I was inside a bass drum. No, I wasn't; I was awake.

There was someone with me, someone in front of me. It was dark and I couldn't see. I felt utterly desperate and hopeless. I felt teary and then I realized I had things I could do.

I reached out and touched a shirt. I grabbed for my bat. I dived for my remote switches. It was all going wrong. Then it went right.

I found them. I switched them. The flashgun went off. I was momentarily blinded but I found my bat and I raised it and I swung it for all I was worth.

It crashed heavily into the soft part of my inner door. It bit deep. It went through.

"My God!" a voice said. "What the hell are you trying to do?"

My eyes and mind cleared simultaneously.

Lieutenant Miller stood in front of me. "Have you gone crazy?"

I blinked. "What the hell are you doing here at this time of night?" I asked.

"Night?" he said. "Twenty past eight may be night for softies like you but for me it's just part of the working day."

"Twenty past eight?" I asked. "Past eight?" I looked around. I saw light edges round the blind over the window. "I was asleep," I said. "I must have fallen asleep."

Miller looked at me like I was crazy. Then asked, "Don't you usually sleep at night?"

I realized I was stiff and sore. "That chair isn't very comfortable." I stepped toward the stove. "Want some coffee?" I tripped on the remote wire to the camera. It fell off the stove and hit the floor with a deadly thud. The flashgun shattered. I moved the pieces to one side with my foot, the least of my problems. "I'm making some anyway," I said.

Miller watched without saying anything. I got water and the percolator and the makings. I brought the combination back to the stove.

Then I turned to him. "Why are you here?" I asked. "Not a social call, surely."

"No," he said as I turned the gas on.

"What, then?"

"I . . ." he began. Hesitated, struggled, inhaled, and spat it out. "I'm supposed to bring you in."

"In?"

"To the department."

"Oh?" I turned the gas off again. It had waked me up better than coffee ever could.

"Gartland wants to see you."

"Is that all," I said. "Well, I don't want to see him." I turned back to the stove.

"Don't make life hard for me, Al," Miller said plaintively. "They've been shitting on me right and left about this because you're making trouble. Don't you give me a hard time, too."

"Nobody is making life easy for me," I said, the plaintive one now. I turned the gas on again.

"He told you to stop working on the case," Miller said quietly. "And you didn't. You told me you would keep me informed if you did any work on it, and you didn't."

"What didn't I?"

"What about Pighee's doctor last night?"

"I was going to call you, but I ran out of dimes. It's the truth."

Miller shrugged. "Gartland wants to see you."

"Jerry," I said, "I already said I didn't want to see him. This thing doesn't add up the way I've been told about it, and I'm going to keep working until I know at least a few more details."

"Like what?"

"Like what kind of project these people are working on that's supposed to be so important."

He looked like he was about to say something. But he didn't.

"Do you know?" I asked him.

Silence again, which this time I took as his not saying no.

"Well, what is it?"

"I'm not supposed to know," he said.

"But you do."

He was quiet for a moment again, but then it burst out. "Only that they're setting up for a bust of just about every major drug distributor in the whole fucking country. That's all. And I call that important."

"How?" I asked. "How?"

He sighed heavily. "I don't know, Albert, but they've been working up their contacts for years."

I just stared at him. "When does the boom get lowered?"

"I don't know," he said. "But soon. And that's why they're so worried about you."

I sat in my chair for a few moments. But then I said, "Is the F.B.I. allowed to break the law, Jerry?"

Exasperatedly he said, "They're working with the heroin to set the real drug gangsters up!"

"I mean, are they allowed to kill people?"

"Kill people? Who?"

"John Pighee, for one. And that other guy, Rackey—I think him, too."

"I didn't know Pighee was dead. When was that?"

"He's always been dead," I said.

He didn't like that. He didn't understand it. "I don't know what you're talking about, Al, but you already know more than you're supposed to."

"It's my face. People just talk to it," I said. "They can't help themselves."

"Come on, get your jacket," he said.

"Why?"

"I already said. Gartland wants to see you."

"And I already said I don't want to see him."

He stood up. "Come on, Al."

"Are you arresting me?" I asked, more than a little surprised.

"Not unless I have to," he said.

"On what charge?" I stood up to meet him.

"If I have to," he said, "because you've been accused of abducting one Marcia Merom." He read from his notebook. "She and a Mr. Seafield came last night late and made a preliminary statement that accuses you of having forcibly removed this Marcia Merom from her place of residence. They say she came to no harm while she was in your power and that you released her, but she is pressing charges. They said they'd come in today and make full statements."

"Where is Seafield supposed to come into this?"

"He says he heard her protesting outside her front door as you removed her through the back."

"Do you believe that crap?"

He smiled an icy policeman's smile. "I believe that Captain Gartland wants to see you."

I picked up my jacket from the chair I'd slept in and put it on. I scratched myself behind my ear. I really didn't want to talk to Gartland; I didn't have anything I wanted to say to him. He thought I was rash and unreasonable. There was certainly no chance of getting him to initiate a real investigation of the Loftus people. The prospect of seeing him made me sorely sad.

I took a step toward the door.

Then I did a rash thing.

I clobbered Miller on the chin with the biggest roundhouse right cross I'd ever in my wildest imagination hit anybody with.

He dropped like a stone. It must have been half the sheer surprise.

It surprised me. I looked at my fist as if it had a life of its own.

I left my office very quickly.

THIRTY-FIVE / I visualized Linn Pighee, pale in her hospital bed, as I walked to the corner on West Maryland and liberated my van from its parking space. But I concentrated soon enough on the problem I had set myself. Staying free for a while and using the time to answer my questions, once and for all.

I'd cooked my own goose, but I needed time to cook a few others and make it a gaggle.

I drove southeast on Virginia Avenue and pulled in at Bud's Dugout. Breakfast is a busy time there. Mom was in full flow, doing everything, which is the way she likes it. Sam was there, too, hovering on the side with a pot of coffee for refills.

I walked straight into the back room, pausing only to drag my daughter with me.

"Daddy, I'm helping!" she said. Then had the presence of mind to look at my face. "Is something wrong?"

"Do you have your car here?"

"Yes. Of course."

"Good. I want you to go into town to my office."

"What's happened?"

"Contrary to what you may be told by other sources, I have broken no laws. Not even resisting arrest, because he never said he was arresting me."

"Daddy!"

I managed a smile. "I left the gas on underneath a pot of coffee. I'd appreciate it if you'd turn it off."

"I don't understand."

"After stopping at the office, I want you to visit Linn Pighee."

"I was going to anyway," Sam said. "After I'd finished helping Grandma wash up."

"When you get back, I want you to call my lawyer."

"You do?"

I gave her his name and phone number. "I want you to call him and tell him to keep awake today. I may need him. He should start checking with the police to see if they have me at two, if I haven't checked in with him before then. O.K.?"

"Yes, Daddy."

I moved toward the door. "I've got to go now."

A good daughter. She asked no more questions.

I waved to my mother as I went by. She had time to scowl at me. Good daughter, perhaps. But bad father.

Miller had had time to think about what happened. His immediate impulse would be to put out a pickup on me. But he would have paused, thought about it. Controlled himself. He'd have gone to see whether my vehicle was in its parking place. He'd have noted its absence, then had the pickup put out. It was the only way he could protect himself.

I took back roads all the way to Beech Grove and didn't encounter any police. I pulled up on the edge of the driveway at Linn Pighee's house. Walked directly to the garage and fished around on the keys she'd given me till I found one for the door. I opened it, got in her car, and drove it out to the road. Then I pulled my van into the garage and closed the door again.

Only when I'd finished getting my vehicle out of sight did I notice that I had an audience.

"Hello, Mrs. Thomas," I said. "How are you?"

"What do you think you're doing here, Mr. Samson?"

"I'm picking up your sister-in-law's car for her," I said. I showed the keys.

"I hope you're not expecting to collect the money for that extortionate bill you sent me, because I'm not going to pay it."

"No, I didn't come out for that," I said. With relief that she was worrying about her preoccupations instead of mine. "I leave that sort of thing to my lawyer."

"Lawyer?" she said with a trace of anxiety. "You're not going to involve lawyers for a little bill like that, are you?"

"Mrs. Thomas, the bill is either big or little. It can't be both."

"Tell you what," she said. "I'll give you forty dollars right now and we'll call it quits. How's that?"

I didn't know whether to laugh or cry.

Instead I said, "All right. As long as it's cash."

"You drive a hard bargain, Mr. Samson," she said, turning toward her trailer.

I followed her. It was little enough time to spend and I didn't have any money on me.

She made me wait outside for a minute before inviting me in.

"You're very lucky," she said, without totally convincing me. "Forty dollars is absolutely all the cash I have in the place." That didn't convince me, either.

She opened a cardboard shoe box, counted out four new tens, and showed me the cardboard was bare. She presented me with the bill Sam had prepared and sent to her. I altered the total figure, wrote in "Discount for cash promptly," and signed it as "Paid."

She put the receipted bill in the box and slipped it into a cupboard behind her.

"O.K.?" I asked. I stood up. The cupboard door swung open. She saw me stare. Beside the shoe box was a metal tube marked with a radiation symbol.

She stood up and closed the cupboard door firmly.

I sat down again. "Mrs. Thomas," I said, "what are you doing with a tube of radioactive material?"

"What radioactive material?" she asked uneasily. She was an appallingly transparent person.

"Your brother gave it to you, I presume," I said.

She narrowed her eyes and abandoned her first defense. "That's right," she said, "but it's no business of yours."

I thought about it for a minute. "No," I said. "Of course it isn't." I stood again, facing her.

"Just a memento of his work. Of him. I've always kept little things from his work. From his first drawings in school."

"I'll be going now," I said.

And I was as good as my word.

But only as far as the Pighees' house. I wanted to use the phone.

I called Maude Simmons, my source of general information, who, in her spare time, works for the *Star*.

"Can you make it brief, Albert? Busy busy."

"This *is* business, Maude."

"Oh."

"I need to know whatever you can find out about some people."

"Go on."

"P. Henry Rush," I said. "Jay Dundree, Lee Seafield, Marcia Janet Merom."

"I don't know any of the names."

"Probably you won't be able to help on some of them. They're fish of varying size at Loftus Pharmaceuticals. Rush is your best bet. He's a director. In his sixties, I'd guess, and said he came to the company in security, after the war. Now he spends his time developing scientific personnel. Doesn't sound like a full-time directorial job to me, but there it is. Dundree, Seafield, and Merom are part of the scientific personnel."

"When do you want it?"

"Fast," I said. "I need it now."

"Emergency rates?" Her interest rose noticeably.

"Within reason."

"How fast is fast?" Her cash-register mind was click-clicking computer-quick.

"I'm talking about minutes and hours rather than days. What time is it now?"

"Well, well," she said. "On to something, are we?"

"It could be, Maude. It could be."

"It's nine-fifty-one," she said. "Are you at home?"

"No. I better call you. Where will you be?"

"Here, of course."

"O.K. How long?"

"Call in for progress reports."

"Good. Say, Maude, do you pay anything for scoops?"

"Scoops?" She mouthed the word as if it tasted bad. "We don't have scoops in this business any more, Albert. We have 'exclusives.' "

"O.K., exclusives?"

"You're not broke and trying to barter with me, are you?"

"Nope. Straight question."

"I don't pay anything for . . . scoops," she said. "Not if I can help it."

Which shows the difference between buyer and seller.

I'd never before hired Maude on her emergency rates. If this was my swan song as a detective—my office, license, and liberty were all at risk—at least I was going out on a high note.

THIRTY-SIX / It was quiet at Seafield's as I drove up to his carriage-house home along the alley that it backed on. I parked and had a look through the garage-door windows. All but one of the spaces were empty. I considered that a good sign. Seafield's T-Bird was not there.

The question was whether he was at work or at the police department. Miller had said they would be coming in "today"; I didn't know whether that meant morning.

I went to the door at the bottom of the stairs to his living quarters.

"Howdy." The voice came from beside the building, and belonged to Thomas Jefferson Walker, Sr. "Looking for Mr. Seafield?"

"That I am, Mr. Walker."

"I know you?" With his head bent sideways, he shuffled so as to get a better angle on my face.

"I was here a couple of days ago. Mr. Seafield wasn't in then, either."

"He keeps unlikely hours. Can't count on catching him any particular time. Hey. I remember you. You came here the other day. Say, I got some coffee on the boil. You care to share some with me?"

"I would," I said, "and I remember your hospitality. But I'm in a bit of a spot. I really need to get into Mr. Seafield's apartment. I think he may have something there that will be important to me." I faced the old man squarely and honestly, and lied. "I'd hoped to catch him in."

"You a friend of his?"

"Not exactly a friend. But we share common interests."

"You one of these federal wheels, are you?"

"Told you about that, has he?"

"My son—he's what owns this place," he said. "We had a problem a while back and he explained it to me."

"What kind of problem?"

"Aw, well," he said reluctantly.

"Last January was this?" I guessed.

"Yeah," he said, brightening. "Know about that, huh?"

"Quite a bit."

"Seafield, he came in here and he was drenching in blood and that. Hell, I never liked him much and I was going to call the police, only he told me to call Tommy, Jr., about it. Tommy, Jr., that's my boy. And he explained. I can keep my peace, that's one thing. You won't see me getting in the way of a government project just for the sake of a loose mouth."

"I'm sure everyone involved appreciates that."

"I expect."

"I'm going to have to ask you a favor, Mr. Walker."

"What's that?"

"I need to have a look around upstairs. You can come in with me, that's no problem."

"Wal, I guess that'll be all right," he said.

I stood quietly while the breeze riffled the summer leaves above me. Walker returned with the key in a few minutes. We walked up the stairs to the carriage-house apartment without exchanging more words.

Apart from a kitchen and bathroom at one end, the space above the quadruple garage had been opened into a single huge room. And it was clear at a glance that Lee Seafield was short of nothing flashy that money could buy. If I'd been more relaxed, I'd have been jealous. I spent my first few minutes walking slowly around the room just seeing what caught my eye.

I noticed books first. A chemistry reference library. And *Teach Yourself Portuguese,* with accompanying records.

Then I saw pictures. A cardboard box filled with snapshots of presumably consenting presumable adults.

One picture attracted my attention specially. Not only because the photographic style and content differed from the others. But because it was of my woman.

The picture I kept in my Never-Touch box.

Against impulse, I left it. It was only evidence *in situ.*

And evidence was in short supply. The rest of the room contained little of interest, or evidence. No weapons, no drug stashes, no canisters with radiation markings.

"Well," I said to Walker, "I can't say this has helped me a lot. Sorry to have troubled you."

A distant voice said, "Lee?"

The voice was sleepy, female, and came from above us.

For all my noting of Portuguese-language records, I'd neglected to realize there was no bed in the room.

Again, "Lee? That you?"

Next to the door we'd entered through, there were ladder steps mounted on the wall leading to an attic. I went to them and climbed up, leaving Walker below.

The attic was a massive peaked bedroom, with a huge bed in the middle beneath a section of roof that had been replaced with glass.

I saw Marcia Merom wallowing in the bed. And she saw me. Her eyelids opened wide; her pupils contracted to a pinhead. She sat up. "Don't touch me!" she said.

"I'll try and control myself," I said, and sat on the edge of the bed next to her. She wriggled away, clutching the sheet. She was surprised and afraid. Ideal conditions to make her cooperative.

"I thought you and Lee were going down to police headquarters to tell them how I'd kidnapped you," I said. "Isn't that the idea?"

"We're going in this afternoon," she said.

"When you get there," I said to her, "you're going to have a surprise."

She repeated her repertoire of disapproving facial expressions.

"I've seen the police already today," I said. "And as you see, I'm still free." Facts, juxtaposed. "I hope you can say the same after you've seen them."

I gave it a moment to sink in. That I knew she'd accused me of abduction meant I had to have seen the police. It wasn't for her to guess that I was on the run from them.

I concentrated on being relaxed and angel-may-care: I find it easy when I know I'm about to lie.

"You and your tall impulsive friend are going to have a little surprise when you go into police headquarters," I said again. "The cops know that this F.B.I. business is all just a con. They are not pleased."

"What do you mean, a con?" An element now of panic.

I couldn't help raising my voice. "That it's all phony. Lies. A cover. That you people are making yourselves rich out of the secrecy that surrounds covert government operations. That you're no more working for the F.B.I. than I am."

"That's not true!"

I looked away, up and out of the glass top to the roof. I saw the leaves of the trees rustling, but couldn't hear them. I turned back to her. "Can you prove you work for the F.B.I.? Do you carry papers or credentials?"

She shook her head. She was worried. "They showed me letters," she said.

"Who did?"

"Henry Rush and Tommy Walker, when they took me into an office and talked to me about it."

"When was this?"

"About six months after I came to work at Loftus. I was really fed up."

"What with?"

"The job was a dead end. I couldn't see myself getting on to anything else for years and years. I saw that Lee was stuck, too, and had been for a long time. There are too many of us."

"Us?"

"Scientists. A whole generation of young ones came in in the sixties, and they're blocking promotion for all of us who happened to be born a few years later. Companies made a big youth thing and cut out all the people who were young too late." She seemed genuinely bitter. I didn't quite understand the grievance. My generation had grown up expecting the voyage to success to be a slow boat.

"What did they say when they took you into the office?"

"Henry and Tommy Walker, they came on very serious, swore me to secrecy. I didn't know what was happening."

"And?"

"They asked me how I felt about my country, whether I was patriotic, whether I could keep secrets, whether there were people who knew me who could vouch for my character. I answered their questions, and then I asked what it was all about."

"A reasonable question."

"Then Henry said, 'I'm going to tell you something very important. I'm going to put my life in your hands.' And he gave me a letter from the F.B.I. that talked about an anti-drug operation called Bagtag; it was all signed and official."

"Who signed it?"

"J. Edgar Hoover. After I read it, Tommy showed me his identification wallet with pictures and everything. He said, 'I'm an agent for the F.B.I.' "

"What did you say?"

"What could I say? I didn't know what it was about."

"Did you think the letter and I.D. were genuine?"

"I'm sure they were," she said definitely. "But who's ever seen that kind of thing?"

"What happened?"

"They wanted me to work with them. I felt honored and important. It changed the whole thing, working at Loftus. And what we're doing is important, too."

"What exactly do you do?"

"We refine drugs, mostly heroin, and then tag them with radioactive markers."

"What happens then?"

"Tommy Walker takes what we make and delivers them to the organizations we deal with. In Detroit, I think. It's taken years, but most of the drugs in the Midwest pass through us now. When we've finally involved all the distributors we can, then bang, the F.B.I. closes in on them and they're holding easily identified drugs. They can check the whole distribution network."

"So you supply refined drugs for the whole Midwest?"

"Tommy is the one who has to meet those people. His is the really dangerous job."

"Except for John Pighee's."

"Well," she said. "Well." She rolled the edge of the sheet.

"Why," I asked, "did Lee kill John Pighee?"

"He wasn't supposed to," she said.

"What was he supposed to do?"

"Just arrange an accident, so we could get him into the Clinic. We were going to keep him sedated."

"Sedated? For months? Maybe years?"

"It was better than killing him."

"But why?" I asked. My chorus refrain for the whole case. "He was one of the . . . group."

"He was," she said, emphasizing the past tense. "He broke the rules."

"What rules?"

"I don't really want to—"

"Look, lady," I said emphatically, "it's gone past what you want or don't want."

"John infiltrated us. Or was taken over by the dealers after he joined us," she said.

"What rules did he break that meant he had to be . . . eliminated?" I said. My voice was rising.

"We weren't supposed to put things on paper," she said. "I . . . saw that he had a book sometimes."

"A book?"

"A notebook. With stuff about the lab in it. He wasn't supposed to do things like that. And when I saw he had some of the calcium—"

"Calcium?"

"Calcium 45. It was one of the tagging materials we use."

"Radioactive?"

"An active isotope, yes."

"Does that come in one of the little metal cans with a radiation symbol on it?"

"That's the outside container, yes."

"And Pighee had one?"

"We weren't supposed to take anything—anything at all—out of the lab. Not notes, not materials." She paused. "So, I *had* to tell Henry about it."

"And Henry decided that Pighee had to be killed."

"No!" she said. "Not killed. Just—just made inoperative. We had a meeting. We decided to get him into the Clinic and keep him sedated, so at least we could think about what to do at more leisure."

"When was this meeting?"

"The afternoon—no, morning. Well, about lunchtime."

"On the day of his accident?"

"Accident, yes," she said.

"My God," I said.

"They'd been infiltrated before," she said. "They said they couldn't waste time."

"So Lee went and killed the guy."

"I think it was an accident," she said.

I shook my head. "Lee was covered with blood when he came back here that night. He was there and close and probably did it with a hammer himself and set an explosion afterwards."

"I don't know that," she said. "But they didn't want him killed. There were insurance problems, keeping investigators out, and all that."

"I can believe there were problems," I said. "Your friend Lee, your colleague, he is not the most controlled kind of person, is he?"

"No," she said.

"Did he kill Simon Rackey? The chemist who, presumably, was the last infiltrator?"

"I don't know," she said, but bent her face into her sheet. To me it meant that he had told her about it. Intimately and in detail.

"So," I asked, "where did Seafield come in with you? Did that start when you joined the team?"

"No," she said. "He had other . . . other arrangements, or whatever, I guess."

"Well?"

"I don't think he thought about me that way. But a week after John's . . . accident Lee came to my place. I let him in. He was quiet and nice. We talked about how things were working out at the Clinic. I gave him a drink." She looked up, through the glass, at the trees, at the summer sky. "He said that I must be looking for a lover now that John was . . . gone. He said that he would fill in, if I liked, until I got someone to replace him. I said no, thanks. I'd get along. And then . . ." She shook her head, and tears formed. "It . . . he . . . it . . ."

"What happened?"

"He did it."

"He raped you?"

She nodded, but said, "Nearly."

"What did you do?"

"What could I do?" she asked vehemently. "I couldn't do anything. Not with the project and being in it. There was nothing . . ." She paused.

"It kept happening?"

"Yes."

"And you don't want it?"

"No," she said. Then corrected, "Not really. I . . . I don't like to think about it, except when we're, when he's . . ."

"You're afraid of him?"

"Yes," she said definitely. "He's so—so rough. And not nice to me. He hurts me and he's never grateful or satisfied or . . . or nice. No, I don't like to think about it."

"But when it's happening?"

"It's different then."

"You bought a gun. To frighten him?"

"Yes."

"Did it work?"

"I haven't had a chance to use it, I mean show it, I mean . . . Well. I don't know whether it will put him off."

"Or turn him on. He doesn't seem the type to shy away from violence."

"No," she said. "He's not."

"Do you think," I asked, "that the F.B.I. lets its agents rape people? Much less other agents?"

"I didn't think they'd know."

"Or murder people?"

She shrugged.

I left.

THIRTY-SEVEN / As I climbed down the wall ladder, I saw that Thomas Jefferson Walker, Sr., was still there. When I turned to him, he was frowning.

We walked down to the front door, and as we stepped outside he said, "It don't do no good, being smart."

"What?"

"It's a disease. People ain't meant to be smart in this world. It gets them nothing but trouble. Tommy, Jr., he didn't get smart from me; I grieve for the boy."

"You heard what she was saying up there?"

"Ain't nothing wrong with my ears," he said.

"You heard what she said about your son?"

"He's smart but he ain't wise," Walker said. He walked away

shaking his head, without even inviting me again for boiling coffee.

About half a mile from Seafield's I found a drugstore. That had a pay phone. Apart from the ten-dollar bills Mrs. Thomas gave me, I had a quarter, a dime, and two pennies. I spent the dime.

"Christ," Maude said, "when you said 'minutes,' you meant it."

It was ten past ten. "It's been more than an hour, Maude. What have you got for me?"

"Very little. Nothing about anybody but P. Henry Rush. I have a contact at Loftus who says he's not very important there. A director without influence, who doesn't push things because he's afraid of being dumped. My contact is checking around about him and the others. Apart from that, I have Rush's home address and phone number, if you don't have them."

"I don't, but I have a phone book."

"Won't do you much good. He's unlisted. But it's up to you."

She gave me the number and an address on Roland Road.

"What about contacts? Police record? Shady stuff?"

"Nothing yet. But I thought you had friends at the police."

"Friends is not what I would call them at the moment," I said, and sighed audibly for her benefit.

"You don't sound very happy."

"I'm not."

"You want me to keep at it?"

"Well, I don't want you to stop. And add a name to the list. Thomas Jefferson Walker, Jr. He used to work at Loftus, but doesn't now. In property and things."

"O.K. Call me again in a couple hours."

I had hoped for a bit more for my ten cents, but you've got to be an optimist to be a private detective at all.

I went out to the drugstore's counterman and asked for change for my quarter.

He acted as if I'd asked for the key to his wife's chastity belt. "Not unless you buy something," he said, shaking his head.

I was stupid enough to play. I looked at the quarter and two pennies in my hand. "What can I buy for seventeen cents?" I asked.

"A Popsicle," he said.

"All right," I said.

He put down the magazine he was leafing through and put out his hand. "Gimme."

I handed him the quarter and the two pennies. He got me an orange Popsicle and a dime.

I left the Popsicle wrapped on the counter and went back to the phone booth. The phone directory gave me the number I wanted.

"Federal Bureau of Investigation. May I help you?"

"Can I speak to an agent, please?"

"One moment, please."

After one moment the same voice said, "May I have your name, please?"

"Are you an agent?"

"Yes, I am. May I have your name, please?"

I gave it.

"And your address, Mr. Samson?"

I gave it.

"All right. How can we help you?"

"There is a man at work who wants me to help him with some rather unsavory things he's doing."

"Unsavory?"

"Illegal," I said. "And I don't want to do it, but he says he is working for the F.B.I. on an undercover project."

There was a pause. "How old are you, Mr. Samson?"

"Forty. Why?"

Bluntly: "Are you sober?"

"Damn right," I said. "It doesn't sound very good to me, either."

"All right. Go on."

"He says it's a very big, important secret project. What I want to know is how I can check out whether he is telling me the truth."

"I can tell you," the agent said. "He isn't."

"He's pretty convincing. And he has some identification."

"F.B.I. credentials?"

"That's what they look like, but I don't know how to tell whether they're genuine. And he has some letters from Washington. Signed and all that. He showed them to me."

"What's this man's name, Mr. Samson?" The voice sounded marginally more interested.

"Rush," I said. "P. Henry Rush." I gave the address on Roland Road. "He's a director of Loftus Pharmaceutical Company, here in town."

I was too eager. The voice said, "You sound like you have something against this man, Mr. Samson. Is that so?"

"Look," I said, "I'm just trying to find out whether I should believe him and help my country or whether he's just trying to take me for a long ride off a short pier. He says the project is too big for your office to know about, but he's got the police believing him."

My agent didn't respond at once. I knew what the silence was telling me, though. It was just possible that what I was describing was for real. Finally, he said, "This is beginning to sound pretty serious, Mr. Samson."

"Do you know anything about this guy? Does anybody there know anything? Is there some way to check?"

"I . . . I don't think it very likely that the man is working for us. We would surely know about any operations in our area. And you can rest assured that the F.B.I. doesn't involve itself in illegal operations. We leave that to the criminals."

"Somehow you don't really convince me," I said.

"But I think it would be prudent if we checked this out."

"I agree," I said truly.

"Can you come into our office here now? Where are you, Mr. Samson?"

I wasn't sure I wanted to go to them immediately. "I'm in Muncie," I said. "But I'll come right in."

I sat in the booth for a few minutes thinking about what I wanted to do. Then faced facts and worked myself up to the hard task I had in front of me.

I walked back to the man behind the counter. He was sharpening a pencil. "That sure is a sharp pencil you got there."

He looked up at me. My Popsicle was gone. That made me mad.

I took a ten-dollar bill out of my wallet. I put it on the counter. I pointed my finger at the guy, which is rude. I said, "I am a dangerous criminal. I am wanted by the police. I want to call them and turn myself in. Give me change for the phone. Give it to me now."

He hesitated. Then he put his pencil down and got me change. I shoved the two quarters back at him and said, "More."

"You want to call the cops, there's an emergency number and you get your dime back."

"Maybe I want to call Dial-a-Prayer," I said.

"Just trying to be helpful." It was the kind of help I'd been getting for a week. I went back to the booth with the makings of ten local calls.

The first was to my office. I wanted a word with Sam. But she wasn't there; Dorrie, on my answering service, cut in on the call, but I hung up without talking to her. I didn't want to leave a message. Sam was probably at Entropist Hospital.

Then I called Miller. "Made it back to your office, then?" Enough had happened to me since our early-morning encounter for me to recall it lightheartedly.

Not him. "You're in trouble, Albert."

"That's what I am reputed to have said to myself when I first realized I'd been born."

"Cut the crap. Get your ass in here. We've got a full county alert out for you."

"For giving you a little push? That's a bit excessive, isn't it?"

"You knocked one of my teeth out," he said.

"I didn't realize. Sorry."

"Where are you?"

"I'm not coming in to headquarters just yet, Jerry," I said.

He didn't say anything for a moment. Then, "You used to be rational. Unless you've suddenly gone berserk, I have to think that you think you know what you're doing."

"I've been finding things out," I said.

"What kind of things?"

"That one of the Loftus scientists killed John Pighee. For instance."

"Did Pighee die? When did it happen?"

"He's always been dead," I said.

"You said that before, but what the hell is it supposed to mean? Has Pighee gone and died or not?"

"Well, his condition hasn't changed, if that's what you mean. But the emergency doctor and Marcia Merom have both told me that he always was dead from the time of the accident, and that they've just kept his heart and vital functions going by machine."

There were a lot of things I could feel pass through Miller's mind. He said, "Can you prove this?"

"To people who start out thinking it's not impossible. But not to your friend Gartland."

"My superior officer," Miller said.

"Does the F.B.I. do things like that?" I asked him. "Or if they do, are they allowed to get away with it?"

"You on about that again, are you?"

"I don't believe things just because somebody tells me. Even your . . . superior officer. Even if he's been told by someone with superior personal credentials. And especially things that don't fit with my concept of the way life is supposed to happen. Somebody is conning somebody here, and unless you people know a lot more than you seem to, you may be some of the people being conned."

"That's not very likely," Miller said.

"What does it take to get you guys to see the noses on your faces?"

"Mirrors."

"Has the Merom woman come in to tell you about how I abducted her yet?"

"No."

"If she does come in, will you interrogate her about her supposed F.B.I. activities?"

"No," Miller said. "Not only is it more than my job is worth, but I don't think it's necessary."

"Will you ask her about John Pighee's real condition?"

He didn't say no right away. So it was possible.

"Jerry, what would it take, exactly, to get you to consider bucking the superior Captain Gartland?"

"More than you're likely to be able to give me."

"Seriously."

"Physical evidence, I guess. The stuff you haven't got."

"You wouldn't consider sending an independent medical man up to look at Pighee's body, would you?"

"On your say-so?" That meant no.

"How about taking the pickup on me off, so I can go and use my van. I'm getting tired of walking."

"It's out of my hands now," Miller said ominously. "But if you come in, you can make your case and we'll see what we can do."

"Why does that not inspire me with confidence?"

I don't know whether he answered. I hung up on him. At least he'd still have people looking for my van, not Linn Pighee's car. Poor old Linn. I wondered if I'd have time to visit her.

I sat in the booth and tried to think. I saw the man behind the counter in the drugstore looking at me. I opened the door and called to him, "I'll be out in a minute, only there's a rat gnawing on my foot." I closed the door again.

Lots of dimes and a phone box in working order. By modern standards, riches. I called my office again, on the off chance that Sam had come back. But Dorrie took the call over after four rings. This time I talked to her.

"Hello, Mr. Samson. There is a message," she said. "Well, sort of."

"From my daughter?"

"No, from a man. He . . . he sounded angry. In fact, he was angry. He said you'd be in trouble when he caught up with you."

"Did he leave a name?"

"No. I guess he thought you'd know."

"It's just there are so many people angry with me now, it's hard to choose."

"Oh, dear," she said. "I've had a bad week with my Rod, but nothing like that."

"Did this man sound like a policeman?"

"Gosh. I don't know. Not really."

"Well, at least that narrows the field to about a hundred."

I used another dime to call Entropist Hospital. There was just a chance that I might be able to catch Sam there, visiting Linn Pighee. I got through to the ward nurse, who was very helpful.

"I'm trying to contact my daughter," I said. "I think she might be there visiting Mrs. Linn Pighee. My daughter's in her late teens with reddish-brown hair, brown eyes, freckles. Ordinary height. The hair is long, looks like a boy's."

The nurse knew her immediately. "Yes, the young lady was here. But she left," the nurse said, "just after I told her that Mrs. Pighee died in the night."

THIRTY-EIGHT / I spent more than two hours at Entropist Hospital. I got no satisfaction. Linn had died unexpectedly. They didn't really know why, and machinery was in hand to arrange an autopsy to find out. I spent a lot of time questioning nurses about the possibility of unauthorized visitors, the chance that someone had come in to . . .

To what? I had trouble explaining my suspicions to them. Afterward I went to their canteen for some coffee, and I had trouble understanding my suspicions myself.

It was pushing one o'clock.

The coffee break made me feel more relaxed, if no less confused. I was either on a compulsive course of self-destruction or I was the only man who saw what was happening. I had no choice but to go ahead. The time for discretion had passed.

I drove out to Roland Road.

I had trouble finding Rush's house. Not because the address was wrong, but because the house was secluded, to put it mildly. There were high unkempt hedges, and the only roadside sign was an unmarked mailbox between the boxes for 112 and 92 Roland Road.

I left Linn Pighee's car a hundred feet from the mailboxes and walked back to the driveway path through the hedges. It was not a rural setting: only about half a mile from the intersection of Interstate 65 and 38th Street. Interstate 65 is the expressway into the city from the northwest side of town; 38th Street is mostly divided highway across the northside.

Behind the porcupine hedge was a ranch-style house. Not apparently special. The line of hedging went all the way around the property.

Isolation was not what I'd expected, but I appreciated it.

I had walked to the middle of the driveway before I realized that I might be behaving rashly. I had assumed there would be nobody there. How the hell did I know?

I became discreet. I moved to what vegetative cover I could find and approached the house slowly. There was no window on the garage door, so I couldn't see if a car was at home. I walked round the house, window to window. I edged cautiously past each frame. There were no curtains or blinds. I saw clearly that there was nobody in any of the rooms.

But there was still the problem of getting in.

For fear of some sort of alarm on the doors, I broke a kitchen window and climbed in over the sink.

I cleaned up the glass and put it in the wastebasket, even removing the few remaining jagged edges of the broken pane. It was not impossible I might want to make a quick exit through the same hole. I was not overconfident.

But a careful walk through the house showed that I was indeed alone. And there was no car in the garage.

I went back to the kitchen and started looking for objects smaller than people. And I tried to get a sense of this man.

The life-style as expressed in his living conditions contrasted with Merom's and Seafield's places. They covered their spaces with small and valuable and flashy things. Most of Rush's things were large.

The kitchen had all the appliances, surfaces, design features. But there was no food. No cooking or eating utensils. Apart from a case of White Rock lemonade and two two-pound boxes of Mrs. Wiggins' Fancy Cookie Assortment, there was nothing to eat at all. There was one glass tumbler.

There were three bedrooms, but the only beds were singles in each of two bedrooms. Both were made, but only one looked as if it had ever been used. There were slippers under it, and a bathrobe on it. There were some blue suits in the closet, two white Stetson hats on a shelf. It was where the man slept. There were some prescription-medicine bottles on a table by the bedside, and a lamp, but no books.

The room with the other bed seemed more clearly an office. Here there was a desk and a telephone. A filing cabinet. Some paper. There were no clothes in the closet.

The third bedroom had a stack of cardboard boxes in a corner but was otherwise bare.

The living room was large and open-plan, but what furniture there was was in a circle at one end. A television set, four deep upholstered armchairs ringing a thick rug over a more basic carpet. But nothing else. No table, no standard lamps, no newspapers, no books.

The only other fitting I found was an American flag in a holder inside the front door.

Nobody spent much time in this house.

To think about what I wanted to do, I sat in one of the armchairs. It was very comfortable, which was balm for the body that housed a troubled mind. It was nearly three o'clock.

I went to the office bedroom and used the phone.

"I hoped it might be you," Maude said. "I haven't found a lot, but I've found something."

"Good," I said.

"Who do you want first? Rush, or the others?"

"Rush," I said.

"He was in Intelligence during the Second World War. For about three and a half years."

"Interesting," I said. "What did he do?"

"I haven't got details, but it wasn't codes or propaganda or evaluation of data received. The implication is that it was in some phase of preparation of operatives."

"Well, well."

"Apart from that, he's deep in Masonics, Legion, and that kind of thing. He's a widower. And about ten years ago he refused to leave the Loftus board when they were doing everything but fire him. Apparently he was in charge of plant security when they uncovered systematic theft by an organized ring of employees. He said he ran security the way Sir Jeff Loftus wanted it, but he nearly went out on his ear, only he had some kind of protection in his contract. They offered him a big lump payment to help him on his way, but he turned it down. He made a deal to stay on at a frozen salary and only in a specialized capacity involving personnel development. It was the same thing that took Sir Jeff out of active company management. O.K.?"

"Yeah. How about Rush's friends and associates?"

"I haven't listed any."

"Don't give me that. The fraternal Hoosier always has friends and associates."

"I don't say he hasn't got them. I just haven't found them. And he's certainly kept very much to himself in the last fifteen years. Since his wife died, in fact. I understand that he's really cut himself off on a personal basis. They say he thinks about work and nothing else, and since his work became isolated, well . . ."

"Can you tell me something else?"

"Give me a try."

"Where does he eat?"

"What kind of question is that?"

"He doesn't eat at home. You say he hasn't got any friends. I just wondered where he eats."

"I can try," she said doubtfully. It wasn't the usual kind of detail she worked on.

"Don't bother," I said. "Just thinking out loud."

Then she told me about the other people I'd asked about: Walker, Dundree, Merom, and Seafield. She didn't tell me anything I'd been wanting to know.

"Should I keep on?"

"Yeah," I said. "But don't tell me how much it's costing me."

"Is it you that it's costing?" she asked. Not out of sympathy but because she was worrying about getting paid.

"Yeah," I said. "My client died last night."

She didn't know whether I was joking.

I said, "Do you get any whiff of Rush or the others doing nasty things? Criminal things?"

"Not yet," she said. "Should I?"

"Certainly possible."

"Can you tell me about it?"

"Not really, no."

"I'll keep a nose out. But you know, Albert, the more you tell me, the more useful I can be."

"When they survive, I tell my clients the same thing every day," I said.

"Do you have clients every day?" She was hopeful, not sarcastic.

I called my office. Again Dorrie intercepted the call. After finding there were no messages, I told her I'd be calling the number again and to let it ring. In case Sam was . . . well, in case Sam was there and just slow on her feet. I called again. I let it ring twenty times, but nobody answered.

I didn't know what to think.

I called Clinton Grillo, my lawyer. He said that Sam had called him in the morning and told him to be ready to defend my rights. He wanted to know what it was all about. I couldn't tell him. I was worried about Sam.

I'd got myself into a melodramatic frame of mind. I was afraid that Seafield had her.

I called Seafield's home number. No answer. I called Loftus Pharmaceuticals. He wasn't at the lab. I called Merom's number. No answer. I called the police.

"Miller."

"Jerry, has Lee Seafield been in there today to back up his story that I abducted Marcia Merom?"

"No," he said. "Neither of them turned up. Where are you, Albert?"

"I'm in Muncie following up a lead."

"And I have three balls," he said.

"Look," I said. "My daughter is missing. I'm afraid that Seafield might have her."

He was just silent.

"Do you understand what I'm saying? I'm afraid he might have kidnapped her, because he wants to get at me."

Quietly, but not sympathetically, Miller said, "How long has she been missing?"

"I'm not quite sure. But two or three hours, probably. She's not at my office."

"So you don't even know that she hasn't gone shopping or something. Do you have any positive reason to believe that this Seafield fellow has her?"

"Not directly. But I've been making trouble for him, and he's impetuous and violent and he's not at work or home."

"Are you at your office or home? You're impetuous."

He didn't seem to be taking me seriously.

"And Linn Pighee died in the hospital last night." He didn't respond at once. "Died . . . or was killed . . ."

"You sound like you've lost control of the game, Albert. Why don't you come on in, relax a bit, and we'll talk about what's going on and what we can do about it."

I didn't sound that terrific to myself. However, "With Seafield and Merom not coming in to back up their story, does that mean you don't have your people looking out for me any more?"

"I'd have called them off, but Captain Gartland wants to see you, too, pretty urgently."

I hung up. I tried to relax. For all I knew, they were tracing phone calls now.

I wasn't particularly rational. But how can you be when you've set your own daughter up for kidnapping?

I called my mother.

"Albert?"

"Sam isn't there by any chance, is she, Mom?"

"No. You sound upset, Albert. What's the matter? Are you in trouble?"

"No, no," I said. "No more than usual. I'm just trying to find out where Sam's got herself off to. I . . . I've got a job I want her to do. She's probably gone shopping or something. Look, can you call my office every now and then, and ask her to call me?" I gave Rush's number. "That's if it's in the next hour or so. Otherwise I'll call you or her."

"Where is she, Albert?" Urgently.

"I don't know offhand," I said, trying to reassure her by being offhand.

"What kind of trouble have you got her into?"

"I have to go, Mom. One thing, if anybody answers the phone here but me, tell her to hang up, O.K.?"

I hung up.

I walked to the kitchen. I rinsed my face with cold water. Trying to shock myself back into reasonability. The water wasn't cold enough to do the job, because it was not nearly as cold as I felt.

I took two cookies from the Fancy Assortment. Then I went back into the office bedroom. I'd come looking for physical evidence; I needed it.

The house was a conventional design, probably not built to order for Rush. I didn't believe that it was likely he'd had hidden safes put in.

The alternate theory is that a good hiding place is better than a strongly defended hiding place.

And there was the question of what it was that needed to be hidden.

The operation was conducted with the minimum of paperwork. But Rush had shown Merom authorizing letters. He had to have those somewhere.

It took me more than an hour. I went through the desk first, then the filing cabinets. Nothing was what I wanted. Particularly the third drawer of the filing cabinet. It was packed tight with folders of newspaper clippings. The clippings didn't seem to have much to do with anything. Random sports cuttings, comic strips, letters to the editors. The rest of his work was involved with complicated financial matters and history of the Second World War. The third filing cabinet drawer just didn't fit.

Until I thought about it.

I took the fat clipping folders out. On the bottom of the drawer was a heavy blue envelope in a plastic bag. The clippings had been there just to sit upon and hide what was underneath.

In the blue envelope were three letters. All addressed to P. Henry Rush. All on headed F.B.I. notepaper. All attached to envelopes mailed in Washington, D.C. All signed by J. Edgar Hoover.

The earliest was dated May 7, 1969. It said:

Agent Walker has reported to me your hesitation to participate in the anti-drug operation he has discussed with you. Be

assured that this project has my fullest enthusiasm and that with your security background and present position you are uniquely qualified to participate in it. To apply your considerable skills to it will assure the likelihood of its success. It is a longterm operation and will require your full commitment. Success means not only reduction in drug availability, nationwide, but augmented fortification for our Country and the Bureau against their enemies and detractors.

The second was dated nine days later.

In response to your further question, it will not be desirable to work with local police personnel. Police security is simply not adequate for protection of a project of this scope and duration. Lives are at stake. Security is paramount. However, if it is necessary to secure your cooperation, you may inform the police official you mention of the establishment of the project. Your work with him in W.W.II has been confirmed and he has been cleared. But his briefing must be a short and general one, in the form of a courtesy, and Agent Walker must be present. Agent Walker is your sole link and he will have complete operational responsibility, and is responsible only to me.

The third was dated twelve days later.

It is with deep gratification that I learned from Agent Walker of your agreement to head the production end of Project Bagtag. The Bureau's success in this operation will usher in a new era of crime fighting as well as renewed Bureau prestige.

The letters didn't make me feel good. I couldn't fault them or the signatures. But I wasn't working in an area where I had any expertise.

I folded up the letters and put them in my jacket pocket. The blue envelope and its plastic bag I put back on the bottom of the filing cabinet drawer. I put the fat files back on top of it.

I went to the living room and sat in one of the deep upholstered chairs. I wasn't ecstatic but I wasn't depressed. I had physical objects that would sort things out once and for all. I was feeling fatalistic. And began to acknowledge the prospect of being wrong.

From outside the house I heard a sound.

I stood up.

I went to the door and listened.

Nothing.

While I stood, someone the other side of the door rang the bell.

I moved. Quietly as I could.

Bell again.

Roland Road was altogether too populated all of a sudden. I eased myself to the kitchen. Hesitated a minute, and instead of going through the window, I unlocked the back door from the inside and slipped out.

"Mr. Rush?"

"What!" Into the verbal arms of a close-cropped young man in a dark suit.

"F.B.I., Mr. Rush," he said. He showed an identification card. "My associate and I would like to have a word with you."

"Your associate?"

"He's out front. He rang your doorbell."

One and one together. "Speak up," I said loudly. "I don't hear very well."

I assembled them in the cluster of chairs at the end of the living room. They were both impressed by the American flag in the hall.

The associate began: "We've had a complaint that you've been impersonating an F.B.I. agent."

"Me?" I said, surprised.

"Yes, sir."

"Ridiculous," I said scornfully.

My back-door agent looked at me carefully. "It does seem an unlikely accusation," he said. "But you can appreciate that we have to make sure. If you wouldn't mind, I'll take a few details and we'll be on our way."

"I'm not even going to ask who made such a ridiculous accusation. I wouldn't want to sully my ears with his name."

My back-door agent said, "Sir, for the record, would you tell me whether you've ever told anybody that you worked for the F.B.I. or that you were working on some project organized by them?"

"I certainly have not ever said I had anything to do with the F.B.I."

I think they believed me. After all, I was telling the truth.

"May we look around, sir?"

I looked puzzled.

The associate said, "It's just routine. With an accusation having been made, if it later came out that you had a machine in the bedroom which printed phony F.B.I. credentials and we'd been here and hadn't found it, we'd look pretty stupid. We'd just like to have a look around."

I walked around with them. They asked only two questions.

In the kitchen: "Where do you eat, sir?"

"At the factory. The government subsidizes meals there, so it's wasteful to eat anywhere else."

And in the third bedroom: "What is in those boxes?" The cardboard boxes in the corner.

I didn't know. "Money," I said.

They left my boxes untouched. They'd only spent five minutes looking around the house. I watched them get in their car, turn it around, and head down the driveway.

I felt like following them, but had to give them a minute to get clear. I was tired of Rush's house. I didn't feel easy there. I wanted to find Sam. I wanted to give the letters in my pocket to Miller. I wanted to sleep.

I spent the minute by going back to the third bedroom before I left. Just for a look to see what was in the boxes in the corner.

I'd lied to the F.B.I. There were four cardboard boxes. Three of them had dusty books and magazines in them.

Only one box was full of money.

Mostly it was fifty-dollar bills, but there were some hundreds and twenties for variety. All nice used cash. My first impulse was to count it.

Then I thought I might take some. Much as I try to ignore money as a fact of life, there are times when it helps. I grabbed a big handful.

But then I remembered where the money had come from. It wasn't the F.B.I. I dropped it.

I was overtaken by the impulse to get the hell out of Rush's house. To go find Sam. To go talk, at last, to the police.

I repiled the boxes in the corner, walked back through the living room, and decided to leave by the front door, the shortest way home.

I stepped onto the front porch.

A hairy forearm crushed my arms to my sides and a flame-hot hand pulled what hair I have on my head backward and down.

"Hot damn!" a voice said beside me. "We don't even set the snare and the goddamn rabbit jumps into it."

Somewhere above, a far more hostile voice said, "I told you that car on the road looked suspicious."

Another voice, sounding tired, said, "You were right, Lee. Bring him on in."

THIRTY-NINE / Two men entered the house before I did. Lee Seafield held me, and after the others had passed from my limited range of vision he cursed at me. "By God, Samson," he said, "you're going to get it."

I had the feeling I didn't want it.

The grip tightened on me, when a voice came back through the doorway. "Bring him in, Lee. Don't hurt him."

"Just give me the excuse," Seafield whispered in my ear, into my very being. He dragged me into the living room.

Henry Rush was sitting in one of the heavy easy chairs. The other man stood at the light switch. "What a day," Rush said plaintively. "Nothing but trouble."

"This one is no more trouble," Seafield said aggressively.

Rush studied me as the other man sat down. Rush said, "I think you're right there. The police want him. They can have him. He won't see daylight again until things are all wrapped up."

The third man said, "Search him, Lee."

Seafield hooked a foot around my ankles and pushed me. My nose hit the floor with a resounding bang, closely followed by a hundred and ninety pounds of too solid flesh. Being searched by Seafield was not a gentle process. But he was looking for a gun, so he passed over the letters I had in my pocket from Rush's files.

Seafield seemed surprised to report that I didn't have a gun. The third man snorted. "These fellas always carry guns. It's what makes them feel like tough guys."

Seafield pulled me up and pushed me against a wall. "He's probably got one of those little ones."

The third man snorted. "A sissy gun, huh? Behind his belt buckle or something."

"Yeah," Seafield said. He turned back to me. "Undo your belt."

I undid my belt.

Seafield pulled my trousers down to my ankles.

"Is all this necessary?" Rush asked tiredly.

"You don't want him shooting the place up, do you, Henry?" the third man asked casually.

Reluctantly, Seafield said, "I don't think he has a gun, Tommy. I really don't think he does."

"You're right," I said. "I don't."

They weren't listening.

"What was he doing here, Henry?" The third man, who had to be Thomas Jefferson Walker, Jr., frowned at Rush.

Rush shook his head. "What did you want in my house, Samson?"

I bent to pull my trousers up, but Seafield hit my arms and said, "No!" He clearly had a partiality for patched boxer shorts.

"What were you doing here, Samson?" Rush asked again.

"Holding a garage sale," I said.

Seafield turned me slightly with his right hand and knocked me flat on my patch with his left. I think that's what he did. I don't quite remember what happened between the point at which the big fist came hurtling toward me and waking up after a count of eighty-seven.

It's not all that unpleasant being K.O.'d; better than a lot of things I can remember.

I woke up saying, "Where's my daughter?"

"What?"

"Where have you bastards put my daughter?"

There was a period of silence. During it, I sat up against a wall and refocused on them.

"What daughter?" Rush asked me then.

"My daughter is missing. One of you . . . criminals kidnapped her."

They were all about to speak when the phone rang. They all hesitated.

"Better get it, Henry," Tommy Walker said. He was a heavyset man with a very thick neck.

Rush walked to a nearby extension. "Hello," he said. Then, "No, Ma'am." Then he held the receiver away from his ear and looked puzzled. "Hung up," he said.

Walker's cheeks glowed. "Now, you shouldn't never tell a lady no, Henry. It just ain't polite."

"Wrong number," Rush said. "It was some girl wanted to know if I was her daddy." Walker and Seafield laughed.

I just choked.

"Lee," Rush said, "you know anything about this man's daughter?"

"No, I don't," Seafield said a trifle petulantly. Then he brightened. "I bet he hasn't got one. Any more than he had an envelope from Pighee."

"Well," Rush said, "whatever your problems with your daughter, Samson, they have nothing to do with us. I don't know what in the world you think we would want with her anyway."

"To keep me quiet," I said quietly.

"You have a powerful strange idea of the sorts of things we do," Rush said self-righteously. "Kidnapping—dear, oh, dear."

"People who murder people seem fair bets if there's a kidnapping going," I said.

All three of them stiffened slightly. But after a moment Rush said, "Murder people, now, is it?"

"Simon Rackey was the first," I said. I was past holding things back.

"Simon?" Rush said. "What are we supposed to have had to do with Simon's death?"

By immediately remembering the name, more than four years later, it seemed to me Rush was saying that I was right.

"Then John Pighee's death," I said.

Rush began, "We have every hope—"

I interrupted, "Pighee is dead in every way but having the certificate signed, you know that. Marcia Merom told me herself."

"I doubt that you will get Marcia to say any such untrue thing before witnesses," Rush said. Seafield smiled and looked pleased with himself.

"And now John Pighee's wife's death," I said.

Rush looked again at Seafield, who sat impassive. "Mrs. Pighee is dead?" he asked.

"She died last night," I said. "Presumably because when her husband is allowed to stop breathing on January 28th next year, you would owe her a large chunk of money. And for economy's sake, not to mention the greed that's got you all into this, you decided it would be better to get out of that commitment."

"I certainly did not know that Mrs. Pighee was dead, and had nothing to do with it," Rush said firmly. "Lee? Do you know anything?"

"Why do you always ask me about stuff like that?" he said. He sounded hurt. "I don't know anything about Pighee's goddamn wife. Why should I?"

Formally, Rush turned to Walker. "Tommy?"

Gravely, Walker shook his head.

Rush said, "As I said, you have some very strange ideas about what we are doing. I assure you, we risk violence only when there are absolutely no alternatives. And plans which involve risk sometimes take courses which are more extreme than we would want." Inadvertently he again looked at Seafield.

"Your bullyboy gets out of hand sometimes, does he?" I asked.

Seafield stood up. "Put your pants on, Samson," he said. "Unless you're afraid you're going to piss in them."

"Sit down, Lee," Rush said.

But Walker overruled him. "No. Get him ready to go out. We've wasted enough time on our visitor. I've got to get on the road."

"Shall I call the police and have them pick him up here?" Rush asked.

"No," Walker said. "Let Lee deal with him."

"Save the taxpayers some money," Rush said. "Take him down to headquarters. They've been looking for him long enough."

"Good," I said. "The police is exactly where I want to go."

Walker looked at Rush questioningly.

Rush shook his head emphatically. "Who'd possibly believe him? They'll commit him to a loony bin soon as look at him. He'll be out of circulation forever. As far as they're concerned, he's a raving lunatic. Hell, he *is* a raving lunatic."

Seafield took me firmly by the arm again. "Come on, cowboy," he said.

He marched me to the kitchen.

"Hey," he called back. "Somebody has broken a window in here."

"Get him out of here, Lee!" Rush shouted back. "Before I do something to him that I'll regret."

FORTY / "O.K., cowboy," Seafield said in the garage. "Let's have the keys to your car out there."

"Why?" I asked.

"Keys!"

I gave him the keys, and started toward the garage door.

"Stop!"

I stopped and turned. He had acquired a piece of rope and was advancing on me.

"Put your hands behind your back," he said.

"Don't be silly!"

"Hands behind your back!"

"You're taking me to the cops. I'm happy to go to the cops," I said. "What's the problem?"

His answer was another big fist hurtling toward my jaw. I let him have the last word.

———

I woke up slowly. Conscious first of a belated surprise. Surprised that Rush, under pressure, was sticking to the F.B.I. story. My version of the tale had a different ending.

I didn't get time to worry about it. My consciousness widened to the point of opening my eyes. Even then, life was still pretty dark. I was face down on the floor in the back of a car. Whose car —Linn Pighee's or Seafield's or Rush's—I didn't know.

My head hurt. I wanted to rub it. But I couldn't. My hands were tied.

I decided to turn over and sit up. But I couldn't. My legs were tied. I squirmed for some leverage or position. There wasn't any.

I bounced heavily as the car came to a stop. I twisted my head to get a hint through a window of where we were. I couldn't see much of a window. In any case, it was nearly dark outside and where we were there was no street-lighting.

I waited for something to happen.

Nothing did. Then the car radio came on. I decided to ask whether it was time to go see the police now and why I was trussed up. It came out "Mmmwhhhhsssmmmmmmnnnmmmmm."

My mouth was taped.

But the sound was enough to attract my chauffeur's attention. "Are we wakies, cowboy?" he asked. I felt a hand on my back. Then the hand pulled testingly on the rope that bound my hands.

"Mmmowowow!" I said.

It let go. "How nice," Seafield said. "Some company for me while I wait."

We waited for more than an hour. I kept track by the news bulletins on the radio. I dozed part of the time. My head cleared some.

"All right," he said, at last. "Time to go visiting." He got out of the car, opened a back door, and pulled me out feet first. He cut the ropes on my feet, then stood me up. I had trouble balancing, and leaned heavily on the car. But I saw we were at the back of Marcia Merom's apartment building.

"I don't want any trouble with you," Seafield said sharply.

It was news to me that there was any kind of trouble I could cause him.

Holding me securely and actually giving me some support while I got my land legs, he led me to the back stairs. There was no one around at all.

We went up to the third floor. Only as we stepped onto Merom's porch at the top did I think clearly enough to ask myself why I was cooperating with him. The fact that he wanted me upstairs was surely reason enough to fight to stay down.

I wasn't thinking clearly enough to answer me.

Then I was. Because I'd thought wishfully . . . because I'd drifted into the acquiescent state of mind. Which worked on the assumption that if I didn't fight, then he wouldn't do anything really bad to me.

But the man was a murderer. And it could hardly be in doubt that he had scheduled me for the next notch on his metaphorical gun.

My God!

From his pocket Seafield took some keys and opened the back door.

Think, think! Keys meant Merom was not at home. Keys meant Merom was cooperating.

I shouted for help through my tape—"Mmmmfmdmdmgh-mmdhfkdkfmmm"—as Seafield pulled me into the apartment. It didn't come out very loud. All a sound like that might attract was the neighborhood cat.

After he closed the door behind us, Seafield said "Come on," and led me through to the living room. He turned on a light, then shoved me down against the bedroom door.

He went back to the kitchen.

I didn't waste the time. I scrambled to my feet and went to the telephone. I nearly sat on it to get the receiver off with my hands behind my back. I lowered the receiver to the table, then squatted again over the dial. I felt for the "O," to get the operator. I got a finger into it and managed to get the dial all the way around first time.

I turned around then and crouched next to the receiver as it lay flat on the tabletop.

A high-pitched voice said, "Operator. What may I do for you—coffee, tea, or me?"

The voice came from the kitchen doorway. Seafield was leaning casually against the frame. Watching me and not trying to suppress his mirth.

"Bit awkward for you, is it?" he asked. "Let me hold it for you."

He came to the table and held the receiver up to my ear and mouth. "Go on," he urged. "Go on."

The phone was dead. I turned away.

"That's right," Seafield said, waving the instrument back and forth in front of my nose. "Last time we were here, you wanted to make a phone call and I pulled the wire out of the wall. And it hasn't been fixed yet, has it? Has it?"

"Mmmrrrmmph."

"No, it hasn't. Now, you didn't think I'd forget something like that, did you?"

He rolled me onto the floor. "Mmrrr."

"But," he said, "what I'm going to do now is fix the phone. Don't get me wrong, cowboy. I'm not going to fix it for you, but at least next time, if you think you've got a chance, then it will be live. Can't necessarily say that you will be, though."

I watched him reconnect the wires he'd pulled out only the day before.

When he finished, he held up the little screwdriver he'd used and said, "See? All fixies."

He went to the phone. I pulled and squirmed at the ropes on my hands, trying to find a little looseness, some way to wriggle free. For the tenth time I didn't find any.

He dialed a number. "It's me," he said. "Henry says that we can't do anything now but get rid of the impurity. You are to help." He paused, then said sharply, "Get yourself over here!"

He slammed the receiver down and walked to the kitchen.

I struggled to my knees and edged toward the phone again.

Seafield reappeared in the doorway, looked at me, and shook his head. "You're game for an old fella," he said.

He walked back into the room and pulled the phone wire out. Before going back to the kitchen he kicked me in the stomach.

It wasn't a kind thing to do.

I heard him open the back door and go out. But a moment later he came in again. And then he was back in the living room with me. He carried a piece of a cement block on a newspaper. He set it down on the floor, returned to the kitchen.

When he joined me again, he had a thick glass wine bottle, empty, in his hand. "This will do nicely, don't you think?" he said.

"Mmmmnnnrmmm," I said, in a conciliatory tone. I raised and lowered my eyebrows invitingly. I wanted to talk.

"Over my dead body," he said.

I didn't like him dwelling on death, so I asked again, "Mmmmrph?"

"You've been such a pain in the ass," he said, waving the bottle at me. "It's hard to be patient. And no matter what happens now, you've gone and busted the sweetest setup a poor country boy was ever likely to stumble into."

"Mmm?"

"Oh, yes, you've got what you wanted. You've busted it up. With people asking questions, it can't possibly stay undercover much longer. But you shouldn't take all the credit. People just aren't as willing to do their country's duty as they were when we started." He shook his head. "Yes," he said, "It's all through. Like you."

"Mmmnn?"

"You better believe it, cowboy."

Despite additional eloquent entreaties, he didn't say anything else to me. Until Merom arrived.

FORTY-ONE / Seafield divided his time equally between sitting in an armchair and pacing around the room. Then we heard a key in one of the locks in the front door. Seafield stood inside waiting for her.

Merom opened the door. He pulled her roughly into the room, and locked the door behind her.

"Hello, honey," he said. He towered over her. With his left hand, he bunched her long hair and pulled it, tipping her face up to his. With his right hand between her legs, he lifted her to the tips of her toes as he bent and kissed her roughly.

Halfway through the long greeting, she put her hands loosely on his waist.

When he unhanded her, Seafield turned to me and leered. The last time the three of us had met in the room he'd had to back down. He was showing me who was in charge, who was the dominant male.

Standing over me, he seemed never to end as I looked up at him, a great rifle of a man who was showing me that his trigger was definitely below the belt.

I tried to look bored. It's hard to attempt anything else with your mouth taped and your hands tied behind your back.

Seafield wasn't finished. "Take off your clothes," he said to Merom.

She hesitated.

He took a slight step toward her, threatening in a couple of centimeters extreme physical violence.

She took off her clothes.

He sat in the chair again and watched for a minute. Then he said, "The idea is this. You've just got out of bed. You've heard something out here and it turns out to be this wicked man who's broken into your apartment."

"Mmmmnnrmm," I said.

Ignoring me, he said, "For protection, you keep this empty bottle by your bed. When you come out to see what the noise is, you bring it with you. Because he's such a coward, he runs for it. But at the back door, on the porch, you catch him and hit him. He stumbles and falls over the railing and hits his head on the cement brick there, which just happens to be at the bottom." He turned to me. "Bad luck, cowboy."

He wasn't leaving my bad luck to chance.

Merom said whiningly, "But, Lee—"

He cut her off. "Shut up. That's how it is. After it happens, you call the police like a good citizen."

She didn't look happy. He looked at her fiercely. "All right, I will," she said.

"Too right you will." Then he turned to me again. "But you've got some time yet, cowboy." He looked at his watch. "Because we've got to wait till it's late enough for the lady to have gone to bed."

They also had to make the bed look as if it had been used. Seafield decided to help Merom with that, but not until he had immobilized my legs again. He tied them and looped a line from them to the bedroom door. On the theory that if I did manage to get free, I wouldn't be able to do it without banging the door and attracting their attention.

I read a book about Houdini once that said he tensed his muscles as he was being tied up so that there would be some slack to play with when he came to try to escape. I tensed my muscles as Seafield tied my feet. Unfortunately, I'm not Houdini.

All I ended up doing was making noise, banging my head against the floor, and pushing at the door. And straining at my bonds so they would leave marks on the parts of my body they were restraining.

But no neighbors complained. And I wasn't all that excited at the prospect of leaving marks to try to catch the eye of the coroner. After a while I just rested. He was going to have to untie me sometime.

And I was getting more rest than he was.

It was nearly midnight when he turned his concern back to me. He untied my feet and pocketed the rope. He stood me up roughly. For a moment the blood left my head. I moaned. He wasn't sympathetic.

He stood me against the wall and hit me twice in the stomach, once with each hand. The great fists felt like meat mallets. Which was unnecessary. I was already tender.

Then he took me to the kitchen and cut my hands free.

While I stood dazed and rubbing my wrists, he opened the back door.

He pulled me by the right arm. "Make a fist," he said.

I wouldn't. So he pushed the back of my open hand through the lowest windowpane.

He brought me in again and closed the door. He looked at my

hand. It wasn't marked enough to satisfy him. He rubbed it in the glass on the floor. That satisfied him.

"Come on," he said, and led me back toward the living room.

Finally, I pulled at the tape on my mouth, and tore it off.

"This is ridiculous," I said.

He pushed me through the doorway and into the room.

"You'll never get away with it," I said, always a quick man to turn a phrase.

"Then that will console you," Seafield said to me.

I saw a shadow behind me and turned to face Merom, who was brandishing her empty wine bottle. I realized from her eyes that she was eager. Which was bad. I'd hoped her initial hesitation was genuine reluctance to commit murder. But she did what she was told. She took orders. And that was bad for me. "You want this yet, Lee?" she asked.

"Good," he said. He took the bottle. He acknowledged that she was completely involved now. "Go put on a nightie," he snapped at her.

She turned, but hesitated. "Don't do anything until I get back."

"Hurry up, then."

She jumped to the bedroom. This was the woman who had been petrified of Seafield when she actually caught me breaking in. She'd feared him. But that was all part of the greater reality that she gravitated to wherever the dominance was greatest. It told me more about John Pighee than I'd found out since I'd started investigating him.

And it also told me how to play things. If she was attracted by power and fear, and if Seafield lived for exercising and inspiring same, there was no room for me in that pairing. It didn't pay for me to be overawed or frightened.

I rubbed my stomach and tried to pick some glass fragments out of my hand.

"All right," I said, "you're going to kill me, but there's no need to rush it and make a messy job." I took half a step forward.

In an instant the bottle was raised.

"Relax," I said. "You've got me. There's nothing I can do."

Seafield studied me and was suspicious. He didn't say anything and he didn't lower the bottle.

I stood still and asked conversationally, "Was Simon Rackey your first?"

He hesitated again.

"It was a good job. The police didn't have the slightest suspicion. I asked them about it. They weren't interested."

"But not my last," he said, finally answering my first question.

"No," I said. "Pighee's wife was your last before tonight."

"I don't know anything about Pighee's wife."

Merom appeared in the doorway. "Is this all right?"

Seafield didn't look. He watched me, keyed to pounce at the slightest movement. "Let's see," he said.

Merom stepped into his line of vision. "What's he so happy about?" she asked.

"He's trying to bluff it out, so I'll relax and he can make a run for it."

"Am I so transparent?" I asked.

"I can see right through it," Seafield said. But not to me. He spoke to Merom angrily. "You're not going to entertain the fucking police in that. Don't you have anything thick and opaque? Use that famous head, why don't you."

"All right," she said, and went back into the bedroom.

"You're going to kill me, right?" I said as I stepped slightly farther forward.

"Right," he said.

"All I want is that you don't make me die unhappy, O.K.?"

"What is this? Last-request time? Last meal? I wouldn't waste the food."

"It's just a couple of questions. Like whether Henry Rush realizes that he isn't really a G-man."

This amused Seafield. He was about to speak when Merom reappeared. He risked a glance at her winter bathrobe, then said, "Go back into the bedroom. Close the door. Get into bed. Turn the TV on low and wait until I call you."

"But, Lee," she whined.

"Do it!"

"I don't want to miss anything and—"

"Do it!"

"—and besides, there was something that I remembered."

I saw her face. She was staring at me.

"Goddamn it," Seafield shouted. "Go to your goddamn bedroom and do what I goddamn told you to."

She didn't want any trouble. She did what she was told. In a moment we heard the drone of the television.

"So she doesn't really know, either," I said.

"For someone so smart, she's fucking stupid," he said.

"And Henry Rush?"

"He thinks he's a cowboy getting revenge for what they did to Custer."

"So he thinks what he told me is the truth?"

"That's right."

"Did you set this thing up?"

"Hell, no," he said. "Much too big for me. This was set up by the big drug boys in Detroit who went through Tommy. He's the one who sold it to Henry. A real patriot, Henry. He'd do almost anything to help the country." Heavy sarcasm.

"And they recruited you?"

"That's it. They saw I wasn't happy stuck like I was. They recruited me and I jumped at it."

"Only you saw through it."

"Damn right."

"And made your own kind of contact with . . . who, Walker?"

He shrugged acknowledgment. His tolerance of my questions was slipping.

"And made your own financial arrangements with him," I said. "Did he know you were already planning to go?"

"Planning to go?" Seafield said.

"I saw the Portuguese books in your apartment. I figured Brazil."

"Quite a place," he said. "Especially for a man with some brains, some knowledge, and some capital."

I nodded.

"Only you've made it necessary for me to go sooner—six months and about twenty-five thou sooner—than I intended."

"What about her?" I asked, and nodded to the bedroom.

"No way." He shook his head. "She's kind of goofy. I don't know whether you noticed."

It was hard for me to keep from telling him a lot of things I had noticed. But a cheap shot could be my last.

I asked, "How did Pighee move in there, with you around?"

"When they brought her in, I didn't think about her. I was kind of otherwise occupied. But then this Pighee guy comes in and he thinks he's hot shit and he spends a lot of time telling me what a compliant piece she is if you handle her right."

"Ah," I said.

"Funny him saying that, when she's the one rats on him and tells us he's up to something."

"What was he up to?"

He shook his head. "In this sort of setup, you can't wait for the details. One thing I'll give him, he wasn't a bad talent scout. Though he didn't even scratch the surface with her."

Merom knocked lightly on the door. Seafield tensed immediately. He'd never moved out of the line between me and the kitchen. I'd never had a chance to run for it. With a bottle in his hand and size, strength, and youth to burn, he would be a certainty in a fight.

"Look," I said, "I'm a little tired. Is it all right if I sit down?"

"Lee?" came the voice through the door. "You haven't forgotten me, have you? Can I come out now?"

"Don't worry about being tired," he said. "I'll take care of that for you."

"You're really going to do it, then?"

"I'm really going to do it." He slapped the bottle in his hand. "All I have to do is think about the money you cost me and I'll enjoy doing it."

"Lee?"

"Almost as much as she'll enjoy watching it."

He stretched a hand to the bedroom door.

I stepped sharply forward, to make him respond to me. He did. I didn't want Merom back in the room.

"Look," I said. "If you're really going to do it, won't you at least let me say my prayers?"

Astonishment passed over his face. "What?"

"If I'm going to die, let me get right with God."

"I don't believe it."

"Please." I put my hands together, palm to palm, to show my good faith.

He smiled. "Say your prayers," he said. A last magnanimity.

I dropped to my knees and then waddled to the couch. My back was to him as I leaned on it.

I heard the door open behind me. Seafield said, "Hey, look at this. He wants to say a fucking prayer." I heard Merom shuffle into the room, grunting at her displeasure at being caged when she could have been playing with the mouse.

I heard her stop shuffling, stop grunting. I heard her gasp. I heard her say, "No, Lee! No!"

FORTY-TWO /   I lunged toward the cushion at the end of the couch. I felt all around under it for the gun that Merom had put there the last time I'd been with her in the apartment. It wasn't there. I couldn't find it.

I couldn't have been wrong, could I? I dived for the cushion at the other end. It couldn't have been under that one. I remembered clearly. But then my fingers found cold hard metal.

I juggled for the handle. Found it. Pulled the trigger as I tried to turn it toward Seafield.

The gun went off into the arm of the couch.

I turned it, pulled at it. It went off again and took a lampshade and a picture frame. I got it up. I saw a big shadow over me, an arm falling. I tried to pull the trigger again. All my strength.

There were crashes. The shadow fell hard on the gun and my hands. Glass sprayed all over me. Everything stung. Light glowed and faded. Seafield—it must have been Seafield—balanced above me.

He seemed to rise, to float, to fall.

Then he sank away to my right. Light came on strong again. I saw Merom standing behind where Seafield had been. She was watching, half curious, half petrified, half smiling. She was covered with blood. Everything was covered with blood. Wall, pictures. I looked to myself. I was covered with blood.

My legs were pinned underneath the huge hulk that used to be Lee Seafield. I knew that he was dead. There was a small pulsing fountain of blood spouting out of his back, but I knew he was dead. Then the fountain stopped. Explosions had ripped him apart. Explosions had taken his life, saved mine. Saved mine.

I looked up at Merom again. She stood exactly where she'd been before. Nothing happened. I watched, wondering if I had hit her. Whether something that had gone through Seafield had hit her.

Then I realized I wasn't holding the gun any more. At least I couldn't feel it in my hand. I looked at my hand. There was no gun in it. I didn't know where it was.

I was afraid again. I pushed forward, growling, and tried to move Seafield's body off me. It wouldn't move. I got panicky.

The gun was beside me, on the floor in a dust of glass. I grabbed it gratefully. I found it hard to grip, between the glass and the blood. I used both hands and turned back to Merom.

She still hadn't moved.

I raised the gun. I pointed it.

I knew in my mind that I was free to pull the trigger if I decided to. I aimed at her heart.

Then I relaxed, and bent my arms.

In front of me Merom began to fall. Then she dropped heavily and hard.

It was as if I'd pulled the trigger when I'd wanted to. As if I'd been the kind of people they had been.

For a while I wondered if I had pulled the trigger.

FORTY-THREE / "Hello, Daddy."

"If it isn't the kid. Hello, kid."

"Lieutenant Miller is outside, but he said I could come in first just for a minute. You're better today, aren't you?"

"I'm awake. They tell me I've been unconscious for two days."

"It's Sunday. They found you early Friday morning."

"So I understand," I said.

"I'm so sorry," Sam said. She began to snuffle.

"Sorry? What for?"

"Grandma said that you went out looking for me. That you thought I'd been kidnapped or something."

"It crossed my mind."

"And that's why you got involved with those people."

"I was already involved with them. They didn't like me very much."

"No," she said.

We both stopped talking for a moment. I was thinking that physically I'd come out pretty whole. Some cuts and a couple of broken fingers.

"I'm supposed to go now. They only gave me a minute."

"O.K., honey," I said. "Look after your grandmother for me."

"I will." She kissed me and left.

Miller entered as Sam left. He didn't kiss me. He didn't even hold my hand.

"Nice of you to stop in," I said. "What's new in the Indianapolis police department? You chief yet? Or are they holding the appointment open for me?"

"We don't usually appoint murderers to be chief of police," he said.

"Murderers?"

He mistook my question, thought I was emphasizing the plural. "That's right. Marcia Merom died thirty-six hours ago."

"I didn't murder anyone," I said.

"What do you call shooting unarmed people to death?"

"Unarmed people who were about to kill me. I call it self-defense."

"Well," he said.

I waited.

"I call it self-defense, too, but Captain Gartland wasn't very happy about it."

"Gartland's not happy when he gets two prizes in his Cracker Jacks, but it doesn't change the facts."

"Fortunately there are some supporting details. Rope marks on your wrists and ankles. Bruising where you may have been beaten. Window glass in your hands."

"Along with broken bones."

"And broken bones. The fact that the gun was Merom's and not yours."

"I don't own one. Maybe I should."

"Everybody else in the world has one."

"You've talked me out of it."

"You know Seafield bent the gun barrel when he hit it with that wine bottle?" Miller asked. He was showing me that he'd reconstructed much of what had happened.

"No," I said. "I didn't know."

"Doctor says he must have hit the gun with the bottle. Broke your fingers on reverberations. If he'd hit your hand, we'd still be picking up the pieces. And all that with three holes in him."

"Three!"

"That's the number after two and before four."

"I couldn't have shot him three times. I wasn't sure I'd shot him once."

"You mean after you finished off the couch arm and the picture on the wall?"

"No comment."

"The gun does hold six shots, you know. And good thing you didn't fire the last one."

"Why?"

"Because with a bent barrel the gun would have blown up on you, that's why. The bullet wouldn't have got out. Things get nasty when that happens."

I lowered my head. "I don't remember very well."

"Gartland may get your license," Miller said. "But you should be all right on any charges."

"You're trying to cheer me up, are you?"

"Don't worry about that cop outside the door. Just a precaution."

"What cop?"

"Well," he said. "We've got a guy out there, that's all. Gartland's orders."

"Terrific," I said. I was getting tired.

Miller saw my eyes fluttering. "You should know that we found those letters."

"What letters?"

"The letters from the F.B.I. to Rush, in your jacket pocket." As he told me I remembered. "The F.B.I. here says they don't think they can be real, but we're checking them out."

"What about Rush?"

"He's been in all day answering questions."

"And Walker?"

"The guy with Rush and Seafield when they caught you in Rush's house? We're looking for him."

"For Christ's sake, don't let him get away, Jerry."

"Is he important?"

"Damn right. He's the link man. He'll be away if you give him the chance."

Miller got up. "I'll let you rest now."

I drifted in and out of sleep. Half my waking periods I thought about happier days. The other half I spent trying to reconstruct how I'd got myself into this.

In the middle of the afternoon, I realized that Linn Pighee was dead. Dead. Linn Pighee, who had slept in my bed, been cared for by my crippled daughter.

"Nurse! Nurse!" I called, I cried, I rang the bell.

A child in white appeared. "What's wrong?"

"She can't be dead," I said. "She can't be."

The child hovered, not knowing whether there was anything she should do, could do. Comfort me, get someone to doctor me, or wait me out. Indecision made her wait. And I subsided.

Later in the afternoon I woke up properly. I asked a nurse to send me someone in authority. I had the head nurse in mind. Instead they sent me Miller.

"You ready to make your statement?" he asked.

"I've been thinking," I said.

"I can see why you wanted someone to mark the occasion."

"John Pighee's wife, Linn Pighee. She died the other day."

"I heard she died," Miller said.

"I need to talk to the guy that did the autopsy."

"*You* need to! Just who the hell are you, then?"

"I've got to know why she died."

"You shot her, too, or something?"

"Look," I said, "I'm not making any statement until you arrange for the guy that did the autopsy to come up here."

"People are supposed to mellow when they get to your age."

"Or get cantankerous. I feel pretty cantankerous."

"All right, all right, I'll go arrange it. But you get your strength up. I've got a stenographer outside. When I get back, we take your preliminary statement, before you shoot yourself. You been shooting everybody else lately."

Forty minutes later, fortified by a glass of orange juice, I started telling them, step by step, how being hired by Mrs. Thomas had led me to the people John Pighee was involved with. It was a long and grisly interview and when I got to the last bit it hit me, hard, for the first time, just what a slender thread of circumstance had made the difference between my being alive and being dead.

"You won't get me knocking the power of prayer now," I told them.

I woke up in the night. I remembered things. I was due to be evicted. My license was in real danger from Gartland. My savings had been stolen. Sam would have to go back soon. I had killed two people.

Killed two people. I couldn't fathom how that had come to happen. I couldn't—in the abstract—conceive how I could do any such thing. But I had. It had just happened. I'd killed to save my own life. It drove home the fact that I was mortal. That Linn Pighee was dead. That Sam would die one day.

I must have been crying out. Somebody came to my bedside in the night. I remember my forehead being wiped, being soothed. I felt better for it. Comforted.

I dreamed again later, but without the same anxieties. Mrs. Thomas burst into my room. I saw her come to my bedside and take my hand and smile from beneath the leather folds of her face. She said, "Job well done," and she patted my head. She didn't say it, but I knew she was congratulating me for shooting Marcia Merom. "She was no better for John than Linn was," Mrs. Thomas said in my dream. "She's well out of the way. When John gets well, we'll try to find him someone else," she said, "someone more like me."

FORTY-FOUR / "Mr. Samson." A gentle urgent voice accompanied gentle urging hands.

"Careful," I said, "or you'll wake me up."

"Mr. Samson, Doctor is here."

I sat up to face a short bald man with an aquiline nose and a droopy mustache. He wore a white coat and a frown.

"What can I do for you?" I asked. "Pulse? Blood pressure?"

"You," he said, "you apparently demanded to see me. I don't know who you are or why you have a police guard on your door, but I don't have much time and I don't have any to waste."

"Ahh," I said. "You're the man who did the autopsy on Linn Pighee."

He did a double take. Then said, "I am."

"What did she die of?"

He decided not to buck the authority that had brought him to my bedside. He just answered, "A bone cancer."

"Not malnutrition?"

"Malnutrition is a side effect."

"How common is it?"

"Not common," he said. "Rare. Even for a bone cancer."

"Why's that?"

"Because the malignancy involves the outside of the bones, not the marrow."

"How does it happen? What causes it?"

"Next time I have an audience with God, I'll ask him."

"That's not quite what I meant. Is it the sort of thing that some kind of radioactive material could cause?"

He was suddenly alert. "Certain beta emitters. Are you saying that this woman worked with radioactive materials?"

"Her husband did," I said. "Did you check for radioactive stuff in her body?"

"I did not," he said crisply. "But I will."

He left me to my dreams. They were no less vivid just because I was awake.

I started causing trouble. I asked for Miller, but he wasn't at the hospital. I demanded a telephone so I could call him.

The nurse didn't want to bring me one.

"Look," I said. "I'm a V.I.P."

"You are?"

"They don't put a police guard on everybody's room in this hospital, do they?"

She thought about it. "Who are you, then?"

"Just bring the phone. Autographs later."

Miller wasn't at police headquarters. I kept the telephone. I told them I was calling a lawyer.

But it wasn't my own lawyer.

"A couple of questions arise," I told Walter Weston, "following the death of Linn Pighee."

"I was shocked," he said. "Stunned." And I believed him, because it had happened to me.

"Do you know that John Pighee is also dead?"

After a pause, he said, "I've talked to the police, who said you'd suggested something of the sort. I'm not prepared to accept it as established until further investigation has taken place."

"Who gets the money and property left by Linn Pighee?"

"If you have an outstanding claim on her estate, then submit it to me and I'll try to deal with it as soon as I can." He hesitated. "Samson, don't underestimate the amount, of your . . . um . . ."

"That's not why I was asking. Is there much to her estate?"

"Not a lot. She was not a rich woman."

"But the house, the money her husband left?"

"Ahh," he said. "That all depends on when—and if—John Pighee dies."

"But he's been dead since the accident seven months ago," I said.

"But not certificated as dead."

"So he inherits from her."

"It would seem so."

"Thanks," I said.

I tried Miller again. Was told he was due soon.

I rested.

Third time lucky. "Tell me, Lieutenant," I said. "If I was to suggest you went to look in a closet somewhere and you found something interesting, would you come and tell me all about it?"

"Albert," he said, sounding tired for so early in the morning, "we got a clown here who works in Missing Persons. He spends most of his time making up hypothetical questions and cornering people to ask them to. I just got caught in the elevator. I'm not in the mood. Do you have something to tell me?"

I told him to go look in Mrs. Thomas's cupboard. "And while you're about it, check out the booze bottles, food containers—that sort of stuff—in the main house."

"Check them out?"

"Start with a Geiger counter. I didn't mean sample them."

"A Geiger counter! What the hell are you on about?"

"Sorry," I said. "You don't like hypotheses, so I can't tell you."
I hung up.

FORTY-FIVE / Miller walked in two and a half hours later.
Before I'd finished my lunch. He looked distinctly happy. I didn't
remember him looking like that since before he made lieutenant.

"You look like a chocolate Cheshire cat," I said. "You just catch
a chocolate Cheshire mouse?"

"I've got a lady outside wants to kill you," he said.

"No wonder you look so happy. Anyone I know?"

"A lady called Dorothea Thomas. John Pighee's sister."

"Ahh," I said.

He handed me a leather-bound book. "I can give you about
twenty minutes with this before I take the lady to her new home."

I nodded. "Thanks," I said.

"I'll be outside." He walked to the door. "By the way, those
letters from the F.B.I. were forgeries and Henry Rush tried to kill
himself. They brought him here; he's five doors down the hall." He
left.

The book was the journal of John Austin Pighee. He had begun
it the day Henry Rush recruited him to work on Project Bagtag.
"I guess the F.B.I. has to do its work somewhere," he wrote. "I feel
the luckiest darn man in the world that it happens to be the place
I'm working. And when this is over, when the culmination of all
the work ahead pays off, I feel sure that the world will want to
know what it owes to people like Henry. That's why I'm writing
this diary. I'll write in it every day. I'll keep it in my sister's trailer
and stop in each day either before or after I go to work."

And he had. The enthusiasm for his work showed. He believed
throughout that he was working for the F.B.I. He felt obliged to

sell the importance of the project, its mission as he saw it, at every opportunity. The man had been a salesman, after all. And in this journal he was silently preparing the product that would be the big sale of his life.

It was clear that he intended to turn the journal into a true-life undercover book. He figured to make his fortune.

From the beginning it was full of personal details about the people involved with him. I suspect that he made approaches to Marcia Merom in the first place only so that he would have juicy details to write about. And write about them he did.

He found her solicitous and flexible. And he claimed to feel alive with her and excited by her. "Which I don't with Linn, my wife, and haven't since our tragedy." The only reference I found to his wife.

The tragedy being the loss of their kids to a car.

But the week before he died, he wrote, "The pressure for secrecy is so steady, so complete, that I haven't even told Marcia about this diary. Should I, I wonder? I don't know. There are depths to her that even I haven't plumbed. Until then . . .

"But I've been worrying," he continued. "When this journal goes to a publisher, will they believe me? I'm wondering if I shouldn't start accumulating supplementary evidence, to prove—against official denials, should they take place—that this is a real operation and not just the product of my fevered imagination. Occasional notes, a few samples of materials we use. That kind of thing."

I called Miller in. "You like?" he asked.

"It would have saved me a lot of trouble if I'd known it existed," I said. "What else did you get out of the cupboard?"

"Some samples of an illegal white powder. And an empty container of some radioactive stuff. Some scraps with notes on them. Some invoice copies. I don't know quite what."

"What about the stuff in the house? Anything radioactive?"

"We didn't go out there with your Geiger counter, if that's what you mean, but we brought a lot of stuff back and we're looking into it. What do you think happened? What's it all about?"

"When I sent you out there, I thought you'd find stuff to show that John Pighee fed his wife radioactive calcium that led to her bone cancer."

"My God. Killed by the dead."

"But I'm not so sure now," I said. "Let Mrs. Thomas in here, will you?"

"Let her in? You sure?"

"Yeah. Come in with her, but stay out of the way."

He shrugged and went out to bring her in. My stock had risen.

Mrs. Thomas came in red and raging; her face looked as if it had just been shorn of fur and was smarting at the abuse.

"You!" she said, and nearly hit me. "You betrayed my trust. It should be against the law to betray a client's trust."

"It is," I said, "except when it involves information relating to a crime."

"What crime?" she asked, suddenly coy.

I held up her brother's journal. "You read this day by day, didn't you?"

She thought about whether she should deny it. Then said, "Yes."

"So when you hired me, you knew this group he was working with was why John was not allowed to have visitors."

"Well," she said.

"But you put me on the scene to pressure them so they would give you money, maybe the money you had been getting from John."

"He would have wanted them to," she said emphatically. "There I was getting nothing, and they were making *her* a wealthy woman for as long as he was sick. It wasn't *her* he cared about."

"No. It was you, and Marcia Merom, but definitely not Linn."

"Definitely not. She was bad enough at the beginning, trapping him with . . . the way she did. But after the children died she was nothing, *nothing* to him."

"She was holding him back. With her out of the way, there were no limits on him."

"She was an anchor," she said.

"Only he wouldn't do anything about getting rid of her."

"No," she said heatedly, "so—" She caught herself.

"So you helped him, as you always helped him, since he was a baby."

She didn't say anything.

"And besides," I said, "if John died—"

"He won't die."

"But if he did, Linn would inherit everything. Unless she died first."

She sat and glared. As clear as a silent confession can be.

FORTY-SIX / Sam visited me in the afternoon. Ray McGonigle was with her. "Hey, man," he said. But stood back as Sam came close and sat at my bedside.

I could see she'd been crying.

"Daddy," she said. "Daddy."

"What is it, kid?"

"I talked to Mummy this morning on the phone. She says I have to go home. I've got to go back to school."

"Of course you do," I said.

"I mean I've got to go now. Ray's taking me to the airport."

"A better father would keep track of these things," I said. In a wave, I felt like crying. But so as not to pressure her I fought it, and won. Then decided I should cry if I felt like it. But by then I couldn't.

"I almost told Mummy I wasn't going back to school," Sam said. "But with only one year to go for my diploma, I think I should probably stick it out this year."

"Of course you should," I said.

"Daddy," she began. But we were interrupted by ructions outside the door to my room. They went on for half a minute while we all watched the door and waited. I had a moment's fearful trembling. It passed through my mind that Gartland had come to the hospital to do a rash thing.

But instead, when the door opened, a short old man walked in.

He carried a cane but hardly let it touch the floor. He was wiry and his hair was bright white.

He came to the bed and, ignoring Sam, said to me, "How's the patient, then?"

I couldn't think of anything snappy to say except, "All right."

"How long are you in for?"

"I don't know."

"Treating you well, are we?"

"Fine."

"Frightful fuss I had getting in here. I told the policeman outside I've been visiting patients fortnightly for twenty-three years and I was damned if I was going to leave anybody out, no matter how dangerous."

"Oh," I said.

He turned to Sam and Ray. "Family visitors. Always good for morale, I think. Well, mend quickly." Abruptly he left.

Ray's excitement carried him halfway to the door. "Do you know who that was? Do you know?"

"I have the feeling," I said, "that I am about to be told."

"That was Sir Jeff! Sir Jeff Loftus himself! Wow!" He looked fondly at the closed door.

"Wow?"

"Imagine an important guy like that taking time to visit patients in a hospital. Wow!"

The way Ray was staring at the door through which the great man had passed, it crossed my mind he was going to take it off its hinges. And fix it.

I said, "Ray, go help Sir Jeff."

"What?"

"It's your big opportunity. He might stumble and you'd be there to pick up his crown. Go on."

Ray hesitated but wanted to follow Sir Jeff as much as I wanted to be left alone with Sam. He went out.

"I was telling you," I said to her, "that you should get your diploma."

Sam sat quietly for several seconds. Then burst on me, "When I graduate, I thought—I thought it would really be good if I came back here and helped you."

"Helped me?"

"With the detective business." She sat up eagerly as she said, "While you thought I was kidnapped, I was out buying the sign."

"Sign?"

"It's a present. To put outside over your door and sell yourself better. It's neon and people will see it, and know you're there."

"I expect they will," I said.

"It says 'Albert Samson, Private Investigator.' And"—real excitement—"it came this morning!"

"It came?"

"They delivered it to the office. It's really lovely. I plugged it in and it flashes!"

"Wow," I said.

"The great thing about it is you can plug another line into it."

"Another line?"

"So it could read 'Albert Samson & Daughter,' " she said. Then she got shy. "If you'd be willing to have me around, Daddy."

"You don't have to ask that," I said.

She didn't say anything. Neither did I, feeling too warm.

"It's a pity," I said, at last.

"What is?"

"That I didn't get my way when your mother and I were fighting about what to name you."

She hesitated. "What did you want to name me?"

"Delilah," I said. "Now, that would be a great sign. 'Samson & Delilah Detective Agency.' "

She smiled. "I can always change my name," she said.

"I could always get another Delilah," I said.

"Why?" Hurt.

"You don't think I'm going to take on a partner with only a high school diploma, do you? I wouldn't consider a partner who didn't have a college degree."

"You wouldn't?"

"Nope." Good deed for the day.

"Oh."

"I've got to maintain standards."

"But you don't have a college degree."

"I don't need another dummy like me in the business. I'm a

luxury I can ill afford. Tell you what, I'll hold the place open for you. How's that?"

"I've got lots of ideas how to make it better," she said.

"It makes me tired just to think of you doing all that thinking." I realized I was tired. I sagged and she noticed it. "When do you go, did you say?"

"I should have gone yesterday. There's a plane in . . ." She looked at her watch.

"Give me your hand, kid."

She bent over and kissed me.

"Keep your detective card dusted."

"I will."

"Your visit was much appreciated," I said. "Knowing I have a grown-up daughter makes me feel ten years younger."

When Sam walked out the door, it felt like the end of a lot of things. But I couldn't get myself depressed about it and for a while I couldn't understand why. I had no money, would shortly have no place to live, and probably no license. I'd killed two people, and a third, a good one, had died. I was alone and childless again.

But the negative blanket of events just didn't envelop me. They were all opportunities, in their own way, to shuffle life's pack. To deal a new hand. Maybe with some of the old cards in it, maybe not.

And I realized what I was really looking forward to was Sam's neon sign. Bright and garish, a flashing silent salesman outside a new office, telling the world, day and night, that I was still in business, still alive.

A NOTE ABOUT THE AUTHOR

Michael Z. Lewin was born in Springfield, Massachusetts, raised
in Indianapolis, and graduated from Harvard in 1964. Before he
wrote his first four novels, *Ask the Right Question* (1971), *The
Way We Die Now* (1973), *The Enemies Within* (1974), and
Night Cover (1976), he taught in a New York City high school.
He now lives with his wife and two children in Somerset,
England.

A NOTE ON THE TYPE

The text of this book was set, via computer-driven cathode ray
tube, in Video Gael, an adaptation of Caledonia, a type face
originally designed by W. A. Dwiggins. It belongs to the family
of printing types called "modern faces" by printers—a term
used to mark the change in style of type letters that occurred
about 1800. Caledonia borders on the general design of Scotch
Modern, but is more freely drawn than that letter.

Composed, printed and bound by
The Haddon Craftsmen, Inc.,
Scranton, Pennsylvania

Designed by Susan Mitchell